"I could make you leave right now, if I wanted."

Elizabeth's face grew still as she studied him.

"I won't do that," Jude said a bit quieter. "I wouldn't turn any woman out on the street, especially Clarence's daughters."

"Thank you for that."

"But I have no interest in having a business partner." *Especially a woman.* "So my proposition still stands. You and your sisters may stay at the Northern, and if you make it until January I will put your name on the deed—and no more talk of buying my share. It's not for sale and it won't be for sale. Are you amenable to my proposition?"

"I agree. My sisters and I will live and work at the Northern until January, when you will add us to the deed. At that time, we will address the terms of our partnership." She held out her hand to shake his.

He took her hand and was surprised at the strength in her grip. She was a confident woman, he'd give her that.

The only thing that worried him was keeping his rescue work hidden. He wasn't ashamed of his work, but most people didn't understand why he did what he did. If she learned the truth, he'd have to explain to her about his past, and that was something that he *was* ashamed of.

Gabrielle Meyer lives in central Minnesota on the banks of the Mississippi River with her husband and four young children. As an employee of the Minnesota Historical Society, she fell in love with the rich history of her state and enjoys writing fictional stories inspired by real people and events. Gabrielle can be found at www.gabriellemeyer.com, where she writes about her passion for history, Minnesota and her faith.

Books by Gabrielle Meyer

Love Inspired Historical

Little Falls Legacy

A Family Arrangement
Inherited: Unexpected Family

A Mother in the Making

GABRIELLE MEYER

Inherited: Unexpected Family

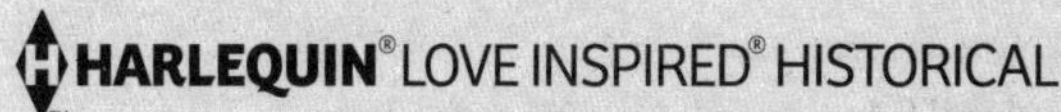

Recycling programs for this product may not exist in your area.

ISBN-13: 978-0-373-42537-2

Inherited: Unexpected Family

This edition published by arrangement with Love Inspired Books.

www.Harlequin.com

Printed in U.S.A.

And Jesus knew their thoughts, and said unto them,
"Every kingdom divided against itself
is brought to desolation; and every city or
house divided against itself shall not stand."

—*Matthew* 12:25

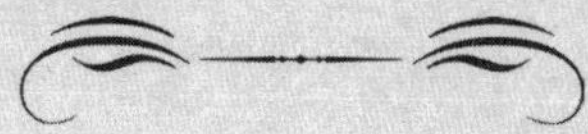

To my dear writer friends, Lindsay Harrel,
Alena Tauriainen and Melissa Tagg.
Thank you for the countless hours of
brainstorming, critiquing and encouragement.
I can't imagine walking this journey without you.

Chapter One

Minnesota Territory
June 26, 1857

There was no telling what awaited Elizabeth Bell and her two sisters when they reached the Northern Hotel. Elizabeth inhaled the humid air, wishing for a breeze as the stagecoach lurched and swayed over the Wood's Tail. They had left St. Paul early that morning and her anticipation had mounted with each passing mile. By night's end she would know how much work lay ahead before they could open the hotel. Maybe, just maybe, they would finally have the lives they had dreamed about since Papa abandoned them four years ago.

The last vestiges of daylight streaked across the sky, casting long shadows over Grace, who sat across from Elizabeth. A sudden bump forced Elizabeth to dig her feet into the floor to stay seated. She clutched Rose tighter on her lap so her little sister wouldn't fall.

"Grace?" Elizabeth spoke quietly so she wouldn't wake Rose.

Grace, just barely nineteen, stared out the window

with thinly veiled hostility, unwilling to acknowledge Elizabeth. She had not wanted to leave their home in Rockford, Illinois, and had made the weeklong trip unbearable. "Could you hold Rose for a bit? I'd like to look at Papa's letter one more time to make sure we're going to the right place."

Papa's letter had been the only correspondence they had received from him in four years, and it had been written on his deathbed. He'd left them a hotel in Minnesota Territory. It was the perfect solution to so many troubles Elizabeth had faced in Rockford. She could get out from under a domineering employer, start over with a fresh reputation and take Grace away from the rough crowd she'd been going around with. If only Grace would cooperate.

She continued to look out the window and didn't bother to respond to Elizabeth's request.

Elizabeth sighed and repositioned herself on the hard bench, causing Rose to stir in her sleep. The four-year-old cuddled close on Elizabeth's lap, her cheek pressed against Elizabeth's shoulder, her soft curls tickling Elizabeth's cheek. Mama had died giving birth to Rose, and Papa had disappeared the moment they finished burying her. His sudden departure had left Elizabeth to provide for her sisters. Thankfully, sweet Rose knew very little about all the pain they had endured and she had no memory of losing either parent.

Elizabeth squinted into the fading sunlight and noticed the first building they'd seen in several miles. She sat up straighter. Was this Little Falls? Their new home? She knew virtually nothing about the town, except for the gossip their stagecoach driver had shared with them—and none of it was good. A failing economy, a gang of desperadoes and a decline in population threatened her plans for the hotel—but surely hard work and dedication would go a long way toward their success.

Anything was better than their life in Rockford.

Another building rushed by, and yet another. The orange sunset sparkled off the Mississippi River in the distance. A sawmill appeared on the banks at the bottom of a hill, with a house and barn outlined in the shadows nearby. Soon dozens of various-sized buildings lined the main stretch of road. A church, a bank, a two-story general store and even a hotel called The Batters House Hotel. Elizabeth hadn't anticipated competition, but hopefully her hospitality would draw customers to the Northern.

Grace's stiff shoulders did not indicate any interest in the new town until a group of men shouted a hello at the passing stage.

Here and there people stood on the wooden boardwalks watching the stage roll by. Some came and went out of buildings, and others gathered in small clusters talking.

Most of them were men.

Elizabeth turned her attention toward the Northern. No doubt the hotel would be boarded up after Papa's death. They might need help prying off the boards to get inside, but maybe the driver would have a tool for them to use. From the date on the letter, and the finality of Papa's words, Elizabeth estimated that he had died about a month ago. She had mourned his loss, but had little time to dwell on what it meant. She'd worked for a week to sell their meager belongings in Rockford and secure their travel plans.

"We should be getting close," Elizabeth said, excitement and trepidation making her voice sound higher than she intended. "The driver told us the stage stops right outside the Northern."

Grace didn't respond, her blue eyes, so like Elizabeth's, focused on another group of men walking in the same direction the stage was headed.

The stage came to a stop outside a large white clapboard building. It was an impressive Greek Revival structure that covered the length of one city block, and looked out of place with the humble buildings in the rest of town. Several lights had already been lit within the pretty establishment, and at least half a dozen men entered through the front door.

Elizabeth frowned. "I thought the stage stopped at the Northern Hotel."

"Maybe this is the Northern Hotel," Grace said in a dry tone.

"How could it be?" Elizabeth handed Rose to Grace, not waiting for her sister's approval, and ducked as she stepped to the door. "The Northern Hotel is supposed to be boarded up and empty."

The driver appeared at the door and pulled it open. "Welcome to Little Falls."

Elizabeth lifted her hem and stepped onto the boardwalk. "I thought the stage stopped at the Northern."

"This here is the Northern." He nodded at the large building.

Elizabeth looked at the structure again. "But how is that possible?" Another group of men approached and stopped outside the door to stare at her.

The driver scratched his head, tilting his hat at an odd angle. "It's possible—'cause it just is."

"But—" Elizabeth gasped. Was someone squatting in

her hotel? Operating it in her absence? She pursed her lips, her heart rate escalating. Whoever was trespassing would soon be turned out, of that she was certain.

Elizabeth went back to the coach to speak to Grace. "I'm going in to confront the squatter. See that our luggage is unloaded properly."

Grace nodded and Elizabeth squared her shoulders. She'd been forced to deal with her fair share of stubborn men in the past four years. One more shouldn't be too difficult…she hoped.

A man standing near the building pushed open the front door and doffed his cap as she marched over the threshold and into the lobby.

The interior of the building was just as impressive as the exterior. Elizabeth paused to let her eyes roam over the white wainscoting, the wide stairway and the floral sofa near the door. In the opposite corner, to Elizabeth's right, was a sturdy counter covered with the same wainscoting. A man stood behind the counter, his back to the door, his head bent over a thick ledger. When he stood straight, Elizabeth couldn't help but notice his height and the breadth of his shoulders under a well-tailored suit coat.

So this was the squatter.

Elizabeth clenched her jaw and prepared for battle. She strode to the counter, ignoring the curious looks she garnered from dozens of patrons milling about the lobby. The air was thick with conversation and the smell of heady cologne mixed with cigar smoke.

She stopped at the counter, but he did not turn.

She cleared her throat, but he must not have heard over the conversation.

Finally, she did something most unladylike and tapped his broad shoulder. "Pardon me."

He turned, his dark brown hair shimmering under the light above his head, his equally brown eyes holding a hint of surprise. "May I help you?"

Elizabeth swallowed the nerves quivering up her throat. My, but he was a handsome man—much too handsome to be a squatter.

But, then again, weren't most scoundrels handsome? Her ex-fiancé, James, had been very good-looking.

She straightened her backbone and lifted her chin. "Who are you?"

Humor twinkled in his eyes. "Jude Allen. Who are you?"

"It doesn't matter who I am. What are you doing in my hotel?"

His humor subsided, just a bit. "Your hotel?"

"You're squatting on my property and I demand you leave immediately before I contact the local authority."

He did laugh this time. "I'd like to see you try to get the sheriff to do something useful around here."

Elizabeth frowned. "Didn't you hear me? You're trespassing and I want you to leave."

He leaned forward, his hands on the counter, all trace of laughter gone from his deep voice. "I don't know if you're trying to be funny or just annoying. If you're here for a room, I'm sorry, but we're full because of the ball." He tilted his head to a set of double doors leading into a ballroom where dozens of people spun about the room.

She put her hands on the counter, too. "I don't want a room—I want my hotel."

He leaned even closer, his voice lowered. "I don't

know who you are, or what you want, but this is my hotel. Has been for two years."

Elizabeth's lips straightened into a tight line. "This was my father's hotel, and he left it to me and my sisters. I don't know who you are, or what *you* want, but this is *my* hotel."

"That's impossible. I don't even know who your father is."

"Clarence Bell, the owner of the Northern Hotel."

His face became still and he slowly stood straight, disbelief lining his handsome features. "Clarence had a daughter?"

She planted her feet. "Three daughters and we're here to claim our inheritance."

They had come so far she wouldn't let this man stand in her way now.

Jude couldn't take his eyes off the beauty before him—the woman who was making such a ludicrous claim. Her sparking blue eyes were filled with determination and certainty. Her gown looked outdated and almost worn through, with frayed cuffs and carefully placed patches. Was she Clarence's daughter or a desperate woman looking for a free ride?

"It's impossible," Jude said. "Clarence never mentioned being married, let alone fathering children." He had never said much at all, which made their partnership ideal.

The door opened and another woman entered the lobby, her chocolate-brown curls and stunning blue eyes indicating she was related to the woman standing on the other side of the counter. She held a sleeping child in her arms and she looked just as exhausted and threadbare as the first.

"I don't know why Papa failed to mention us," the first woman said—though her tight lips and stilted voice suggested she wasn't surprised. "But, regardless, we are his daughters and heirs to his hotel."

The conversation in the lobby stilled as several people stopped to listen to their exchange. Jude was highly respected as one of the first business owners in Little Falls. He'd built the American Hotel in 1855, but it had been nothing compared to the impressive Northern. When the Northern had come up for sale just a few months later, Jude sold his smaller hotel to Mr. Batters. He didn't have enough money to buy the Northern, so he'd taken on a business partner, Clarence Bell. The man was moody and taciturn—though he was a good businessman. He'd taken over the bookwork and behind-the-scenes operations, while Jude worked at the front of the hotel with the customers and staff. It had been a good partnership—until Clarence fell ill and died a month ago.

Jude had assumed he was the sole owner of the Northern after Clarence's passing...apparently he'd been wrong. But how could he be sure? "Do you have proof? Did Clarence have a will I'm not aware of?"

"I have a letter."

"A letter? That's all you have to prove you're his heir?"

"What else do I need?"

"A legal document, at the very least. A birth certificate, a will—something substantial."

She anchored her gloved hands on the counter, her voice level, her jaw firm. "My father abandoned us four years ago. The only thing I have from him is a letter."

How could Clarence have abandoned his own children? “Where is the letter?”

She opened the reticule dangling from her wrist and pulled out an envelope as the other lady approached.

The second woman stood behind her sister and surveyed the room with disdain wrinkling her brow. It was hard to imagine these beautiful women were Clarence’s daughters. They looked nothing like him. The man had been unkempt and disheveled, to say the least. Why had he never mentioned a family?

The first lady handed the letter over to Jude. It was addressed to Elizabeth and Grace.

“I’m Elizabeth,” she said. “This is Grace.” She indicated the other woman. “And the child is our youngest sister, Rose.”

Jude lifted his eyes from the letter and looked at each of the women, his gaze stopping on the sleeping child.

He looked back at the letter and, sure enough, it was Clarence’s handwriting. He’d know it anywhere. And the letter seemed legitimate, written the day before Clarence had died. He apologized for leaving them four years ago upon the death of his wife and asked for their forgiveness. He’d planned to invite them to Little Falls once he had enough money to send for them, but he’d used it all to buy the hotel. As a way of recompense, he offered the hotel to his daughters.

Pain began to pulse in the back of Jude’s eyes as he lowered the letter. This couldn’t be happening. He had gone into the hotel business for one reason only: to rescue defenseless women from prostitution. The profits from the hotel allowed him to help them escape and then give them a job while his cook, Martha, taught them domestic skills. Over the past two years, they had rescued ten women, including his current maid, Violet. The other nine had either married or found jobs far from where they had been enslaved to their former profession.

Jude was driven to redeem the sins of his past, but no matter how many women he rescued, he could never bring back to life the one woman he wanted to save, but couldn't.

His mother.

What would the Bell sisters think when they met Violet or found out what he did with the proceeds from the hotel? Clarence hadn't liked it, but he'd allowed Jude to continue if it didn't interfere with the business. There was no way the prim and proper Miss Bell would approve—and, as 50 percent owner, she would have a say…if she found out.

Jude handed the letter back to Elizabeth, resolve strengthening his voice. "I plan to speak to my attorney in the morning."

She put it back in the envelope. "What's there to discuss? We own half of this hotel."

Jude cringed. It couldn't be true. What did they know of running a business? "I don't believe this letter will hold up in court. It's not a legal document—just a piece of paper written when your father wasn't in his right mind."

"His right mind?" Elizabeth spoke the words in a sort of hushed anger. She looked over her shoulder at her sisters and then around at the room of men watching them. She lowered her voice. "Mr. Allen, I do not believe we are in a frame of mind to argue this further tonight. I propose we both visit the attorney tomorrow and sort this out."

"Fine."

She stared at him.

He stared back.

The little girl roused in Grace's arms and lifted her head to look around the room. She, unlike her sisters, had golden-blond hair and deep-brown eyes—the same color as Clarence's. They blinked with sleep and came to rest on Jude. She studied his face and didn't look away, even when she reached for Elizabeth.

Elizabeth took the child and then addressed Jude. "We are all tired. Will you please show us to our father's room?"

Martha appeared from down the hall where she spent most of her time in the kitchen. She wiped her knotted hands on her apron, her concerned gaze hopping from one Bell sister to the other and finally landing on Jude. Her droopy bun hung loose at the back of her head and wisps of graying hair poked out around her face. She was one of the hardest workers Jude had ever met, which was one of the many reasons he trusted her explicitly. She watched all of them closely, but didn't take a step forward to interfere.

"Your father's rooms are occupied," Jude said.

"Then we'd like whatever you have available. My sisters are tired."

How could he refuse Clarence's daughters a place to stay, especially the child? But where would he put them?

"Jude." Martha finally approached, a frown of disapproval on her face. She had become his surrogate mother over the years and he felt her chastisement now. "Are these Clarence's daughters?" She didn't wait for his answer. "They're tired and grieving and should have their papa's rooms. You can sleep on one of the sofas in the parlor."

Elizabeth looked at once relieved and irritated. She addressed Jude. "*You're* the one occupying my father's rooms?"

Jude had given the master's suite to Clarence when they had purchased the establishment, but he'd moved in after Clarence passed. "I will give them to you and your sisters for now, but as soon as we clear up this mess, I'll see you on the next stage out of town."

"Hush, now," Martha said in her no-nonsense way. "All that can be worked out later. I'll show them to their rooms." Martha turned to the Bell sisters. "Don't mind Jude. He's just surprised, is all. I'm Martha Dupree. I'm the cook around here, but I'm more like the mama hen." She chuckled at her own joke as she pulled the women close around her. "I'll show you to your rooms and Andrew can bring up your things." She glanced at Andrew, the stagecoach driver.

He dipped the brim of his hat and headed out the door.

Martha ushered the ladies up the stairs, clucking all the way about how tired they looked and how hungry they must be.

At least two dozen men stood around the lobby, watching their ascent with keen interest, no doubt wondering who the pretty strangers were and when they'd get a chance to meet. The town was young, only a few years old, and like many frontier settlements the single-male population far outnumbered the eligible females. It was probably a good thing they were going up to his room. With a ball going on, they'd soon be bombarded with attention and they didn't look energetic enough to deal with that sort of problem.

A thought struck Jude and he scrambled to get out from behind the counter. He raced up the stairs and ran down the hall, but he was too late. Martha had already showed them into his room.

He had to get his journal before they noticed it lying open on the secretary. It was full of details about his mission work, his contacts throughout the territory and notes about several women who were in need of help.

If they saw what he did, he was sure they would not think very highly of him or the women he rescued. Most proper young women didn't.

He and Martha worked hard to keep their mission work a secret from the citizens of Little Falls. It would be much harder to keep it hidden from two women and a child living under his roof.

Chapter Two

Elizabeth didn't know what to expect, but she wasn't prepared for the fine sitting room they entered.

Martha lit a tall lamp using a match from a box on the fireplace mantel and the room filled with a soft glow.

The walls were papered in tiny blue flowers and the trim was crafted of beautiful red oak. Two tall windows allowed the stars to be visible in the fading dusk, and a small fireplace sat empty on this warm night.

"The bedroom is over there." Martha indicated a door on the right as she picked up a man's shirt hanging over the edge of a wingback chair.

A cursory glance around the room indicated Mr. Allen was not tidy. A lone shoe peeked out from under a table, a pair of suspenders hung from a lamp and a journal lay open on a secretary with a few crumpled papers nearby.

"I'll just grab Jude's things and then you can get sett—"

"I'll take care of my own things." Jude walked through the open door and went to the secretary, where he snapped the book closed. With quick hands, he picked the discarded paper up off the desk and then went around the room gathering his personal items. Though he was tall, he moved about with surprising grace. His suit was pressed, his shoes shining and his hair combed into perfect submission. It was clear Mr. Allen liked his appearance in order—so why the disheveled room?

"I'll get my things out of my bedchamber and be on my way," he said as he entered the other room and closed the door.

"I'll grab the clean linen while we wait for Jude. It's just down the hall." Martha bustled out of the sitting room, leaving Elizabeth alone with her sisters.

"I'm tired, Lizzie." Rose laid her head against Elizabeth's shoulder.

"We'll be in bed in just a moment." She swayed back and forth, holding her sister close while Grace went to the window and stared outside.

After a few minutes, Jude's bedroom door opened and he held a small trunk on his shoulder. "Tell Martha I'll sleep on one of the sofas in the ballroom parlor tonight."

"I heard you well enough," Martha said as she walked back in. "You go on now. I need to get that wee one in bed."

Jude left the sitting room as Martha led the way into the bedroom. "How are you holding up, lovey?" she asked Elizabeth. "Clarence was a good man. Though he could be surly at times, to be sure, I'm still grieving our loss."

Elizabeth allowed the first smile to warm her lips at Martha's frank assessment. She remembered Papa in much the same way, though Mama had always tempered his bad moods with her gentle manner. "I'm doing much better now that I'm here."

Martha nodded and patted Elizabeth's hand as she guided her into the bedroom. "The three of you should fit comfortable-like in this room, though it might be a tight squeeze in that bed." Martha set the clean linens on a bureau and clasped her hands together.

The room held a bed, a bureau, a rocking chair and a large green trunk that had belonged to Papa.

Martha noticed the trunk, too. "Jude was meaning to bring your pa's things to the attic." She went to the trunk and lifted the lid. "I think there will be a few things in here you'll like to have."

Elizabeth slowly followed her to the trunk, unsure if she could face more memories of her father. She had been angry and hurt when he left them, and then overwhelmed with the burden of her responsibilities. In her head, she wanted to believe she had forgiven him—but her heart wasn't as certain.

Martha pulled out a daguerreotype and handed it to Elizabeth.

Elizabeth set Rose on her feet and ran her fingertip over the cool metal. "Mama." It was the only picture they had of their mother, and Papa had brought it with him when he left. "I almost forgot what she looked like."

Grace stood just inside the door, her detached gaze looking anywhere but at the picture.

"Mama?" Rose asked, tugging on the sleeve of Elizabeth's dress. "Is that my mama?"

Elizabeth bent to show Rose the picture for the first time. The lantern light flickered over the image, making it appear lifelike.

"She looks like you." Rose glanced up at Elizabeth. "She was pretty."

"Grace and I look like Mama." Elizabeth put her hand on Rose's cheek. "You look more like Papa's family."

Martha had remained quiet as she watched them, but now she made a clicking noise with her tongue. "Poor dears. I'll get this linen changed so you can go to sleep."

Elizabeth helped her strip the bed and then put on the clean sheets. Andrew came into the sitting room with their luggage and soon they were all set for the night.

Martha looked around one more time and then said to Elizabeth, "If you need anything else, I'll be in the kitchen at the back of the hotel until the ball is over."

"Thank you." Elizabeth closed the door of the suite behind her, then she returned to the bedroom and found Grace helping Rose unbutton her dress to change into a nightgown.

It was just Elizabeth and her sisters, alone again. She looked at both of them, feeling, as always, that she had somehow failed. "I had no idea Papa had a partner. It changes all my plans."

Grace glanced up at her but didn't say anything.

Elizabeth took a deep breath and put on a smile for Rose's benefit. "I'll trust God that it will work out just fine. He didn't forsake us in Rockford and He won't forsake us here, either."

"Speak for yourself." Grace pulled Rose's dress off over her head. "The way I look at it, He didn't do us any favors before and He won't do us any favors now. We're no better off than when we were in Rockford—at least there we had friends." She went to Rose's trunk and took out a nightgown, her movements quick and awkward.

It didn't pay to argue with Grace when she was in this frame of mind. The friends Grace had in Rockford had been leading her in a direction Elizabeth didn't want her to go, but Grace did not agree.

Instead of fighting, Elizabeth untied the ribbon under her chin and removed her bonnet with deliberate care. Rose watched her older sisters closely, and though Elizabeth could not control how Grace acted, she could control her own behavior.

Grace slipped Rose's nightgown on over her head and began to unlace her boots. "What will we do?" she asked Elizabeth. "Will we stay?"

"Of course we'll stay." Elizabeth squatted down to help remove Rose's boots. "This is our hotel and I plan to operate it to the best of my ability."

"How?" Grace sat on the bed. "We might own half the business, but no man will allow you to have a say in how he runs his establishment."

Elizabeth took off Rose's stockings and turned down the bedcover. She motioned for Rose to climb in. Thoughts of her old employer, Mr. Brown, filled her with terrible memories. He owned the general store Elizabeth had worked at in Rockford, and he had come to depend on her for all aspects of the store's operation. She had done everything from stocking the merchandise to managing the books, and he had never once given her credit. When someone complimented his store, he'd boasted about his business acumen.

The job had kept her and her sisters fed while Grace had finished school, and she found she had a natural knack for the work, but she had been forced to resist his advances from the first day. It had become harder and more wearisome with each passing month, especially when his wife assumed Elizabeth had been guilty of appalling things at the very end. Each time she said she was leaving, he would increase her pay and treat her better for a time. Truth be told, there were so few jobs available for a woman with her limited education, she couldn't give up the work, no matter how difficult it was.

She had looked forward to doing as she pleased with the hotel business—but now she would be forced to bend to another man's will. Would Mr. Allen be just as horrible to work with?

"There's only one thing to be done," Elizabeth said to Grace with more confidence than she felt. "We will need to raise enough money to buy Mr. Allen's share of the hotel."

Grace stopped working on her boots and looked up at Elizabeth. "Why would we want to do something like that? Why don't we sell our share to Mr. Allen?"

"Mama and Papa spoke of owning a hotel for as long as I can remember, but they never had enough money to pursue the venture," Elizabeth said. "We can't give up on their dream now—especially when Papa wanted it this way."

"Their dream?" Grace asked with sarcasm in her voice. "Or yours?"

"Of course it's their dream. Don't you care about their legacy?"

Grace scoffed. "I don't give a fig about this hotel or Mama and Papa's dreams. Papa abandoned us and I don't owe him a thing."

Elizabeth's chest tightened and she wanted to cover Rose's ears. It had been this way with Grace since their father left. Before Mama died, Grace had always been sweet and kind—a little mischievous, but never mean. The best thing for her would be to find a good husband, and the sooner the better. She needed to be settled in her own home and getting on with her life. She didn't need to be saddled with their father's hotel and a little sister. Those were Elizabeth's responsibilities. She had forfeited her own happily-ever-after when she chose her family over James. What man would want her with all her responsibilities now? Isn't that what James had said? She came with too many problems.

Her sisters deserved better, and she would do whatever she could to ensure their happiness. She would find Grace a good husband as soon as possible and provide for Rose to the best of her ability.

Elizabeth met Grace's gaze and she knew her face revealed the depth of sadness she felt.

For a moment, it looked as if Grace might soften, but then she inhaled a breath and kicked off her second boot. "Do whatever you want. I don't care."

Rose looked up at Elizabeth, searching for reassurance. The unconditional love in her big brown eyes was the reminder Elizabeth needed to keep fighting for Grace, for her parents' dream and for her own future.

Elizabeth winked at Rose and gave her a smile. "It's time to sleep."

"I forgot to say my prayers." Rose climbed out of bed and knelt on the floor. She said her nightly prayers and then got back into bed.

Grace had put on her nightgown and sat beside Rose. "How will we raise enough money to buy Mr. Allen's share? It could be thousands of dollars."

"Maybe we can get a loan from the bank." Elizabeth tucked the covers in around Rose. "Regardless, we'll have to do extra work to pay for it. I'll speak to Mr. Allen about all of that tomorrow. For now, get some sleep and don't worry."

Rose yawned. "I'm thirsty, Lizzie."

Grace lifted the sheet and snuggled into the bed without looking at Elizabeth.

"I'll get you something. But don't leave this room," Elizabeth said to Rose. "Stay here with Grace and I'll come right back with something for you to drink."

Rose nodded, a solemn promise in her trusting eyes.

Elizabeth kissed her forehead and left the bedroom through a door that led directly into the dark hallway. She stood for a moment, wondering where the kitchen might be. Martha had said it was at the back of the hotel.

She walked down the hall to where a swatch of light lit up the stairway at the end. The sound of laughter and music made her feet itch to dance. It had been years since she'd gone to a ball. James had not approved of dancing, and after he left, her name had become sullied by Mrs. Brown's accusations, so no one had extended another invitation.

It would feel good to twist and twirl around a dance floor again, especially if she was in the arms of a competent dancer. For a fleeting moment, she thought of Mr. Allen's strong form and graceful movements and wondered if he was any good at dancing, but the question soon faded when she remembered how much he irritated her.

Hopefully she could sneak in and out of the kitchen without being noticed.

She wasn't in the mood to see him again tonight.

Jude stormed through the dining room and entered the kitchen. The aroma of freshly brewed coffee and warm cinnamon bread wafted up to meet him. But even that didn't improve his mood.

"What am I going to do with them?" he asked Martha as soon as the swinging door closed.

"I don't imagine there's anything you *can* do with them." Martha lifted a steaming pan of bread from the oven. "They're here to stay."

Jude pulled out a stool and took a seat—but he couldn't stay still, so he stood and shoved it back under the worktable. "They can't stay here."

The door opened and Violet entered. Her bright-red hair would make her stand out in a room—but it was the worldly set of her shoulders and the hardened look in her eyes that made people take a second glance. "Is the coffee ready?" she asked.

Martha nodded to the pot on the stove. "Just now. Bring me the empty one from the ballroom when you come back and I'll get more going."

Violet moved to the stove without another word. Though Jude had rescued her six weeks ago and had been nothing but kind, she still didn't meet his gaze. She skirted around him like he might reach out and grab her—but he didn't take it to heart. It was the same with almost all the women he'd liberated these past two years. They knew almost nothing about compassion and decency. For many, their only experience of men was abuse and neglect. He was the first man who'd respected them and treated them with care. It would take her some time to trust him.

Violet left the kitchen with the coffee and the door swung closed again.

"The way I see it," Martha said, setting the loaf of cinnamon bread on the cooling rack near the window, "Clarence's daughters own half this hotel and there's nothing you can do to change that fact. God knows what

He's doing. He doesn't make mistakes. Though we don't understand some of His choices, He's still sovereign and much smarter than the rest of us."

Jude rubbed the back of his neck. He usually appreciated Martha's wisdom and perspective, but at the moment, he'd rather she keep them to herself. "There has to be a way to get rid of them."

"Ack!" Martha clicked her tongue. "Go on with you. Those women are in need of a home and this is all they have. They're not that much different than the women you rescue."

"There's a world of difference between them—besides, this hotel can't support all the women living here!" They could barely support Martha and Violet. "I need to find a way to get them to leave. I'm going to see Roald Hall tomorrow and find out if that letter has any legal value."

"And what if it does?"

He didn't want to contemplate the validity of the letter. How could he hide his rescue work if they ended up staying? Surely, once they met Violet, they'd start asking questions. What would happen when he brought in the next lady? And the next?

Frustration made him pace faster. "I don't know why such pretty women aren't married."

Martha turned away from the window, her hands on her hips. "Did you ever stop to think that maybe they don't want to be married?"

"Well they should—and soon. At least then they might give up on the idea of running a hotel."

Martha took another pan of bread that had been cooling at the window and brought it to the worktable. She turned it onto a cutting board. "You probably won't have to wait long. There's nary a bride in this town that had to wait more than a fortnight to be engaged."

Jude paused, the first glimmer of hope rising. "You're right."

"I usually am."

"If I do a little matchmaking, I could probably have them engaged by the end of this week."

Martha harrumphed. "If they had attended the ball, they would have had at least a dozen proposals tonight."

It was true. So true, in fact, the men in town had placed an advertisement in several papers back East seeking brides. They had claimed there were a hundred eligible bachelors for every single woman. To his knowledge, no one had answered the ad—yet—but it only proved how desperate and lonely the men were in Little Falls.

He simply needed to introduce Elizabeth and Grace to the best husband candidates and they could be out of his way in no time.

"Martha, you're a genius."

The door opened slowly and Elizabeth Bell poked her head through the opening. She paused when she saw Jude.

For the first time since her arrival, he was happy to see her. Maybe he could still get her into that ballroom tonight and start the introductions. He moved forward and opened the door wider. "Come in."

She took a tentative step over the threshold as she looked around the kitchen.

Martha wiped her hands on her apron. "What do you need, lovey? Are you hungry? There's leftover roast beef and fresh cinnamon bread, right out of the oven."

"Could I have a glass of water for Rose, please?"

"Water, you say?" Martha stood on tiptoe to reach one of the glasses. Her short stature was a constant irritant to her, so Jude reached over her head and grabbed a glass for her. "Thank you." She straightened her shirtwaist. "How about some warm milk for the little one?"

"Milk would be even better." Elizabeth's voice hinted her relief. "She's had none since we left Rockford a week ago."

"Then milk it is. I'll grab some in the cellar and be back in a jiffy."

Martha exited the kitchen leaving Jude and Elizabeth alone.

She looked at him for a moment and he studied her, perplexed all over again by how Clarence could have such a beautiful daughter. But, more important, how could he convince her to go into the ballroom with him?

She looked away and played with the frayed cuff at her wrist.

"The ballroom is full tonight," he said. "We have the best orchestra in the territory right here in Little Falls. They'll play until midnight, at least, maybe longer if the dancers insist."

"I imagine it's good for business."

"It is." He smiled, trying to draw upon all the charm he'd mastered as a business owner. "Do you enjoy dancing, Miss Elizabeth?"

She lifted her blue-eyed gaze and blinked. "I do enjoy dancing, Mr. Allen."

Her answer encouraged him. "Would you—?"

"Here we are." Martha returned much sooner than he would have liked—or expected. "I left the milk on the shelf in the lean-to and thought I'd put it in the cellar later. Good thing I didn't." She placed a kettle on the stove. "The milk will be warm in a minute."

"It isn't necessary to heat the milk." Elizabeth took a step toward Martha. "I can take it as it is. Rose won't mind."

"Nonsense. Everyone benefits from warm milk before bed."

"If you enjoy dancing," Jude said, "would you care to join the others in the ballroom?"

Elizabeth stared at him and Martha turned with the milk in one hand and the kettle in the other. "Look at the lady, Jude. She's tuckered out."

Martha wasn't making this easy for him.

"I thought Miss Elizabeth might enjoy a little entertainment after her long journey."

"Even if I would, my ball gown is tucked away in my trunk and in need of some updating." Elizabeth touched her cuff once again. "It's been years since I've gone to a ball."

"All the more reason to go tonight."

"I should be with my sisters."

Martha tossed him a look of disapproval and then went back to the milk.

"They'll soon be asleep." Jude tried again. "You can stay for as little or as long as you'd like."

Elizabeth glanced over her shoulder toward the door that would lead them to the ballroom, and she looked like she might concede—but then she shook her head. "Not tonight. I'll need all the strength and mental clarity I can muster when we meet with the attorney and go over the books tomorrow. I'm sure there will be a hundred things we'll need to discuss about the operation of the hotel."

The thought of talking business with her made him crabby. What did she know of such things? "Fine." He gave her a curt nod. "I'll see you in the morning." He walked past her and out the kitchen door. He might not get her into the ballroom tonight, but he'd be sure to invite every bachelor he knew to come by tomorrow.

He would marry Elizabeth Bell off to the first man who turned her head, and then he'd get on with the work that really mattered.

Chapter Three

Elizabeth looked in the mirror the next morning, well before the sun had crested the horizon. Dark circles hung beneath her eyes and weary lines edged the sides of her mouth. Though she hadn't slept well in weeks, she had tossed and turned all night, trying to think of a way she could earn enough money to buy out Jude Allen.

More than anything, she wanted to be in control—not only of the hotel, but her life. So many decisions had been made for her since Mama had died. It would have been nice to have a say in her future for once. But before she could think of saving money, she needed to know if she had any legal right to the hotel.

Not wanting to wake her sisters, Elizabeth found her father's letter, put it into a pocket in her skirt and left their rooms. Worries about the legality of the letter had plagued her all night long. Surely it was enough to claim her inheritance—it had to be. She had used every penny they'd made on the sale of their things in Rockford to make the trip to Little Falls. There was nothing left to go elsewhere. They'd be destitute.

Casting aside the troubling thoughts, Elizabeth tiptoed down the dimly lit hall, not wanting to disturb their guests. More than two dozen doors spread out on either side of her, and snores could be heard escaping from several rooms.

The hotel was clean and orderly, the furnishings were well cared for and everything about the place spoke of top-quality craftsmanship. How much would it be worth if she wanted to purchase Mr. Allen's share?

Elizabeth descended the front stairs and found a man seated behind the counter, his keen gaze following her every step. As she approached, he stood and nodded a clumsy greeting. He was a tall man—taller than most she'd ever met. His beefy hands and balding head were the first things she noticed about him, but despite his size, a simple kindness emanated from his hazel eyes.

"Good morning, miss." His voice hinted at a lack of education. "Are ya one of them Bell sisters?"

"I am Elizabeth Bell." She extended her hand and watched in amazement as it was swallowed up inside his.

"I'm Pascal Doucette." He pumped her hand up and down.

She pulled her hand away and held it by her side—surprised it had returned to her unharmed from his massive grip. "Are you the night watchman?"

"I am, miss. But I do lots o' other things for Mr. Jude."

"What things do you do?"

"Well, I watch out for the ladies."

Elizabeth frowned. "What ladies?"

"Violet—and the others when they lived here."

"Who is Violet?"

"The lady Mr. Jude brought here." Pascal stood a little straighter, his eyes going round. "Didn't Mr. Jude tell you about them ladies?"

She shook her head. "Will you tell me?"

Pascal took a step back and put up his hands, concern deepening the wrinkles on his high forehead. "There's nothing to tell, miss. Nothing, at all."

What was he talking about? Who was Violet and where had Jude brought her from? "Does Violet work in the hotel?"

Pascal looked all around the lobby, everywhere except at her. He reminded her of a cornered animal and she decided to leave him be for the moment. Soon enough she'd have Mr. Allen answer her questions.

"It was a pleasure to meet you, Mr. Doucette."

"Call me Pascal, same as everyone else."

"All right, Mr. Pascal." She left him and walked down the hall, past the double doors leading into the ballroom, past a few single doors she assumed were sitting rooms and into the large dining room. At least two dozen tables were scattered about, and ferns filled every corner. A bank of windows lined one wall facing the street, with sheer curtains draping from brass rods. White linen cloths covered the tables and a single, unlit candle stood in the center of each.

Elizabeth was surprised to find that she wasn't the first person awake. Already there were three men seated in the room, steaming cups of coffee and large plates of flapjacks before them.

She felt their gazes as she passed through and pushed open the swinging door into the kitchen.

The aroma of coffee filled the room and she inhaled a deep breath. The smell invigorated her and gave her some much-needed energy.

"Morning, lovey. You're up early." Martha stood at the stove turning a flapjack. "Couldn't sleep?"

Another woman sat in the room, polishing silverware, but she paused in her work to stare at Elizabeth. She had bright red hair and brown eyes. At first glance, Elizabeth assumed she was a young woman, but the lines around her hard eyes made her look much older.

Martha glanced at the woman and then wiped her hands on her apron. “Miss Elizabeth, I’d like you to meet Miss Violet.”

“I’m pleased to meet you,” Elizabeth said, offering her hand.

Violet put out her hand and shook Elizabeth’s with a force that surprised her.

So, this was Violet. Something about the woman didn’t settle right in Elizabeth’s mind. “Do you work here?” she asked.

“Yes, miss.”

It was a simple answer and Elizabeth waited for more of a response, but none came. “What do you do?”

Violet continued to polish a spoon. “Whatever needs to be done. Mostly I clean.”

“Don’t let her modesty fool you,” Martha said with a merry laugh. “She’s invaluable to us.”

“How long have you worked here?”

Violet looked to Martha and Martha hurriedly said, “Long enough to know she’s one of the best maids we’ve ever had.”

So far, Elizabeth had counted three employees at the hotel—four, including Mr. Allen. Were there more?

The door swung open and Mr. Allen appeared with a freshly shaved face, the pleasant scent of cologne preceding him into the room.

He scanned the kitchen and his handsome gaze stopped on Elizabeth. “Pascal told me he met you and that you came in this direction." He let the door close behind him. "I see you've also met Violet."

"I have." She took a step closer to him and said quietly. "Are there any more employees I need to know about?"

"Not that I'm aware of."

Martha placed a flapjack on a plate. "Will you have some breakfast before you go see Mr. Hall?"

"Mr. Hall?" Elizabeth asked.

"Roald Hall," Jude supplied as he took the plate from Martha. "My attorney."

Elizabeth touched the letter in her pocket, hoping the law would be on her side.

They ate in the kitchen, and when they were finished, she followed Jude out of the hotel and into the bright sunshine. The morning was cool, though humidity hung in the air and promised to bring more warmth later.

The Northern stood on the northwest corner of what appeared to be a main intersection. Wide streets fanned out in all four directions, the hard-packed dirt filled with deep wagon ruts crisscrossing from one side to the other. Dozens of clapboard buildings, some complete with false fronts and others fashioned in the same Greek Revival style as the Northern, lined every street, with wooden boardwalks connecting them together. It looked like many of the frontier towns they had passed on their way from Illinois to Minnesota—but it boasted something most others lacked: the rushing waters of the Upper Mississippi River.

"Mr. Hall's office is near the ravine." Mr. Allen motioned for her to cross the road.

"Ravine?"

"It's an old river bed running through the eastern edge of town."

They crossed the street, and as soon as they rounded a building on the corner, she was able to glimpse the landmark he'd referenced.

A bridge crossed the ravine, with wooden walkways on stilts extending out from either side to four different stores.

Elizabeth tried to keep up with Jude's long strides, her boot heels clicking on the boardwalk. He was much taller than she and appeared to be just as eager to speak to the attorney.

Before long, Jude stopped in front of an unremarkable building and pushed open the door. He held it for her to enter and she passed by with nary a glance in his direction.

The law office of Roald Hall was not much to speak of. A wide desk, two bookshelves and a few wooden chairs were the only items in the room.

But the man behind the desk lit up the space with a gregarious smile. "Welcome! Come on in." He stood and waved them inside. "To what do I owe the pleasure of this visit?" He looked at Elizabeth, his grin growing wider.

"Roald, I'd like to introduce you to Miss Elizabeth Bell." Jude nodded at Elizabeth. "Miss Elizabeth, this is Mr. Hall—my attorney."

"It's a pleasure to meet you." Elizabeth offered her hand.

"Bell?" Mr. Hall shook her hand and looked from Jude to Elizabeth. "As in Clarence Bell?"

"Clarence was my father," Elizabeth said.

Jude planted his feet and crossed his arms. "I wasn't

aware of it, but apparently Clarence had three daughters, and according to Miss Elizabeth he sent a letter from his deathbed bequeathing his share of the hotel to them."

Mr. Hall rubbed his square jaw, his gaze assessing Elizabeth. "Do you have the letter?"

She dug it out of her pocket and handed it to the attorney, her hands shaking as she clasped them together. Her future depended on that letter. It was the most precious and valuable thing she owned at the moment—yet, was it enough?

Mr. Hall read the letter, nodding now and again as he perused its contents. Finally, he lowered the paper and looked at Elizabeth. "I don't see why this letter wouldn't hold up in a court of law."

She wanted to collapse in relief.

"However, you'll have to gather several other documents to prove you are Clarence's heir. You'll need your birth certificate and his death certificate for starters. You'll also need to find documents with his handwriting to prove he wrote this letter." He handed it back to Elizabeth, his face grim. "It could take months, or even up to a year to gather everything you need and present it to a judge."

"A—a year?"

"Not to mention a great deal of money for legal fees."

She didn't have a penny to her name. How would she pay for legal fees?

"And," Mr. Hall continued, "until then, Mr. Allen isn't required to house you and your sisters. You'll need to find somewhere to live."

Elizabeth sank into a chair nearby and tried not to let panic overwhelm her. She'd been in a similar situation right after her father had left, before she found work with

Mr. Brown. She had been so desperate to keep her sisters alive and there hadn't been any work to speak of, she'd almost sacrificed her virtue. Would she be required to make that choice again?

Jude watched Elizabeth collapse into the chair, her shoulders rolling forward in defeat. She hadn't received the news she'd hoped for—yet neither had he. It was clear these were Clarence's daughters and they had nowhere else to go. He wouldn't sit back and let the worst happen to them, no matter what it might cost his business. What kind of a man would he be? Especially when he spent his life protecting defenseless women just like her.

The Bell sisters weren't all that different from the others, after all. They were victims of their circumstances and forced to make the best of their lives. Some women went into prostitution to provide for themselves and their families—but Elizabeth had been able to avoid that trap. She was clutching her father's letter as if it was a lifeline, and in many ways, it was.

"I have a proposition, Elizabeth."

She glanced up, yet didn't really look at him.

"I have no doubt Clarence wrote that letter," Jude said, "and regardless if it's binding or not, I'd like to propose a solution."

"What?" Her gaze finally focused on his face, though mistrust lay deep in her eyes.

Roald also looked at Jude, though with more calculation than Elizabeth.

"Shall we take a walk and discuss the terms of the agreement?" Jude asked her.

"W-What kind of an agreement?" She stood slowly and looked at him like he was about to propose a tryst.

"It's a proper agreement," he said quickly. "I'll not ask anything immoral of you."

Her cheeks filled with color and he looked away from her. If only she knew who she was talking to.

Elizabeth offered her hand to Roald. "It was nice to meet you."

Roald bent over her hand in a great show of aplomb. "The pleasure was all mine. I do hope we meet again soon."

Could Roald be the one who would capture Elizabeth's attention? It wouldn't be a bad match. Roald was loud and boisterous, but he made a decent living and was a good man. Yet he didn't seem right for Elizabeth. She was almost regal in her bearing and she deserved someone who would complement her graciousness and not draw all the attention, as Roald was wont to do.

Jude opened the door and waited until Elizabeth passed.

"Sorry for troubling you," he said to Roald.

Roald's eyes were on Elizabeth. "No trouble at all."

Jude joined Elizabeth on the boardwalk. She watched him warily and he wondered if she had trusted any man since her father left her.

"What is your proposition, Mr. Allen?"

The street bustled with people and several men stop to stare at Elizabeth. "Would you like to take a walk as we discuss my idea?"

She nodded and he led her up Broadway, past the Northern and toward the river.

"I am sorry about your loss," he began. "And I'm sorry that your father left the way he did. I wish he would have told me about you and let me know he was offering his share of the hotel to you, but he didn't and I've made plans and adjustments accordingly."

She was silent as she walked beside him. He wished he knew what she was thinking.

"So I have a proposition. I will allow you and your sisters to continue living at the Northern, if you work for your room and board—"

"My father didn't intend for us to simply work there," she said with frustration in her voice. "He intended for us to be owners."

"You didn't let me finish." He tipped his hat at an acquaintance, but didn't stop to chat, though the young man looked like he wanted an introduction. "This town is rough—too rough for a sensible woman. I don't know what your father was thinking when he wrote that letter. The frontier is no place for an unmarried lady to make her way."

Elizabeth stopped and put her hands on her hips. "Are you saying I'm too weak to endure the frontier?"

He also stopped. "It's nothing personal. Most women would struggle."

"I'm not most women."

"Maybe not, but you'll be hard-pressed to make it through the year. After winter sets in you'll be stuck—if you make it that long. So here's my proposition. If you can make it until January, I will put you and your sisters on the deed. If, before that time, you decide life in Little Falls isn't what you had hoped, I will pay for you and your sisters to go back to Rockford. I don't have enough to buy your share of the hotel, but I have a little saved that could set you up in a comfortable place to live." He hoped it wouldn't come to that. If she and Grace were married before then, he wouldn't have to pay for them to go back. They would all be happy then. Elizabeth and Grace would have homes with husbands to provide for their needs, and he'd have his hotel.

She started walking again, her shoulders stiff. "I think you underestimate me, Mr. Allen."

"Call me Jude."

"I'll make it until winter," she said with certainty, "and beyond. You're stuck with me until I can earn enough money to buy your share of the hotel."

"Buy my share?" He reached out and grabbed her arm to stop her.

She looked down at his hand and up into his eyes, a pretty scowl on her face.

"It's not for sale," he said.

She lifted her chin. "Everything is for sale."

"Not my hotel."

She pulled her arm out of his grasp. "It's my hotel, too—or, at least, it will be when I am still here in January. As soon as I have enough money saved, I intend to buy your share. It might take me a long time, but I have no intentions of going anywhere or doing anything else."

Jude clenched his jaw. "I could make you leave right now, if I wanted."

Her face grew still as she studied him.

"I won't do that," he said a bit more quietly. "I wouldn't turn any woman out on the street, especially Clarence's daughters."

She swallowed and some of her bluster faded. "Thank you for that."

"But I have no interest in having a business partner." Especially a woman. "So my proposition still stands. You and your sisters may stay at the Northern, provided you work for your room and board, and if you make it until January I will put your name on the deed—and no more talk of buying my share." He started walking again. "It's not for sale and it won't be for sale."

She walked beside him, but she didn't say anything until they reached the river and stopped to watch the logs float past. The waterfall was to their left, with the dam, sawmill, gristmill and cabinet shop on the eastern bank. Abram and Charlotte Cooper's home was at the bottom of the hill where their boys were running around in the yard.

Jude turned to face Elizabeth. The sun played with the highlights in her hair and bathed her face. Her blue eyes reflected the water, and the wind toyed with the tendrils of hair playing about her cheeks. He had to steel himself against letting his thoughts wander. She was a beautiful woman, and he couldn't deny he was attracted to her, but he had no unrealistic hopes about winning her affection. She was destined for another man and the sooner the better.

"Are you amenable to my proposition?" he asked.

She finally looked up at him. "It's not what I had hoped when I came to Little Falls, but it's far better than the alternative." She nodded. "I agree."

"Good. Martha can use you and Grace in the kitchen and dining room. You'll also need to help clean."

She stood a bit straighter. "I will gladly help with the cooking and cleaning, but I would also like to look over the books, if I may."

"Are you good with sums?"

"I worked at a general store for the past three and a half years and I was in charge of all the bookwork."

"I will happily hand over the accounting to you."

After Clarence died it had fallen on Jude's shoulders, and he'd be the first to admit he did a poor job.

"Then it's settled. My sisters and I will live and work at the Northern until January when you will add us to the deed. At that time, we will address the terms of our partnership." She held out her hand to shake his.

He took her hand and was surprised at the strength in her grip. She was a confident woman, he'd give her that, and if she had experience in business then she would be an asset. He might be a little more concerned if he wasn't convinced that she and her sister would be married well before January.

The only thing that worried him was keeping his rescue work hidden. He wasn't ashamed of it, but most people didn't understand why he did what he did. If she learned the truth, he'd have to explain to her about his past and that was something that he *was* ashamed of.

He let go of her hand and indicated the road that would take them back to the Northern.

"May I look at the books immediately?" she asked as they walked.

"I give you full permission to do whatever you'd like with them." Toss them in the river, for all he cared. They had been a bane to him this past month.

"And may I make a few suggestions regarding your budget?"

"If you can find a way for us to spend less and make more, then by all means."

They continued on to the Northern, and when they walked inside, Rose jumped off the staircase's bottom step and flew across the lobby into Elizabeth's arms.

"Where have you been, Lizzie? I've been waiting for you all morning."

"Does Grace know you're down here?" Elizabeth asked.

The girl nodded, her eyes solemn, and then the nod turned to a shake of her head. "No."

Elizabeth dropped her forehead to her sister's. "You know you're not supposed to leave Grace's side. She's probably worried."

Rose noticed Jude watching her and she burrowed her head into Elizabeth's chest as she peeked out at him. "Who is he?"

Elizabeth looked up. "This is Mr. Jude. He lives here, too."

"Is he nice?"

Elizabeth studied him. "I don't know—I didn't think so, at first, but then he did something very nice today."

Rose pulled back from Elizabeth's chest and she smiled. "What did you do, Mr. Jude?"

Jude swallowed. He had never spent time in the presence of children before and didn't quite know what to think of this one.

"He gave us a home," Elizabeth said.

"He did?" Rose studied Jude closely, her wide eyes blinking slowly. "Thank you, Mr. Jude."

He had no frame of reference for how to address the child, so he simply nodded. It didn't feel right to accept her appreciation when he would be finding them another home as soon as possible.

Chapter Four

He thinks the frontier is too rough for an unmarried lady. The thought still riled Elizabeth hours after she and Jude walked home from the attorney's office. She pulled a clean apron from her trunk and snapped it with a flick of her wrists to get the wrinkles out. With quick movements, she tied it around her waist and smoothed down the material.

"Too weak, indeed," she muttered to herself and then looked over her shoulder to make sure she hadn't woken Rose, who was taking a nap.

Her ex-fiancé, James, had thought the same. He assumed he was rescuing her from a life of poverty and shame when her father had abandoned them—and she had been so overcome with fear at the time, she almost believed him. But he wanted her without the responsibilities of her two younger sisters. If she had married him, she would have had to leave them. She could never have done that. Not only because she had promised Mama she would take care of them—but because she could never sacrifice her sisters' well-being for the love of a man.

No. She had broken her engagement to James and

faced her fears. In the process, she had realized she was a lot stronger than she—or James—had given her credit for. It hadn't been easy, but she had done it.

And she'd do it again at the Northern Hotel. January would come and go, and she'd still be there, waiting to see her name on that deed.

A quick look in the mirror confirmed that her hair needed to be repinned. She had helped serve lunch and cleaned the dishes afterward in the hot kitchen, while Grace kept an eye on Rose. When all was finished, Rose had been put down for a nap and Grace had gone to clean one of the guest rooms with Violet. Elizabeth had asked Jude for a tour of the property to assess what needed attention so she would have an understanding of how the business worked when she looked over the books. There were always ways to cut spending and generate revenue.

She pulled out all the pins and combed her hair with her fingers, then she twisted the thick mass at the back of her head. With practiced fingers, she replaced all the pins and looked at her work. She shouldn't care so much about her appearance with Jude, but she wanted him to think of her as a smart, competent and organized woman. Maybe, if he recognized her worth, he would put her on the deed sooner than January.

Elizabeth left her bedchamber and walked into the sitting room to get a piece of paper and a pencil out of the secretary to take notes. Jude had removed his journal and pulled papers out of the drawers the night they had arrived, but perhaps there were still a few supplies left for her. She opened the first drawer, but found it empty. The second and third were also empty. If she didn't find something, she could always ask if he had paper at the front desk.

Elizabeth opened the last drawer and paused when she glimpsed an envelope crushed into the back. She pulled it out, thinking it could be salvaged for her notes. There was no name or return address on the envelope. She smoothed it down, opened the flap and pulled out a letter. The slanted handwriting was not her father's, but maybe it was Jude's. She quickly scanned the simple contents.

Take the young woman tonight. Proceed with caution and all haste.

It took a moment before the weight of the message hit her. Who would write such a sinister note? And more importantly, who had received it? Was it a joke to frighten her? Jude had said she couldn't survive the frontier—was this his way of making a point? But how could he have placed the letter in the secretary without coming into the room? He wouldn't have done that without her permission.

Would he?

That left her to assume the correspondence was legitimate. But what did it mean? Was someone stolen? Was Jude involved?

The wall clock chimed the hour. She needed to meet Jude in the lobby, but questions continued to fill her mind with horrible assumptions.

Elizabeth put the letter back in the envelope and slipped it into the pocket of her apron. She didn't want to leave it out for her sisters to find—yet what would happen if she showed it to Jude and demanded answers? He would probably deny all knowledge of the note, or make an excuse to pacify her.

On second thought, she went back to her room and placed the letter in the bottom of her trunk, under her personal items. She'd do some investigating of her own before she approached him. She could always talk to Martha and Violet and ask if they knew of any suspicious behavior. If something didn't seem right, she'd take the letter to the authorities.

Elizabeth scurried out of her room, raced down the hall and descended the stairs. Jude stood in the lobby, speaking with a customer. The other man shook Jude's hand and left the building.

When Elizabeth stopped at the bottom of the steps, out of breath, Jude turned, his eyebrow raised. "Do you always make such a dramatic entrance?"

She forced a smile and tried not to look wary. "Not always."

"Shall we get started on the tour?"

"May I have a piece of paper and a pencil to take notes?"

He nodded and went behind the counter to grab her requested items. "Are you always so thorough?"

She took the paper and pencil. "Always."

He smiled and walked her down the long hall to the right of the main stairway. "We have one of the finest ballrooms west of the Mississippi River," he began without small talk and pushed open the wide double doors.

They entered the echoing hall and Elizabeth took in a surprised breath.

Beautiful parquet floors gleamed from the sunshine streaming in through the tall windows. Large mirrors reflected the creamy yellow paint on the walls and three chandeliers hung suspended from the high ceiling overhead. A raised platform stood at one end, where the orchestra probably sat during the balls.

"It's amazing," Elizabeth said.

"I like to hold a ball each month. It's good for business and morale. We'll also be hosting the Fourth of July Ball."

"Do you charge an admission fee?"

"No."

She scribbled a note on her paper.

"What?" he asked.

"We could bring in revenue if we charged a small fee."

He frowned, clearly not convinced. "The balls always fill up the guest rooms."

"Which is good," she said. "But not good enough. Do you charge for refreshments?"

"Of course not."

She scribbled another note. "We'll have to change that, too."

Jude put his hand on the paper and she looked up. "I won't let you come in here and change everything, especially since the Fourth of July Ball is less than a week away."

"You said I was in charge of the books and I could do anything that would bring in revenue." She pulled the paper out of his grasp. "We shook on it."

"Within reason."

"This is within reason."

He stared at her for a moment and then said, "We can talk about it after the Fourth of July Ball." He led her out of the ballroom and down the hall toward the kitchen.

As she made notes about the peeling wallpaper and the cracked glass in the back door, she couldn't stop thinking about the letter tucked inside her trunk. What did she really know about Mr. Allen? Her father must have trusted him...shouldn't that be good enough for her?

"How did you and my father come to be partners?"

He showed her the back staircase that led to the upper rooms. "I met Clarence when he first came to town working for the Little Falls Company as a carpenter. The company was started by Abram Cooper and two other men to establish Little Falls. They construct buildings, build roads, operate the mills and sell property. I owned the American Hotel—what's now the Batters House—and Clarence lived there. He told me he had always wanted to go into the hotel business, so when I sold the American to buy the Northern, I asked if he was interested in becoming partners."

"How long were you partners?"

"Two years." He climbed to the top of the back stairs and stood to the side to let her pass in front of him into the hallway near her bedroom. "Your father was a good man and I was sad to see him go."

She bit her bottom lip as she listened to him speak. He seemed truly genuine. If her father had been in business with him for two years, and still felt it safe enough to send for her and her sisters, shouldn't that be enough for her to trust Jude? It would have to be. She couldn't walk around suspicious of his every move.

"We have twenty-four guest rooms in all," Jude said as he opened the one across the hall from hers. It was currently unoccupied. "There is a bed, a bureau and a rocking chair in each room." He closed the door and stepped across the hall to open another. A set of stairs led up to the third floor. "It's a large, single room under the rafters. Martha and Violet sleep there. If you'd like to see it, you can ask Martha to show you."

Elizabeth wrote more notes. The guest room drapes needed to be cleaned and the quilt on the bed needed to be patched. She looked up and found Jude trying to see what she wrote. She tilted the list up. “Where does Pascal sleep?”

“In the barn loft. He takes the overnight shift at the front desk, so he sleeps during the day.” Jude took the back stairs down to the main level. “I’ll show you the barn. We have one of the best in town. Some of the local men rent space from us to house their animals. For a small fee, Pascal feeds them and mucks out the stalls.” Jude pushed open the back door. “We also own twenty-five acres of cornfields, so I keep our tools and equipment in the barn, as well.”

She paused. “Cornfields?”

“On the outskirts of town.” He held the door open for her. “There are several business owners in town who have wheat and cornfields to earn a little extra income and provide for the community. It brings in much-needed money to pay for a couple months of mortgage over the winter when business is slow.”

She scribbled notes as fast as she could and then stepped into the shadowed alley between the hotel and barn. “You reap and sow the fields yourself?”

“With help from Pascal—yes.” Jude closed the back door and started toward the barn. It was covered in the same white clapboard siding as the hotel.

A tall man passed on Broadway and paused. He waved hello to Jude and entered the alley at a leisurely pace.

Jude turned to Elizabeth. “I’d like to introduce you to a friend.”

Elizabeth had met so many men at lunch, she was sure this one would be yet another she’d soon forget, but they were all potential customers, so she acquiesced. "All right."

The man approached, and the first things Elizabeth noted were his kind eyes and his handsome smile. She found herself offering him a genuine smile in return.

"Miss Elizabeth Bell, this is my good friend Reverend Ben Lahaye."

"Reverend?" Elizabeth looked at Jude. "You attend church?"

"Only on Sundays," Reverend Lahaye said with a grin. "Jude wouldn't miss a chance to hear me preach."

Jude grinned. "If I missed your sermon on Sunday, I wouldn't know what to banter with you about the rest of the week."

Reverend Lahaye took Elizabeth's hand and offered a slight bow. "It's a pleasure to meet you, Miss Bell. I've already heard much about you and your sisters."

"The pleasure is mine, Reverend Lahaye."

He let her hand go. "Call me Ben. I wouldn't know how to answer to Reverend Lahaye." He was an attractive man, with high cheekbones and a wide mouth. If she wasn't mistaken, he looked Métis. She'd read about the people who lived mostly in northern Minnesota and southern Canada. They were descended from French fur-trading fathers and Chippewa mothers. She wouldn't know it by his clothing, which looked much like Jude's, or even his hair, which he cut just below his ears, but in his features she saw Indian ancestry, and his last name indicated he was also French.

"Will you be joining us this evening?" Jude asked his friend.

"If Miss Bell will be here."

Elizabeth looked between the two men. "I don't know where else I'd be."

"Splendid," Ben said. "I hope you'll save a dance for me."

"A dance?" Hadn't there been a ball the night before?

Jude shifted on his feet. "I've invited a few friends to the hotel this evening to welcome you and Grace to Little Falls. I thought you might enjoy a little dancing."

He'd remembered her comments from the night before and planned a dance for her? His thoughtfulness surprised and delighted her—much more than it should—and she offered him a smile. She would enjoy the opportunity to dance again.

She looked at Ben. "I'll save the first dance for you."

It would be too forward to ask Jude for a dance, but maybe she'd get to find out if he was good on his feet, after all.

Jude stood in the lobby after supper, waiting for Elizabeth and Grace to come down the stairs. Rose had been put to sleep and Violet had agreed to stay in their sitting room for the evening to keep an ear on her. Pascal would watch the front desk and Martha would keep the coffee and refreshments going—though after Elizabeth's comments earlier in the day, he wondered if she'd approve.

The doors opened and a group of Jude's acquaintances entered. "Where are the *mesdemoiselles* you told us about?" Pierre LaForce's French accent punctuated each word. "I have come to sweep them off their feet."

"They'll be down shortly," Jude said. "Make your way to the ballroom."

The men moved on and Jude paced across the lobby. He had invited about fifty men in hopes that several of them would catch the eye of each Bell sister. No doubt word had spread and others would come, but he couldn't control the numbers. Single women were so scarce in the territory, they might attract dozens more.

Another group entered and Jude sent them on to the ballroom.

Jude looked at the wall clock and paced across the lobby. If the Bell sisters didn't come soon, the men would get anxious and Jude would have trouble on his hands.

Finally, two sets of feminine boots appeared at the top of the stairs under two brightly colored hems. For some reason, Jude's heart rate picked up speed as they made their way down the steps.

Elizabeth and Grace had gone up to change as soon as supper was over, but now they descended and Jude couldn't take his eyes off Elizabeth. She was the prettiest woman he'd ever met. Yet, it was more than her looks that attracted him. Her eyes were filled with intelligence and she had a drive and a determination that he admired. She carried herself with a graceful mixture of confidence and humility. She wore a blue gown, tight at her slender waist and belled down to the floor. Her dark-brown hair was done up in ringlets with a blue ribbon woven through the curls. Delicate earrings dangled from her earlobes and matched her necklace.

Her sapphire eyes caught the light and sparkled when she looked his way. Color filled her cheeks—but was it from excitement or was she embarrassed to catch him admiring her?

The innocence of the thought warmed him and made him smile. He'd spent most of his life around women who no longer blushed at being noticed by a man. It was refreshing to be near one who wore innocence and purity like a garment.

The door opened again and another group of men entered.

Elizabeth and Grace looked their way.

Catcalls and whistles pierced the air, and while Elizabeth's blush deepened, Grace seemed to thrive on the attention.

"Gentlemen," Jude said above the noise. "I'll kindly ask you to be respectful or you'll have to leave the hotel."

"I'm not leaving until I get a dance," said Alec O'Conner.

"Then I'd advise you all to keep your remarks to yourself and head into the ballroom." Jude leveled him with a serious gaze. "Or you'll be on your way out."

The men grumbled their agreement and walked toward the ballroom.

"How many friends did you invite?" Elizabeth asked Jude.

"A few dozen or so." He offered his arm to her. "Shall we?"

She gingerly wrapped her hand around his arm and he tried not to notice how good she smelled.

"I don't know about you," Grace said as she smoothed the front of her green gown, "but I'm beyond excited to dance again."

Elizabeth wiggled her fingers just enough for Jude to notice. "Me, too."

He hadn't kept track of how many men had entered the hotel—and he was surprised to find at least eighty standing before them when they entered the ballroom.

Already, the fiddle and mouth organ were being put

to use, but no one was dancing. How could they? There were no other women in the room.

Another catcall filled the ballroom, followed by whistles and shouts of approval.

Elizabeth tensed at his side and her hand gripped his arm tighter. “This is what you call a few friends?”

He grinned. “I have more.”

She glanced up at him and smiled at his joke.

“Gentlemen,” Jude called, putting up his free hand.

The room quieted as eager eyes roamed the women from head to toe.

“I would like to present to you Clarence Bell’s daughters, Miss Elizabeth and Miss Grace.” Jude indicated each woman. “They have just arrived in Little Falls and will be living and working here at the hotel. They are here to enjoy an evening of visiting and dancing. As you can see, there are only two ladies and far too many men—”

“I’ll say,” said a man in the back and the group broke out in laughter.

“So you won’t all get a chance to dance,” Jude continued. “Be gentlemen and don’t forget your manners.”

Jude nodded toward the stage and met the fiddler’s gaze.

The music started up again and the men swarmed around the ladies. Jude extracted his arm from Elizabeth’s grip and took a step away.

Her gaze found his and he smiled, satisfied that his job was done for the moment. “Have fun.”

“Where is Reverend Lahaye?” she asked over the din.

It pleased Jude to know she had remembered Ben. Of all the men Jude knew, Ben was the most worthy of her attention. Jude looked around the room and spotted Ben near the mirror, not pushing or demanding attention.

Just like Ben.

For once, he'd like his friend to be a little more aggressive. Maybe he'd have a wife by now if he was.

"He's over there," Jude said to Elizabeth.

"What?" Elizabeth mouthed—it was too loud for him to hear the word.

Without thinking, Jude took her hand and began to tug her out of the crowd.

She maneuvered through the throng. Her hand was warm beneath her glove. When they were beyond the thick of it, she stood close and smiled up at him. "What did you say?"

Jude was so taken with her smile, he couldn't think for a moment. "I don't remember."

Her smile slowly faded as she became serious. "I asked if Reverend Lahaye is here."

"Oh." Jude pulled his gaze from hers and pointed across the room. "He's being inconspicuous by the mirrors."

At that moment Ben noticed them and left his sanctuary.

"Where are the women?" Elizabeth asked as they waited for Ben.

He hadn't even thought to invite other women. His only concern had been to get the single men in the door.

"There you are," Jude said to Ben. "Elizabeth has been looking for you."

She pulled away from Jude's hand and shook Ben's.

Jude's skin was hot where she had touched him—but it cooled considerably as she gave her full attention to his friend.

"I've been looking forward to our dance," she said warmly.

Ben grinned down at her. "I hope I'm not too rusty."

They moved away without another word to Jude, their heads bent toward each other as they laughed and took their place on the dance floor.

Jude was soon joined by dozens of men who were forced to watch the ladies waltz with other partners. The dance floor cleared off and the music began in earnest, but Jude's temporary victory over Elizabeth and Ben diminished when he spotted Grace and her dance partner.

Hugh Jones, one of the most notorious desperadoes in Little Falls, held Grace as if he already had claimed her—and perhaps he had. Several break-ins and fights had been attributed to his gang, but the citizens were helpless to stop them—just as the other men were helpless to stop him from dancing with Grace now.

Sheriff Pugh was rumored to be one of the desperadoes and he didn't bother to enforce the law. Judge Barnum tried to hold them accountable, but without the support of the sheriff, it was pointless.

The gang members rarely showed their faces in the Northern, but they were frequent customers at Dew's place, a brothel and saloon south of town, near the river.

Why had Hugh come? Was it simple curiosity to meet the Bell sisters? Or was he looking for trouble?

Hugh's cronies peppered the edge of the dance floor, waiting for their turn to dance with Elizabeth and Grace. They would have to contend with over eighty prospective grooms who stood nearby—not to mention Jude, who suddenly felt a deep responsibility to make sure Clarence's daughters married well.

Chapter Five

Elizabeth rubbed her temples as she squinted at the ledger and put in the appropriate numbers from a receipt. A soft breeze blew in through the open window of her sitting room and ruffled the green pages of the book.

She had wanted to work on the books yesterday, but getting ready for the dance had prevented her from finding the time. Now, hours after they had come home from church and finished the lunch dishes, she was in her room working to balance their accounts and fix all the errors Jude had made in the past month. She didn't like to work on Sundays, but she was eager to get a better understanding of the business.

Memories of the previous evening made her smile when she recalled all the fun she'd had dancing. Ben had proven to be an entertaining partner and she'd enjoyed their one dance, but the others had been just as eager to please her.

Jude had stood on the outer circle of the dance floor all evening and watched. Not once had he approached her to dance and it had disappointed her more than it should. The one sour note in her evening had been the inordinate amount of time Grace had spent with a gentleman named Hugh Jones. He had monopolized her time and Grace had allowed it.

The clock chimed three times. She should go down and help Martha with supper preparations, but for some reason spending time in the ledger, adding and subtracting from the figures her father had entered, made her feel close to him. It had been years since she'd felt any sort of bond to the man who had walked out of their lives and left her to pick up the pieces.

She looked back at the last column she'd added and paused when a strange noise filled the air from outside. It sounded like a drum—yet it was playing a beat she'd never heard before.

Elizabeth stood and walked to the window that looked out over the tops of the buildings all around her. The Northern stood higher and prouder than most. Her mother would have loved this hotel. It was exactly what she and Papa had dreamed of owning.

The sound grew louder and soon a chant rose above the drum—yet she couldn't see anything from her position at the back of the hotel.

"Lizzie!" Rose ran into the room from the hallway. She had been spending the afternoon with Martha, who had invited her to go on a walk. "Come quick! Mr. Jude said I must ask you if I may watch the war dance."

"War dance?" Elizabeth's chest tightened at the ominous name. "What are you talking about?"

Rose ran across the room and took Elizabeth's hand, pulling until they were standing in the hallway. "It's right outside our front door!" Rose squealed in delight.

"There's a war dance in front of the hotel?" Concern

filled Elizabeth as she raced down the hall with Rose close behind. "Where is Mr. Jude?"

"He's in the lobby waiting for me."

They came to the stairs and descended to the lobby, where a crowd of guests had gathered at the windows. Jude stood among them, his gaze directed outside.

Elizabeth lifted Rose and pushed through the crowd. "Pardon me."

A young man moved aside just as Jude turned toward her.

"Is it all right if I go outside now?" Rose asked.

"No, you may not go outside." Elizabeth held her sister tight and addressed Jude. "What's happening?"

"There's no need to worry. It's just a war dance."

"No need to worry!" Her voice was louder than she intended and she glanced around her to find several people looking in her direction. She spoke quieter. "A war dance?"

"It's not really a war dance. They've already been to war and now they're celebrating." He stepped aside and motioned out the window. "The Chippewa are not here to hurt us. Have a look."

Elizabeth walked to the window and looked outside. Directly in front of the Northern a large circle of Indians danced to the rhythm of a drum. A man sat on the ground with a drum positioned in front of him and he beat it with a stick. In the center of the circle, three young women held long poles with hoops at the end. These poles were beautifully ornamented with ribbons and bells and scraps of red cloth. In the outer circle, at least a dozen men and women danced in single file, crouching low and then jerking upright, lifting one foot and then the other. They stepped out on their toes and then came down on their heels in a movement that looked awkward, yet mesmerizingly beautiful at the same time. Their leggings and tunics had tassels and other colorful ornaments dangling from them.

"They wear bells on their clothing, so it makes noises when they dance." Jude spoke from right behind her. "It really is perfectly safe."

Someone opened the door and a few people left the lobby to stand on the porch.

"Would you like to go out and see it closer?" he asked.

She put her hand to her throat and shook her head. "No, thank you."

The noise grew more intense and another peek outside revealed that more Indians had joined the dance and now several townspeople had come out to watch.

Sunshine beat down and the dancers began to glisten with sweat. More than one warrior was among them. Their feathers bounced in their hair and their loincloths rippled around their waists. They looked fierce. If this was a celebration, why did no one look happy?

Some had hatchets hanging from ropes at their waists and more than one wore a rifle slung over his back.

Rose wiggled out of Elizabeth's arms and tugged on her skirt. "Let's go out and see, Lizzie."

"No." Elizabeth shook her head. "I don't want you out there."

"Are you afraid?" Jude asked.

Everything inside her demanded that she run back to her room, lock her doors and cover her ears until the sound went away. But then she remembered his earlier implication that she was too weak to withstand life on the frontier. This was part of that life. She couldn't show fear now. If she did, she'd just prove him right—and she couldn't do that.

She straightened her back. "I'm not afraid."

Rose's face perked up. "Then we can go?"

Elizabeth glanced outside and saw numerous children in attendance. "I suppose."

Jude looked surprised for a moment, but then he opened the front door wider. "After you."

Elizabeth took Rose's hand and walked through the door with her chin held high, though her knees were shaking beneath her gown.

He watched her closely, the planes of his handsome face quirking into a half smile—something she chose to ignore.

Instead, she skirted past him on the porch and forced herself to watch the dancers.

After he closed the door and joined her, she asked, "What are they celebrating?"

"Victory over their enemy, the Dakota."

"Why do they celebrate here, and not in their own village?"

"Little Falls sits in a contested zone between the Chippewa and Dakota. They celebrate here to claim the territory—and, I suspect, to keep us aware of their presence. Do you see the young ladies in the center?"

She nodded. The women were beautiful with their dark hair flowing freely to their waists.

"Each hoop they carry represents the death of an enemy warrior. In this case, there were three Dakota who were killed in their recent raid."

A shudder ran the length of Elizabeth's spine.

Rose strained to leave her side, but Elizabeth held her sister's hand tight. "It's time to go inside, Rose."

Jude turned with her. “I didn’t mean to upset you.”

She shook her head, her whole body ill. How could they celebrate killing?

He took a step closer. “Are you all right?”

No, she wasn’t all right. She was terribly frightened. Why had she thought this place was the answer to all her prayers? Things had been so much safer in Rockford. Never once had she seen an Indian victory dance. Here, Jude and everyone else acted as if it was a common occurrence.

She glanced into his face and saw his concern. He truly thought she was too weak for life in Little Falls—and he should know. What other atrocities would she face?

But what were her choices? She had to succeed here, because she and her sisters had nothing in Rockford to return to. She would have to pull herself together. A strong woman wouldn’t behave like this. “I’m fine.” She straightened her shoulders and forced herself to look back at the dancers.

“Are you sure? You don’t have to watch.”

Rose moved her head this way and that to get a better view of the dancers, so Elizabeth picked her up to see over everyone’s heads. “Yes, I’m sure.”

He nodded, but didn’t move away from her. After a few moments, he spoke. “Despite how this looks, they are friendly.”

She didn’t respond. How could she? She had little comprehension of Indian life.

“Their enemies are the Dakota in southern Minnesota, not us,” he continued. “They fight back and forth. The deaths they’re celebrating are the restitution they’ve gained for the death of three of their warriors from a few weeks ago." He put his hand on the small of her back. "I really am sorry I frightened you. Would you like to go back inside?"

His touch surprised her—not only because he reached out to comfort her, but because it was so tender.

His brown eyes were full of compassion, and a strange feeling stirred within her. "It wasn't your fault—and I really am all right."

He dropped his hand back to his side and cleared his throat. "The last time they danced—"

The dancers stopped hopping and jumping, and threw up their arms. With a wild cry, they gave three of four whoops, placing their hands over their mouths and taking them away quickly.

Elizabeth grabbed Rose by the shoulders and was about to race into the hotel when they returned to the normal rhythm and continued shaking and moving in the circle.

The longer they stood there, the harder it was to watch the Indians dance—especially when Elizabeth allowed her eyes to wander to the women holding the poles in the center of the circle. "It's time to go back inside, Rose. I need to help Martha with supper."

Rose's bottom lip protruded, but she didn't put up a fight. They went back inside the hotel, Elizabeth's whole body shaking with the pulse of the drum. She doubted she'd be able to sleep peacefully tonight.

She looked over her shoulder and found Jude watching them. He offered a reassuring smile and then pulled the door closed, staying outside to watch.

They had only known each other for two days, but already she sensed in him a kindness that was hard to come by in a world that had treated her poorly. The letter she'd hidden in the bottom of her trunk still troubled her, but there had to be a good explanation. Surely she had read more into it than was intended.

At least that's what she continued to tell herself.

Nearly everyone had come out to watch the Indians dance, as they usually did. Jude stood by and watched for a few more minutes, speaking to friends and neighbors. Several Chippewa who lived and worked in Little Falls were participating in the celebration.

The traditions of the Chippewa never failed to amaze Jude, even if he didn't fully understand them. They had taken the lives of three Dakota warriors because they were avenging the blood of their fallen men—but it meant the Dakota would now seek revenge for the three who had died this very day.

He felt bad that Elizabeth had been so shaken by the dancers—and that he'd been the one to explain the reason for the celebration. He had touched her back in a spontaneous gesture to comfort her, yet the contact had made him all too conscious of how she affected him. Even now, his hand still tingled and he had to rub it to ease the sensation.

The night before, as he'd stood in the ballroom and watched her dance, he'd enjoyed himself far too much. Hopefully one of the gentlemen had made an impression on her. No doubt several would be coming by to court her and Grace. He expected a full dining room for all three meals until both were married.

He sighed and looked back at the dancers. He should go inside and fix the hinge on the kitchen door that Martha had been bugging him about for almost a week—

yet he needed some space from Elizabeth until he could clear his head.

Jude walked east on Broadway. The streets were quiet, with everyone watching the dance. Many of the storekeepers had even closed their shops to go and observe the scene. Even though there had been other dances like it, they never failed to amaze the citizens of Little Falls.

Movement down an alley caught Jude's attention.

A group of four men entered the back door of Harper's Emporium; one of them cast a glance over his shoulder to the opposite end of the alley.

Jude pressed against the side of a building, hoping he had not been seen.

It was hard to make out the faces of the men, but he had a feeling he knew who they were. No doubt Hugh and his men were using the distraction of the Indian dance to loot the store.

Anger seethed inside Jude's chest. Roger Harper was a good man who worked hard. Something like this could close his store and force him to file for bankruptcy. It was hard enough to keep a store open with the economy as tight as it had been for the past two years.

Jude wasn't armed, but he couldn't stand back and let this happen to another business owner in Little Falls—especially in broad daylight. He refused to let fear stop him from doing what was right.

He approached slowly, not wanting to startle the men, knowing they probably had weapons.

One of the men exited the store with a bag over his shoulder.

"What's going on?" Jude asked.

The man jumped and pulled his pistol from his holster. "What do you want?"

Jude put up his hands to let him know he wasn't armed. "I'd like to know what you're doing."

Hugh stepped out of the store next, his fingers hovering over his pistol. "It's none of your business, Allen."

Jude slowly lowered his arms. "Maybe it's not, but Roger Harper is a friend."

Hugh stared at Jude for a minute and then motioned his head toward the other man. "Mick, go inside and clear everyone out. We're done for now."

Mick put his pistol back into the holster and disappeared inside.

Hugh took a step toward Jude. "I don't know what you think you saw, but I'd advise you to keep it to yourself."

"I know exactly what I saw."

"Do you?" Hugh was so close, his stale breath filled Jude's nostrils. "I've seen a few things myself."

Jude frowned as the other three men filed out the back door of Harper's Emporium. Each man carried a sack slung over his back. One or two cast a glance at Jude as they walked calmly down the alley toward their waiting horses.

"I know a thing or two about your *maids*." Hugh's voice became low and threatening. "And I know a few people who don't like what you're doing. I'd watch your step. All I'd need to do is mention your name to the right people and no one in your hotel would be safe."

Jude tried not to show Hugh how close his words came to their mark. The women under his protection had no one in the world to trust but him. He couldn't put them at risk. "You have no idea what you're talking about."

"Don't I? I'd especially watch out for Jack Dew." Hugh narrowed his eyes. "He suspects what you've been doing and he said he'll kill you if one of his ladies goes missing. No questions asked."

Jude would never admit anything to Hugh—but he couldn't back down now, either.

"Roger Harper doesn't deserve to be robbed. He's a hardworking man with a family to support—"

"My men got families to support, too."

"At least Roger is doing it honestly."

Hugh took a step forward. "You really want to mess with me?"

Jude clenched his jaw, anger and frustration warring within his chest. "Keep your men away from the honest folks and we'll have no trouble."

"Keep your mouth shut and we'll have no trouble—and neither will your prostitutes."

"They're not prostit—"

Hugh turned away and mounted the one remaining horse, drawing it to the side to face Jude. It pranced on anxious feet and Hugh had to hold the reins tight. "Say hello to Grace for me. I look forward to seeing her again real soon." His smile was anything but gentlemanly as he spurred his horse down the alley.

Jude hadn't realized his fists were clenched until they began to ache.

He strode out of the alley and walked back to the Northern. There was little he could do to bring justice to Hugh Jones for what he'd just witnessed. If he told the sheriff, it wouldn't be dealt with, and if he told Roger Harper, the man was liable to take the law into his own hands and get hurt in the process. Whether Jude said something or not, everyone would know who was guilty.

A few guests still stood in the lobby, watching the dancers from a safe distance, so Jude pulled Pascal aside and spoke quietly. "I need you to be extra vigilant. Don't do anything that would make the ladies worry, but keep your eyes and ears open to suspicious activity—all right?"

Pascal nodded. "I'll do everything in my power to keep those ladies safe."

"I know you will." Jude clapped the man on the shoulder and walked down the hallway into the parlor that connected with the ballroom.

He closed the door and crossed the room to where his piano sat, waiting to be played. He lived a simple life with simple pleasures. Every spare penny he earned went into his hotel and mission work. But there was one thing he owned that had cost him a great deal of money.

His piano. The instrument that brought him more joy than almost anything else. He played it almost every night, especially when he was upset. As a boy growing up in a brothel in St. Louis, he hadn't had the luxury of going to school like other children. His mother had been a prostitute and he'd never known his father. The only male figure in his world was the brothel owner, who had been distant.

Jude had dreamed of getting his mother out of the brothel and into a home of her own, promising himself that as soon as he was old enough he would get a good job and provide for her. But she died at the hands of a drunken client when Jude was twelve. With no education and no other family but the women who worked at the brothel, Jude had quickly taught himself how to play the piano so he could stay employed. His piano skills had made him irreplaceable to the owner.

Jude sat on the stool and laid his fingers on the cool

ivories. He wanted to play, but he was afraid he'd disturb everyone, so he just touched the keys.

If he had been a single man with no one to protect or worry about, he would have done all he could to make Hugh pay for his crimes. But he had the safety of everyone in the hotel to consider. Having Clarence's daughters under his care was a little different than the others. Their innocence and faith in him was something he didn't want to lose.

Elizabeth's trust was a gift he wouldn't take lightly, either. After he had offered to let her and her sisters stay, she had looked at him differently, as if he was the first man who had done her a kindness in a long time. When she looked at him he wanted to stand taller, do better and be stronger. He'd never felt that way about anyone in his life. It had always been him against the world and he hadn't worried too much about trying to impress anyone. Now…now he wanted her to think highly of him—and to like him.

Jude pressed down on the piano keys in frustration. He had no business entertaining any thoughts about Elizabeth Bell. She would never approve of his mission work, and besides that, he had nothing to offer except for a hotel that she could rightfully claim a share of, anyway. His last name wasn't even his. It had been the name of the man who owned the livery near the brothel where he had grown up. The man had been kind to Jude once—only once—and it had meant everything to Jude, so he had used the man's last name. If Elizabeth knew the truth about him, she would never look at him the same way again. He was destined to be single for the rest of his life. It was the fate he'd accepted when he answered God's call to rescue prostitutes.

Someone needed to marry Elizabeth, if for no other reason than so Jude could stop thinking about her.

Chapter Six

Five days later, Elizabeth held the thick hotel ledger in her hands as she walked down the hallway to the first room at the top of the main staircase. It had taken her almost a week to go over the accounts in fine detail and come up with a budget that would help them cut costs and earn more income. It had been hard to find the time between cooking, cleaning and entertaining the young men who flocked to the hotel every evening, but she had worked late each night and sneaked in moments throughout the day.

She had finalized the plan that morning, but she'd been putting off a visit with Jude all day, knowing he wouldn't like her suggestions. If the hotel was going to support all of them, there would have to be sacrifices made.

Elizabeth knocked on the door and waited for Jude to answer. She hadn't seen him since breakfast, which was odd because he usually mingled with the guests during mealtimes.

After a moment, he pulled the door open and, for the first time since she'd met him, his appearance wasn't in perfect order. His hair looked as if he'd been running his hands through it, giving him a tousled look, and his cravat was untied. He had taken off his suit coat and rolled his shirtsleeves up his muscular forearms. He looked disheveled and extremely attractive.

She dropped her gaze, hoping her cheeks didn't look as red as they felt.

"Do you need something, Elizabeth?"

She couldn't find her voice, so she extended the ledger and tried to gather her thoughts. "I-I've finished going over the books. Do you have a moment to discuss some things?"

He glanced over his shoulder at the mess on his desk. "I am a little busy right now."

She pulled the ledger back to her chest and finally met his gaze. "When might you have a chance? Tonight?"

"Not tonight. I've invited Ben and Roald for supper. I was hoping you and Grace would join us."

She would enjoy seeing Ben again, and Mr. Hall would be a nice distraction for Grace, who had been preoccupied with less-desirable men this past week. "Tomorrow, then?"

"I don't know when I'll have a free moment. Tomorrow is the Fourth of July and we'll be busy all day. I am planning to leave town directly after church on Sunday."

"You're leaving?"

"The day after tomorrow."

"Are you traveling for business? If you are, I'll need to take account of your expenses and adjust the budget accordingly."

He hesitated and then said, "I'm traveling for personal reasons. I'll use my own money."

"How long will you be away?"

"Hopefully I'll return by the end of this week. If you need anything, Martha and Pascal will be here to help." He paused and looked like he was trying to decide if he should tell her more. "I might be hiring another maid next week."

Another maid? What was he thinking? "The hotel can't afford another maid—besides, that's one thing I wanted to talk to you about. We already have too many employees. I was going to suggest that you let two of them go. Now that Grace and I are here, we can replace the cook and the maid, or even the night watchman."

He frowned. "I won't let anyone go. They're like family to me."

"But they're not family and this is a business. If you want it to succeed, you must cut some costs."

"I won't turn them out. Martha is like a mother to me and Pascal is invaluable for security and all the odd jobs he does about the place—not to mention working in the cornfield."

"What about Violet?"

"I can't fire Violet." He ran his hand through his hair. "I brought her here and it would be disastrous if I let her go now. She might return to her former employer and that wouldn't be good for anyone."

Elizabeth was confused. "Who is her former employer?"

Jude became still and didn't answer Elizabeth for a moment. "It doesn't matter. I'll find Violet another job when she's ready."

What was he hiding from her? "Fine, but the sooner the better. I looked over the ledger from the past two years and the numbers are falling steadily. If things don't turn around soon, I don't know how we'll make the mortgage payments through the winter—even with the income from the corn."

"We'll find a way."

"Only if you listen to me and follow the plan I've created." She hoped he understood how serious she was. "I insist you do not hire another maid. Grace and I are more than enough help."

"I need to return to my correspondence. Is there anything else you need?"

Was his correspondence anything like the letter she'd buried at the bottom of her trunk? She looked over his shoulder and tried to see what he was working on, but it was impossible—especially when he stepped into her line of sight.

"There is one more thing." She pulled a piece of paper out of her apron pocket. "After our tour the other day, I created a list of repairs from the most important down to the least."

He took the paper and glanced at it briefly. "It looks very thorough."

"I've also budgeted for some of the repairs. You'll see a little star by the ones that we can afford to do now. I put dates beside the others when I foresee we'll have enough cash to afford those."

He studied her with fascination. "I'm impressed."

Her cheeks grew warm again and she took a step back. "I'll see you at supper." Before he could say another word, she walked down the hall toward her room.

His door closed a few moments later and she paused in the hall. Why was he acting so strange today? He was clearly distressed. Did it have something to do with his travel plans?

It was time she did a little investigating and spoke to

Martha and Violet about their employer. If he was hiding something from her, maybe they could help shed light on what it might be.

Elizabeth returned the ledger to her room and then walked down the back stairs to go to the kitchen. Martha had asked Rose to help make biscuits for supper, and no doubt Grace and Violet were helping in some way, too.

She passed by the back door and saw Violet sitting on the stoop with her back to the hotel. The young lady had managed to avoid Elizabeth at every turn—but there was nowhere for her to go now.

Elizabeth pushed open the screen door. It squeaked on its hinges, causing Violet to look up from her work. She sat with a large bowl of peas in her lap.

"May I join you?" Elizabeth asked.

Violet shrugged.

Elizabeth sat on the wooden step beside her. "May I help with the peas?"

"Suit yourself." Violet's speech was much like Pascal's, uneducated and filled with a strange lilt Elizabeth didn't recognize.

Elizabeth took a handful of the crisp pods and put them on the apron covering her lap. "I've always loved shelling peas. It's such a mundane job, but it's so relaxing."

"It's a job, same as the others," Violet said in an even tone.

Elizabeth popped open a pod and reached over the bowl to scrape the little green peas out. "Do you enjoy working at the Northern?"

Violet readjusted the bowl on her lap. "It's just fine."

"Have you worked in many hotels before?"

Her hands stilled over the bowl. "No."

"Where did you work before here?"

The peapod she'd been shelling was still in her hand and Violet didn't move. "Lots of places."

Elizabeth shelled a few peas, trying to think of a different approach. "My parents always wanted to own a hotel, but I dare say I don't know much about running this kind of business. I appreciate Jude's experience, though I know very little about him and the work he did before starting the hotel." She paused. "How did you come to work for Mr. Allen?"

This time Violet gripped the bowl and stood. Peas rolled over the lip of the bowl and bounced down the stairs. "I'll see if Martha needs my help."

"You sit yourself down." Martha stood just inside the screen door. "I don't need help and you don't need to be running off."

Violet obeyed Martha's orders and resumed her spot on the steps.

Martha opened the door and took a seat between them. There was just enough room for all three.

The older lady grabbed a handful of pods and placed them on her own lap.

"Now," Martha said. "What would you like to know, lovey? I'm sure you're full of lots of questions about the hotel and the people who work here." She chuckled. "I imagine you'd like to know more about Jude, too."

The way she said the last sentence made heat rise in Elizabeth's cheeks. "I'd like to know about all of you."

"All right, then." Martha worked with expert fingers, popping the pods open, running her thumbnail down the inside and dumping the peas into her apron. Her bun drooped and her clothes were a bit rumpled, but she was a kindhearted woman. "First, I'll tell you a little about me. I was raised in Rhode Island, in a large family. I married young and moved west with my husband, Ernest. We went to St. Louis and started a restaurant and hotel, much like this one. We couldn't have babies of our own, so I took in whatever stragglers I came across and over the years I ended up raising a passel of kids in one way or another."

She opened a pod with much more care as she continued. "My Ernest died suddenly. The doctor said it was his heart. So I was left alone in the world. All the little ones I'd raised had gone off on their own. Some still wrote or checked in, but most got on with their lives." She ran her thumb along the pod and tossed it away. "I was lonely and had no interest in running the hotel by myself, so I sold it and started to look for a way to be useful." She laughed, but it wasn't a humorous sound; rather, it was full of pain. She looked at Elizabeth. "When you ask God to show you the hungry, the hurting and the oppressed, He does, with startling clarity."

Elizabeth looked down at her paltry pile of peas. She was humbled by this woman and what she had asked God to do with her life. All of Elizabeth's own dreams and goals seemed to pale in comparison.

"After some time, I found Jude's establishment. He was in need of a cook, so I went to work for him."

"In St. Louis?" Elizabeth asked.

"Yes."

"So he'd been in the hotel business in St. Louis, too?"

"I'll let Jude tell you about himself when he's ready," Martha said. "I could never do his story justice."

What did that mean? Elizabeth frowned as she studied Martha. Though she was being open and honest, Elizabeth still felt she was hiding something.

"When Jude decided to come to Minnesota Territory and open a hotel, I came with him." Martha smiled and patted Violet on the knee. "Jude heard Violet was in need of a job, so she came to us about six weeks ago. She's quick and smart, and has been an asset to the hotel."

Violet didn't look up. "Martha's been teaching me my letters and numbers."

"You've caught on faster than most." Martha was quiet for a moment and then she said, "Violet, could you run inside and start the coffee? It's Friday night, so we'll probably need more than usual."

Violet didn't hesitate, but handed the bowl of peas to Martha and went back into the hotel.

Martha waited for the sound of Violet's steps to disappear, then she looked at Elizabeth. "Violet has withstood much pain in her life and Jude brought her here to learn some skills to make a better way for herself. Not only is she learning to read and write and do her sums, she's also learning how to cook and sew. It's our hope that she'll find a good job or maybe a good husband."

Elizabeth had more questions now than ever before. "Have there been others?"

Martha's smile held joy, but also grief. "There have been others—but not nearly as many as we want to help."

"Where do you find them? How did you start—?"

"I simply asked God to show me where I could be the most useful and He led me to Jude's door. The rest is Jude's tale to tell."

Elizabeth's respect for Jude continued to grow, and his desire to help was honorable, but they were running a business and they couldn't afford to take on more employees—no matter how desperate those women were.

* * *

Jude paced in his small room at the top of the stairs as the scents from supper wafted up to meet him. His stomach growled, but he had no interest in eating. If he hadn't invited Ben and Roald to supper, he wouldn't even bother going down.

Both ends of his cravat lay untied over his shoulders and he tugged on them as he walked over to the small desk to look at the note one more time.

Sally. Reed's. Duluth.

A woman named Sally was in need of rescuing at Reed's brothel in Duluth. Jude had been there twice before to investigate and let the women know there was help if they needed it. Not all the women accepted or trusted him. They had been enslaved in their trade for so long, they didn't believe there was hope—or they simply didn't feel worthy of his help.

But now a woman named Sally was reaching out. Jude's informants were all over the territory. Some were women he had already helped to escape, some were the husbands of rescued women and others were people like Ben who cared deeply about helping those in need. There was no way of knowing who had sent this particular message, but that was part of their plan for anonymity. He didn't want anyone hurt or placed in danger helping him.

He'd already told Elizabeth he was leaving. Now all he needed was to figure out where to take Sally. It would be too hard to explain Sally's presence at the hotel so soon after Elizabeth told him they needed to let the others go.

A knock at his door was soon followed by Martha's voice. "Jude?"

Jude opened the door, a little surprised to find her there. She rarely came to his room unless it was an emergency. "What's wrong?"

"Nothing too serious." She glanced down the hall and lowered her voice. "Elizabeth was asking Violet questions today."

His senses became alert. "What did Violet say?"

"Nothing, but that was the problem. She was skittish, so I answered Elizabeth as best as I could without divulging too much information. I told her we bring women here to teach them and help them find other positions. I didn't tell her where they came from, though." She leaned in. "She asked me about you."

Jude gripped the doorknob, more concerned about Elizabeth's response than he should be. "What did you say?"

"I said you'd tell her in your own time."

Jude turned away from Martha and ran his hand through his hair. "That probably made her more curious than ever."

Martha smiled. "Don't worry, lovey. I could see her admiration for you had grown considerably after she learned what you're doing for Violet."

Jude stopped pacing. Her admiration had grown? Just as soon as the hope emerged, it dwindled. What would happen when she learned the truth, that he was a prostitute's son and that he'd owned a brothel before coming to Little Falls?

"I know you're going to Duluth in a couple of days. If you need to bring the lady back here, it will be a little easier to explain to Elizabeth now."

It might be a little easier, but it still wouldn't be easy,

especially because he'd put her in charge of the finances. "Thank you."

"I'll see you at supper." Martha left the room and closed the door.

His mind wandered back to his previous conversation with Elizabeth. He should have taken the time to meet with her and go over the books. He could have justified his need to bring on another maid.

The other slip of paper he'd received that day caught his eye: Elizabeth's repairs list. Many of the things she'd listed were things he'd overlooked, which told him she was perceptive and detailed. It wouldn't take her long to put all the pieces together and start asking the right questions.

Could he marry her off before that happened?

The ticking clock brought him out of his thoughts and he faced his reflection in the mirror. Ben and Roald would soon arrive and he'd need to play host.

He tied his cravat with nimble fingers and combed back his hair. Not for the first time, he wondered if he resembled his father. The man he never knew.

The vivid memories of his mother had faded long ago and all that remained were shadowed recollections. He did recall her sky blue eyes and her blond hair, though. He imagined she'd been lovely when she was young, but age and melancholy had dimmed her beauty. She had died before he could ask her how she'd ended up in such a horrible profession, but after hearing the sad stories of so many others, he'd decided he'd rather not know.

Looking at his dark hair and eyes, he assumed he resembled his father, but would he recognize him if he saw him on the street? And if he did, could he look him in the eyes, knowing he was the kind of man Jude was trying to protect other women from now?

What was his name? Was he married? Did Jude have brothers and sisters? Was he even alive?

The questions had taunted him for years, but he shoved them back where they had come from. He'd learned long ago not to dwell on questions he could never answer.

Jude finished dressing and left his room. He walked down the steps to the front lobby, where Ben and Roald were already waiting. His two friends stood near the sofa talking in serious tones, no doubt about the latest break-in that had happened at the livery.

Jude approached and heard Roald's comments. "I don't know how much longer I'll be able to keep my door open. I can't afford to live on my paltry income, especially if I want to take on a wife."

"Why do you think your business is struggling?" Ben asked.

"No one is spending money right now. My biggest client is the Little Falls Company and they're not doing well, either."

Ben noticed Jude's arrival and his smile turned to a look of concern. Could he tell Jude was troubled this evening? "Looks like you've got a few burdens tonight, as well," Ben said.

"Nothing that won't resolve itself in time." He shook Ben's hand and then Roald's. "For now, let's forget our troubles and enjoy a nice meal with friends."

"Sounds good to me," Roald said, rubbing his hands together. "Will Miss Grace be joining us?"

"I believe both Grace and Elizabeth will once they've served the other guests. Violet will manage after that."

Ben stood a little taller and adjusted his cravat.

Jude led them to the dining room, where Elizabeth, Grace and Violet were serving their patrons. The room was full with single men, all of them vying for a little attention from the ladies. Jude had reserved a table in the corner, near the windows, away from the kitchen.

"Have a seat," he told Ben and Roald. "I'll see if they need some help." He was walking toward Elizabeth when Hugh Jones entered the dining room.

Hugh glanced around the lobby and laid his eyes on Jude. "I'm here for Grace."

Grace must have noticed his arrival, too, because she left the table she was serving and walked over to Hugh. "Welcome back."

Hugh's self-satisfied smile landed on Grace. "Hello, sweetheart."

Elizabeth paused in her work, her concerned gaze flickering between Jude and Hugh.

Hugh leaned closer to Grace. "Would you like to dine with me this evening?"

Grace didn't hesitate. "I'd love to."

"Grace." Elizabeth maneuvered around the tables separating them and stood next to her sister. "We've already agreed to have supper with Mr. Allen and his guests."

"I didn't agree to anything."

Elizabeth's cheeks filled with color. *"Grace."*

"There's a table right over here." Grace led Hugh to a table with two empty seats. "I'll get a couple plates of food for us."

Elizabeth stood in stunned silence.

"Why don't you go sit with Ben and Roald?" Jude asked her. "I'll see if Martha and Violet need more help."

"We're almost finished serving," Elizabeth said quietly, looking down at her hands.

"Good." He looked around the room. "Where is Rose?"

"She's in the kitchen with Martha."

"Do you think she'd like to join us for supper?"

Elizabeth looked up at Jude. "Do you think Ben and Mr. Hall would mind?"

Jude shook his head. "Not at all." He nodded toward their table. "Go have a seat."

Elizabeth walked toward Ben and Roald, and Ben pulled out a chair for her.

Thankfully they were gentlemen and wouldn't make a scene about Grace.

Jude strode over to the kitchen door and pushed through, needing to talk some sense into Clarence's second daughter. If her father had known who Grace would be cavorting with, he would never have invited her to Little Falls.

"Grace." Her name came out much rougher than he intended.

She jumped and spun around from the worktable, where she'd been filling two plates with roasted chicken and mashed potatoes.

"Do you realize what kind of a man Hugh Jones is?"

Grace turned back to the food. "He's charming, fun to be with and he doesn't care what others think of him."

"Apparently not. He's responsible for break-ins, gambling and—" He couldn't tell her he was a frequent visitor at Dew's place.

Grace continued to fill the plates, but didn't say anything in response to Jude's accusations.

Martha worked at the stove, but he knew she was keeping an ear on their conversation.

Violet stacked four plates onto her right arm and lifted another with her left hand. She exited the kitchen without a glance behind her.

Jude had forgotten about Rose. She sat on the floor in the corner of the kitchen with some of Martha's pots and pans. She looked as though she had been pretending to make supper—but her large brown eyes were now focused on Jude and Grace. Concern lined her face and Jude felt responsible. He shouldn't have talked so freely about Hugh in front of the child.

He squatted before her and smiled. "Rose, would you like to join Elizabeth and me for supper?"

"She's fine to eat in here with me," Martha said. "I was just about to dish her up a plate."

"Where would you like to eat?" Jude asked her.

Rose looked from Grace to Martha to Jude. "With Lizzie."

"That's a good choice." Martha winked at Rose. "I'll make up some plates."

Grace took the two she had filled and walked out of the kitchen.

Rose's gaze followed Grace, her usual smile nowhere to be found.

Jude tried to coax a smiled out of her, but it didn't work. She stood to watch Martha.

"And what's the matter with you, lamb?" Martha asked Rose. "Don't you like chicken and mashed potatoes?"

Rose nodded, her eyes solemn.

"Then maybe you don't want to dine with Mr. Jude, is that it?"

Jude stood and the child looked at him, but she didn't respond.

"Then it's Grace you're worried about."

"Yes."

"You don't need to worry about Grace," Jude said.

"Is Mr. Hugh bad?"

"He's hurting, is all." Martha placed a piece of chicken on each plate. "He doesn't know how to deal with his pain, so it turns to anger sometimes."

"Will he get angry at Grace?"

Jude hoped he wouldn't.

"Mr. Jude and Mr. Pascal will keep her safe." Martha scooped potatoes onto the plates. "Won't you, Jude?"

Rose turned her trusting eyes to Jude. "Will you keep Grace safe?"

Jude had rescued many women and he'd done a great deal to keep them safe—but he'd never felt more obligated than he did now. The weight of the request, from such a small child, was heavier than any other. "I will do all I can to keep her safe." He couldn't resist. He reached out and tweaked her nose. "I'll keep you safe, too."

A smile finally warmed her face, causing her eyes to sparkle. "What about Lizzie?"

"I'll keep Lizzie safe, as well."

"Thank you, Mr. Jude."

"Go on with you now." Martha laughed. "Bring these plates to our guests before they get cold."

"May I help?" Rose asked.

Jude handed her a plate. It looked much too large for her, but she pinched her tongue between her lips and concentrated as she walked across the kitchen.

Jude picked up the other four and pushed the swinging door open to let her pass into the dining room.

Elizabeth sat at the table with Ben and Roald. She looked beautiful with the candlelight sending shadows dancing over her face. A radiant smile tilted her lips as she devoted her attention to Ben. It was clear they enjoyed each other and the knowledge was bittersweet for Jude.

"What do we have here?" Roald asked when he caught sight of Rose.

"A little waitress in training," Ben said with a laugh.

Rose placed the plate on the table in front of Elizabeth and grinned. "I helped."

"I see that. Good job, Rose." Elizabeth looked up at Jude, her smile now glowing for him.

He had promised Rose he'd protect her and her sisters, but who would protect him from his growing attraction to Elizabeth?

Chapter Seven

It had been hours since supper had ended, yet Grace was still entertaining Mr. Jones in the dining room.

Elizabeth paced in the lobby, her feet growing tired and her head pounding. If the man was any sort of gentleman, he would not monopolize Grace's attention.

Pascal sat at his usual place behind the front counter and Jude had long since disappeared on some sort of errand. Roald and Ben had said good-night and Rose had been put to bed.

The front door opened and Jude appeared. He looked surprised to see her in the lobby. "I thought you'd be asleep by now."

"Grace is still in the dining room with Mr. Jones."

Jude glanced down the hall and his jaw tightened. It was clear he did not approve, either.

"What do you know of this man?" she asked. "If he has honorable intentions toward Grace, I need to know. If he doesn't—I need to know that, too."

Jude took off his hat and hung it on a coat-tree near the front door. He approached Elizabeth and put his hand on the small of her back, leading her into the sitting room across from the front desk. It was a fancy parlor, with a large fireplace, a woven rug and two divans covered in dark brocade. Sheer curtains, like those in the dining room, hung on brass rods.

Elizabeth tried to be patient as she waited for Jude to speak. She had been sure they were leaving Grace's unsavory friends behind in Rockford. She hadn't even considered the fact that her sister would find more in Little Falls.

"Unfortunately, I do know a lot about Mr. Jones," Jude said in a low voice. "And none of it is good. Frankly, I'm surprised he'd show his face here at all."

It was just as she had suspected and feared. "Can you ask him to leave? I need to talk sense into Grace. Tell her to stay away from him." Yet, would it matter? She hadn't taken Elizabeth's advice in Rockford.

"I will ask him to leave—but I don't believe this is the last we'll see of him."

Elizabeth closed her eyes briefly. She'd been so preoccupied with the hotel this past week, she hadn't made any progress in finding her sister a husband. They had met more men than she could count, but she hadn't been paying close enough attention to know if they were worth pursuing.

Ben and Mr. Hall were good men. Tonight, she would sit down and make a list of all their obvious strengths and weaknesses and then compare them to Grace's to see if they would be compatible. She'd also go through the list of men they'd met so far and see which ones would be good candidates for Grace. She had a distinct disadvantage, since she was new to town. It would be so much easier if she had someone who knew the men already.

Maybe Jude would help—but how did she go about

asking? In all truth, she hardly knew Jude, yet what little she did know suggested that she could trust him. "I have a favor to ask."

"Of course."

"This may seem untoward, but I would like help finding Grace a husband." Embarrassment clouded her vision for a moment and she had to look away. What kind of woman asked a man to help her find a husband for her sister? But Grace's future depended on her success. "I fear Grace will make a horrible mistake if left to her own devices. I need to help her, and soon."

"I'll do what I can."

"We need someone with the right type of personality to attract her."

"I have a few men in mind."

"Are they good men?"

He smiled and his eyes softened at her request. "The very best. Leave it to me. I'll help you find someone for your sister."

She bit her bottom lip, afraid she might cry. This was the first time since her father left that she'd felt she had an ally against the world. "Thank you."

"Maybe you should wait to thank me until after I find someone."

"I trust you will. And Grace will thank you, one day." She was sad to think of Grace leaving to start a life of her own, but it was for the best. "She needs to get on with her life."

He studied her for a moment. "What about you?" he asked softly.

She looked down and played with the cuff of her sleeve, a nervous habit she'd had since she was a child. "What about me?"

"Do you want to get on with your life, too?"

"I am getting on with my life. That's why I'm here."

"That's not what I meant. Don't you have dreams of marriage and your own family someday?"

His question made her throat feel tight and her lungs too small to take a deep breath. She hardly knew him, yet he was asking such a personal question. But it wasn't his question that troubled her as much as the answer her heart wanted to give. Yes, she'd dreamed of having a husband and children one day…but all of that had changed when her mother died and her father left. Who would want her and Rose now? James hadn't. She was better off staying single and working hard to one day buy Jude's portion of the hotel. It was the only way to have control of her future.

"I gave up on that dream years ago. I'm choosing to focus on Rose and my work here."

"Is that really what you want? When you look back at your life, will you be satisfied with your decision?"

Elizabeth lifted her chin. "I don't see how it's any of your concern. I hardly know you."

He stood so close she could smell the cologne he wore. It was filled with masculine scents that made her senses swirl.

"Maybe it's not my concern," he said slowly. "But I somehow feel responsible for you and your sisters, since your father called you here."

Responsible? She had been the only one responsible for so long, she wasn't sure if she liked having someone else feel responsible for her.

"Thank you for your concern." She moved away from him. "But all I want to do is focus on my sisters right now." Her nerves were so tightly wound, she was afraid she might say or do something she'd regret. "I'll go check on Grace now."

"I'll come with you and ask Hugh to leave."

"Thank you." She left the room and he followed.

They entered the dining room and found it almost empty. Only a handful of men sat at a table near the kitchen door playing a game of cards. Violet filled their coffee mugs, but as soon as Elizabeth and Jude entered, she retreated to the kitchen.

Grace sat with Mr. Jones at the same table they'd been occupying all evening. Their heads were tilted together and Grace was laughing at something Hugh must have said. He watched her with undisclosed hunger.

The look made Elizabeth's skin crawl.

Jude didn't pause, but went right to their table.

Hugh slowly stood and Grace's back stiffened.

"Grace," Elizabeth said. "It's time to say good-night."

"I'll say good-night when I'm ready."

"You're ready now. Jude is going to close the dining room for the night."

Hugh winked at Grace. "That's my cue to leave, sweetheart." He put his hat on and gave her another heated look. "I'll be back."

On his way out the door, he cast a hard look in Jude's direction.

The other men left the dining room, as well, and Elizabeth offered polite smiles until all were gone.

Grace turned on her then. "I've never been more humiliated in my life, Elizabeth. Really. You and Jude are not my parents."

"If you'd stop acting like a child, I wouldn't have to parent you," Elizabeth countered.

Grace narrowed her eyes. "I will see who I want, when I want."

"Mr. Jones is not a good man." Elizabeth lowered her voice and looked around the room. Jude stood nearby, watching. She sensed he would come to her defense if she needed him. The thought gave her more courage. "The man is dangerous, Grace. You're best to forget about him now and find someone else—"

Grace didn't wait for her to continue, but turned and left the dining room.

Elizabeth had no energy left to fight her sister. They were back where they had been in Rockford.

Jude came to her side. "What can I do to help?"

"Just find her a good husband—and tell Mr. Jones not to come back." It was the only thing that would save Grace.

As soon as Elizabeth went upstairs, Jude strode to the lobby and grabbed his hat.

"Are you going out again, Mr. Jude?" Pascal looked up from a drawing he'd been working on.

"I am." He went over to the counter and lowered his voice. "I'm going to Dew's place. I need to speak to Hugh Jones before I leave for Duluth and I have a feeling he's down there. If I don't come back in an hour, you know where to look for me."

Pascal nodded, used to such instructions from Jude.

Jude left the front of the hotel and stepped into the darkness of night. The streets were empty and the moon shone bright, casting shadows against the sides of buildings, creating eerie shapes and distorting objects. He wore his pistol this evening, knowing it would be foolish to go without protection. Thanks to Sheriff Pugh, the town was lawless. It was every man for himself and Jude took that responsibility seriously.

He went around to the barn and saddled Lady with the aid of a lantern. He put out the light and led Lady from the barn, wanting to be done with his task.

Dew's place was south of town on the banks of the river, not far off the Wood's Trail. The road ran from Pembina to St. Paul and it was the same route the stagecoach took. It was the only road leading into Little Falls from the north or the south. Jude took it now, riding past the church and graveyard, past Abram's home and sawmill, and headed out of town.

Lady's steady gallop brought him to Dew's place in short order. There were six or seven horses tethered to the rails outside. Jude recognized some of them and easily identified Hugh's mount.

The place served as both a saloon and brothel. Jude hated setting foot inside, but there was no way to avoid it if he wanted to confront Hugh.

Jude pushed open the door and entered the dingy interior. The building had been constructed so quickly and so poorly, it looked like it might fall down under a strong wind. Large cracks let in the moonshine from outside and he imagined it didn't provide much protection during the frigid winters.

A few men glanced up when he entered, but most kept their faces lowered, no doubt afraid of who might enter and recognize them. Jude was known as one of the upstanding citizens in town, but that didn't mean much to brothel owners. Some of their best clients were upstanding citizens. He should know. When he was barely twenty, he'd purchased the brothel where he'd lived his whole life. At the time, he'd done it because the women who worked there were the only family he had and he believed he was protecting them. But eventually, after Martha had taught him the truth, he was disgusted at the life he'd led.

It had appalled him who came into the brothel week after week. Some were family men, community leaders and the like. Men who appeared pious and devout on Sunday, walked about town with their wives on their arms on Saturday afternoons after darkening the brothel doorstep on Friday evenings.

Forgive them, Father, for they know not what they do. It was his constant prayer when he walked into a brothel. It was the only thing he could concentrate on when he witnessed the atrocities they brought upon the women and their families. He hadn't known any better until Martha entered his life—at least, he hadn't been taught better. All he'd ever known was brothel life—yet, some of these men had an advantage over Jude. They had been raised by godly women who had taught them right from wrong. Still, it was not his place to judge, but to pray that their eyes would open to their depravity.

Jack Dew watched Jude closely, his beefy hands wiping down a glass with a dirty cloth. He didn't blame the man for being suspicious. Jude had made his stance clear on the brothel—yet experience told him that a man who condemned a brothel publicly might support it privately. No doubt Dew was wondering if Jude was that kind of man.

"Are you looking for someone?" The scar on Dew's face puckered when he scowled at Jude.

Jude scanned the interior and his eyes met the steely gaze of the man he'd come looking for. "I found him."

Jude walked across the small room to the table where Hugh sat with his cronies.

He watched Jude closely, contempt wedged into the lines of his brow.

Two interior doors led out of the main room. One opened and a man Jude knew from town stumbled out, clearly drunk. His clothes were disheveled and his gait was awkward. He didn't look right or left as he pushed his way out of the building.

The door began to close, but just before it did, Jude caught the gaze of a young woman. Her brown hair was in a mass of curls around her shoulders. She was prettier than most he saw in brothels, and if his instincts were correct, she was new to her trade. She lacked the troubled look of a woman buried beneath years of pain and suffering. In her eyes he saw fear and shame, but it wouldn't be long until she hardened against every last remnant of self-respect and hope. If only he could get to her before it was too late.

She closed the door and Jude focused again on Hugh.

"Are you here to start something, Allen?" Hugh took a long drink of the amber liquid in his foggy cup.

"I'm here to end something." Jude didn't bother to sit. He wouldn't be there long. "I want you to stay away from Grace Bell."

Hugh's eyes were already lazy from the alcohol. "Who are you, her father?"

"I'm as close to a father as she has. Clarence Bell entrusted his daughters to my care, so I'm here on their behalf." It wasn't quite true, but Hugh didn't need to know the details of their arrangement.

Hugh snorted and suddenly he looked a lot more sober than he had a moment before. "I thought I already dealt with you." He stood and came face-to-face with Jude, his breath reeking of whiskey. "I'll see anyone I please."

"You're not welcome in my hotel." Jude didn't back down. "If you enter again, I'll have Pascal throw you and your friends out. I thought I'd save you the embarrassment of Grace watching that happen."

Hugh looked Jude up and down, a sneer on his lips. "That won't stop me from finding a way to see her."

Maybe it wouldn't, but at least it would allow Grace some time to get to know the other men who came to the Northern.

"You've been warned." Jude turned away, but Hugh snaked out his hand and grabbed Jude's arm.

"Now let me warn you." Hugh flexed the muscles of his jaw. "Watch your back, Allen."

Hugh's cronies laughed and Jude gritted his teeth. He knew there would be repercussions, but he had to take a stand.

Jude yanked his arm free and walked up to the counter.

"I'd like some time with the new girl." Jude indicated the door he'd watched the man exit a moment ago.

Dew looked him over with mistrust, but then he nodded. "It'll be a dollar."

"A dollar?" The price was an extravagant amount of money for Dew's place.

"She's new," he said, by way of explanation.

Jude didn't want to garner too much attention, so he slipped the man a dollar and walked to the door.

No one paid much attention, except Hugh, who stared him down with a snarl.

Jude pushed open the door and entered a small room with a single glass window facing the Mississippi River.

The woman stood near the window, looking outside, and didn't bother to turn when he entered the room.

A chair sat in one corner, a bed in another and a bureau in a third. There was nothing warm or welcoming about the room.

The space brought back memories Jude would just as soon forget, so he pushed them aside and decided not to waste any time. He had come into the room for one reason only, to tell this woman there was a way out for her. Paying for her time was the only way to get a chance to speak privately with her—just as it was with all the other women he had visited the past three years.

"Miss?" Jude took a step into the room and closed the door.

She finally turned, but didn't quite look at him. With a shy dip of her shoulder, she started to cross the room toward the bed.

He put out his hand. "Don't."

She stopped and met his gaze, but didn't say anything.

"I'm only here to tell you I can help."

Her brows furrowed. "What are you talking about?"

"I can help you escape here," he spoke quietly. "I've helped other women, all over the territory. I can help you find a better life."

She pulled her wrapper over her shoulder and didn't meet his gaze. "You're not the first man who's made that promise. Almost every man I meet says the same thing—but they usually promise to take me home with them."

"I have no desire to take you home." This conversation was like so many others. "I used to own a brothel, but then I realized I was wrong to profit off the lives of women. Now I own the Northern Hotel and I help women like you escape prostitution. My cook, Martha, teaches them necessary skills and then I help find them jobs far away from where they worked before. I could help you, too."

She frowned, her eyes full of pain. "Who are you and why are you telling me this pack of lies?"

"I'm Jude Allen—and it's not a pack of lies. I've helped ten women in the past three years. If you want out, I can help you, too."

She took a step back, suspicion in her eyes.

"What's your name?" he asked.

For a moment, she looked like she wouldn't say, but then she whispered. "Gretchen."

"If you ever need help, you can get word to me through my friend, Reverend Ben Lahaye. We'll get help here as soon as possible." Ben had given him permission to use his name. Sometimes it was safer than someone coming directly to Jude. "I know you're scared and uncertain, but trust me when I say there's a way out."

She didn't respond but continued to frown, and he sensed she was sorting through all he'd said.

"Good night, Gretchen. Don't forget. Contact Reverend Ben Lahaye if you need help."

He didn't wait for her to speak, but opened the door and left her alone.

More men had come into the saloon and Hugh was now engaged in a game of poker. No one noticed as Jude slipped out the front door and got on his horse.

He hoped Gretchen would heed his advice and reach out for help.

The life she was living was no life at all.

Chapter Eight

The next morning, Elizabeth sat across from Mr. McGovern, one of the local bankers, and waited for his laughter to subside. His office was lavishly decorated in rich walnut and leather. His desk was immense and so was his mustache. It wiggled as he laughed at her.

She'd come to ask if she would qualify for a loan to buy Jude's portion of the Northern Hotel in January, but she'd hardly made her request known when the man started laughing.

He looked at her over the rim of his spectacles and wiped tears from his eyes. "Why did you really come, Miss Bell?"

Elizabeth tried to maintain her dignity. "For the reason I just stated."

His shoulders continued to shake as he shook his head. "Really, Miss Bell." He stood and came around the desk, putting his hand under her elbow to help her stand. "It's been a distinct pleasure to meet you, but I'm not in the business of loaning money to unmarried ladies—especially for business purposes. It's been my experience that women are too fickle to operate a real business." He prodded her toward the door. "Now. Why don't you focus on raising a nice family, instead? You'll offer more to society by bringing up good young men to lead the next generation." He winked at her and gave her a pat on her shoulder. "I do hope we run into each other again soon."

Elizabeth stood speechless. Every muscle in her body was tight with anger. If Jude had come in for a loan would he have been denied?

She didn't bother to thank Mr. McGovern for his time, but walked out of the bank with her head held high. How would she ever raise enough money to buy Jude's half of the hotel…that is, if she could convince him to sell?

It was July Fourth and the streets were filled with people coming into town to enjoy the afternoon festivities. The banks and most of the stores would close at noon to allow everyone to attend the speeches, participate in the contests and visit with their neighbors, far and near. At the Northern, Martha, Violet and Grace were busy preparing food to be served for lunch and supper. Martha had sent Elizabeth to the grocer's to get a few supplies. Elizabeth hadn't intended to go to the bank, but she had walked by and been drawn in on a whim. Frustrated to have wasted her time, she hurried along the boardwalk to get back to the Northern.

The day was hot and humid. Elizabeth fanned herself with her gloved hand, but it offered no relief. Sweat dripped down the nape of her neck and slipped into the crevice of her back. Thankfully Mr. Fadling had offered to have the groceries delivered for her, or she would have had a difficult time hauling them back in the heat.

But it was impossible to let her spirits lag as she witnessed all the festivity on the street. A fenced-off area on Main Street held a dozen squealing piglets, greased down and ready to be chased. Mr. Green stood at the lemonade stand under the awning of his hardware store, squeezing the yellow citrus fruit and laughing loudly at a joke shared by an onlooker.

A podium had been placed on the porch of the Northern Hotel, ready for the round of rousing speeches, sure to excite even the youngest among them. The Ladies' Improvement Society busily set out baked goods to be auctioned off before lunchtime, while Mr. Harper stood at the front door of his emporium handing out firecrackers to a group of children.

Many of the people on the street had been hit hard by the economy and the local trouble with Hugh's gang, but every one of them wore a smile of anticipation. Regardless of their personal plight, their patriotism and fervor were high.

Grace appeared on the boardwalk, pushing her way through the crowd toward Elizabeth.

"I can't find Rose," Grace said when she was close enough to be heard.

Panic raced through Elizabeth and she grabbed Grace's arm. "What do you mean, you can't find her?"

"I've looked in every room and every corner. I even looked in the cellar and the attic. The others are looking for her in the barn and outbuildings."

Elizabeth gripped her skirts and started running toward the hotel. "How did this happen?"

"I was rolling out dough for biscuits and she was right beside me. She said she had to use the privy, so I let her go. When she didn't come back, I went to look for her."

Elizabeth scanned each face as she ran. Rose could

have gone anywhere. The lure of the activities outside the hotel would have been too much for her to resist.

They approached the Northern and Jude rushed out the front door, his gaze scanning the street.

"Have you found her?" Elizabeth asked.

He shook his head. "No. I was just going to the river."

"The river?" Grace's face turned ashen. "Do you think she's drowned?"

"Don't borrow trouble," Elizabeth said. "I'll go with Jude and you keep looking around town."

Grace nodded and didn't look back as she continued up the street toward the school.

Jude came down the steps. "I have a feeling she's down by the log boom."

Elizabeth's chest squeezed tight as she followed his lead. "Why would she go there?"

"Martha said when she took Rose on a walk last week, they saw children playing on the logs and Rose had wanted to join them."

Elizabeth began to pray like she'd never prayed before. She must find Rose and return her safely to the hotel. She'd made a promise to Mama and she wouldn't let her down.

The humidity made it hard to breathe as Jude ran toward the river and the log boom. Elizabeth tried to keep up, but she lagged behind. Jude took her hand and pulled her along, knowing she would want to be by his side if he found Rose.

They turned left on Wood Street and rushed past Abram and Charlotte Cooper's front door. The boom held the yet-to-be-milled logs in the millpond. It attracted the local children, who loved to race across the tightly packed logs, jumping from one to another before the log turned.

It was a dangerous game and had cost a twelve-year-old boy his life last year. Jude prayed Rose wasn't at the river, but a sinking feeling weighed down his heart.

"Rose!" Elizabeth yelled her sister's name as she pointed wildly toward the millpond.

There, on her knees, balancing on a log near the riverbank was Rose. She was the only child in the millpond. All the other children were probably playing on Main Street, waiting for the festivities to begin.

Thankfully, the log looked fairly secure, as it was pressed against the bank, but Rose was moving toward the center of the pond, where the logs were scattered with nothing to keep them stable.

"Jude," Elizabeth pleaded as she tugged on his hand. "Save her!"

Jude let Elizabeth go and ran across the sawmill yard. "Rose!" He called her name, but she didn't seem to hear.

She continued to crawl across the log and he ran faster. If he didn't get to her in time, she could go under and it would be almost impossible to rescue her from beneath all those logs.

His chest felt like it would burst as he ran down the riverbank as fast as he could go.

"Rose!" he said again, and this time she turned, but as she did, she lost her balance and tipped to her side.

Elizabeth ran close beside Jude and he heard her scream her sister's name.

Rose tried to hug the log, but it was easily four feet in diameter. Her legs were in the water as she clawed at the tree bark, screaming and crying for help.

Jude jumped onto the log and rushed across it, balancing to stay on top. "Rose," he said again. "Hold on. I'm almost there."

"Mr. Jude!" Rose cried as her right hand slipped off the log and she batted violently at the water.

The log shifted beneath his feet, almost sending him into the water, but he held on and finally reached her. He grabbed her other hand as it slipped from the log. "Hold on, sweetheart." He tugged at her arm and pulled with all his strength, remembering the promise he had made to keep her safe. The river tried to yank her from his hands, but now that he had her, he would never let go, even if it meant going under with her.

He lifted her into his arms and held her tight. "You're safe, Rose. I have you."

Her cries filled his ears as she clung to him, her clothes dripping water down the front of his.

Elizabeth stood on the riverbank, her hands clasped over her mouth. Tears streamed down her cheeks as she waited for Jude to teeter back across the log.

"She's safe," Jude said breathlessly, as he passed Rose to Elizabeth.

Elizabeth wrapped her arms around Rose and lifted her eyes to the sky. She said "Thank you," over and over, but he couldn't tell if she was thanking him or God.

Jude put his hand on Rose's shoulder. "Let's get her back to the hotel to warm up."

"I don't know what I would have done without you."

He put his other hand on the small of Elizabeth's back and led her up the embankment.

Charlotte Cooper appeared at the door of her house. She rested her hands on her protruding stomach as she watched them cross the yard.

"Bring her into the house," Charlotte called. "We'll dry her things by the stove."

Elizabeth looked at Jude and he nodded. "You'll like Charlotte."

They walked to the Coopers' front door and Charlotte welcomed them in with concern tilting her brow. "What happened?"

"She was missing and we found her playing on the logs," Jude said.

Charlotte shook her head. "Poor dear, she's freezing cold. Bring her into the kitchen. Abram and I were just sitting down to enjoy some coffee with Ben before we head up the hill for the celebration."

They walked across the main room and followed Charlotte through a door and into a hot kitchen. Abram and Ben were seated at the table, coffee mugs in their hands. Abram and Charlotte's young daughter, Patricia, sat in a high chair beside her father, playing with a wooden toy. When Jude and Elizabeth entered, both men rose.

"The little girl was playing in the log boom," Charlotte said to her husband. She turned to Elizabeth. "Bring her near the stove. We'll hang her clothes up to dry." She looked back at her husband. "Abram, will you run and get her one of the boys' nightgowns?"

Abram left the kitchen as Elizabeth knelt before the large potbellied stove and set Rose on her feet. The little girl shook uncontrollably, but whether it was from cold or fear, Jude didn't know. His own hands were still shaking from the whole ordeal.

Ben stood beside Jude and put his hand on Jude's shoulder. "You look like you need a strong cup of coffee."

"I could definitely use one right about now."

Ben went to Charlotte's cupboard and pulled out two mugs. He filled them from the large coffeepot sitting on the table and Jude took it gratefully.

Abram reentered the kitchen a short time later and handed the long nightgown to his wife. On his heels were the Cooper's three sons, Robert, Martin and George. The oldest, Robert, was deaf. Compassion filled his eyes and he signed something to his father.

"She'll be all right," Abram said as he signed back. "But this is a good reminder not to play near the river."

All three boys nodded as they looked at the little blond-haired moppet. The nightgown was huge on her, and Elizabeth had to roll up the sleeves for Rose's hands to poke through.

"Thank you," Elizabeth said to Charlotte as she took Rose in her arms again.

"You're most welcome. I'm Charlotte Cooper and this is my husband, Abram."

"I'm pleased to meet you. My name is Elizabeth Bell and this is Rose."

"Yes, I know." She smiled at Ben. "Our friend here has told us all about you."

Elizabeth's cheeks filled with color and Ben's eyes shone. "To be fair," he said. "I also told them about your sisters, too."

"These are the Coopers' children," Jude said quickly. He nodded at each one. "This is Robert, Martin, George and Patricia."

Charlotte smiled at Jude and rested her hand on her stomach. She didn't mention the unborn child, since women rarely spoke of such things, but the glow in her cheeks was all the mention needed.

"I'm happy to meet all of you." Elizabeth took the mug of coffee she was offered and looked at Jude. "I will need to get word to everyone at the hotel that we found Rose. I'd hate for them to worry longer than necessary."

"I'd be happy to go," Ben offered.

Jude stood. "No, I'll go." He'd rather Ben stay with Elizabeth a bit longer.

"Are you sure?" Ben asked. "You still look a little shook up."

"I'm fine." As Jude started to walk toward the door, Elizabeth reached out and took his hand.

"Thank you," she said.

He paused and squeezed her hand in return. Her touch meant more than her words, but he couldn't find his voice, so he simply nodded.

Rose cuddled next to Elizabeth, but she looked up at him with those big brown eyes and he couldn't stop himself from squatting down to face her.

"Please don't ever go near the river without an adult again," he said. "We were all very frightened."

She shook her head, large tears forming in her eyes. "I won't."

Jude took one of her small hands in his—the one he'd grabbed when he pulled her out of the water—and saw the red marks his grip had left from rescuing her. He gently rubbed them and placed a kiss there. "I'm happy you're safe."

Rose leaned forward and fell into his arms, almost knocking him over. She wrapped herself around Jude and hugged him tight.

For the first time in Jude's adult life, tears stung the backs of his eyes and he had to force them away.

"Thank you, Mr. Jude," she whispered.

He cleared his throat, afraid he might not be able to respond, but he managed a weak "You're welcome."

Rose pulled away and reached for Elizabeth. Jude handed her back and then stood.

Without another word, he left the Coopers' home, afraid his emotions would become too powerful to control in front of his friends.

Jude walked back to the Northern with the heat pounding on his back. He shoved his hands in his pockets, his gaze intent on the dirt road. In all the years he'd faced danger, he'd never been more afraid then when he saw Rose on that log. His heart still hadn't returned to a steady rhythm, and the farther he walked away from the Coopers', the more he wanted to go back and make sure she was truly okay.

He couldn't imagine what would have happened if he had been too late or was unable to pull her out of that water. The very thought made the panic return.

Grace stood on the porch of the Northern and rushed out to meet him. "Is she all right?"

"Yes, she's safe with Elizabeth at a neighbor's home."

Grace closed her eyes briefly, then forced a stoic face. "Good. We can get back to our other work now."

Jude entered the hotel and found Martha in the lobby, her face pale. "Where is the little love?"

"At the Coopers' with Elizabeth. We found her in the millpond and I had to pull her out of the water."

"Thank You, Lord," she prayed. When she finished wiping the tears from her cheeks, she said, "Will you go back to the Coopers'?"

Jude shook his head. "Ben's there. He can bring them home. I have too much to do today." It could be hours before Rose's clothes were dry enough for her to put them back on, and no doubt Charlotte was making Elizabeth feel welcome in her home while Ben charmed her with his easygoing nature.

"Why don't you just go back and get them?" Martha asked. "I can tell you want to."

"It might be hours before they're ready to come. Ben will bring them home."

"Nonsense. I'll run up and get a dry dress for Rose and you can go back and get them now." She started up the stairs.

"What's the point?"

Martha put her hand on the rail and turned to look at him. "You don't fool me, Jude Allen. I can tell you care about Elizabeth and Rose, and you want to see them back here as soon as possible."

"Of course I care about them. I feel responsible since Clarence sent them to me."

"So go and get them."

Jude nodded hello to a patron who came down the stairs and exited through the front door. There was work to be done, but it would wait for him. "Fine, I'll go. But only because you seem just as anxious to get them back as I do."

Martha chuckled. "Go on with you."

Jude waited for her to get one of Rose's dresses and then he left for the Coopers'. The whole way back, he chastised himself for returning. He wanted Ben to have as much time as possible with Elizabeth, didn't he? Ben hadn't been stopping by as much as he could, though he seemed happy to see Elizabeth whenever they were together. He resolved to talk to Ben and encourage him to court Elizabeth as fast as possible.

Jude pushed open the back door into the Coopers'

home and found Ben standing near the stove, pouring coffee into two mugs. No one else was in the kitchen.

Ben smiled. “I didn’t know if you were coming back.”

Jude walked over the threshold.

“Everyone is in the front room,” Ben said. “I came in here to refill Elizabeth’s mug.”

Jude didn’t want to put off what he had come to say. “I’d like you to start courting Elizabeth.”

Ben took longer than necessary to finish what he was doing. He finally looked at Jude. “Now, why would I do that?”

“To get to know her, of course!” Jude glanced at the closed door leading into the front room. He spoke quietly. “I need to find the Bell sisters suitable husbands so I can get on with my mission work. I gave Elizabeth control over the budget and if she discovers what I’m doing with the money, she’ll want me to quit. Elizabeth poses a risk for my future plans.”

Ben stepped away from the stove and held the mugs in his hands. “I agree that Elizabeth poses a risk to your future—but not in the way you think.”

Jude crossed his arms. “What do you mean?”

“I see the way you look at her. I’d be blind not to notice.”

“Don’t be ridiculous.” Anger tightened his chest and he looked away from Ben. “I’m not looking at her any different than anyone else.”

“Are you sure?”

“Of course I’m sure.”

Ben became serious. “Then you’re serious about me courting her? If you’re interested, I won’t—”

"I told you I'm not."

Ben studied him for another moment, and then he nodded. "I'll ask her."

"Fine." Now that he'd accomplished what he'd set out to do, Jude had no desire to continue this conversation. "I'll see if she and Rose are ready to head back to the Northern."

He didn't wait for Ben to respond, but walked around him and into the Coopers' main room.

Elizabeth and Charlotte sat in rockers positioned on either side of the fireplace. Abram sat on a chair nearby, his daughter in his arms, while the boys played jacks in the corner. Jude swallowed the sudden jolt of longing that clogged his throat. He had never experienced a loving home with a mother and a father. And, until this moment, he hadn't allowed himself to think about all he'd missed. He had always believed God had chosen a different path for him and he'd accepted it long ago.

But when Elizabeth looked up at him and Rose saw his return, their smiles tugged at his heart and made him long to be a part of a family for the first time in his life.

"You're back," Elizabeth said with a smile that made his insides ache.

He held up Rose's dress. "I thought you might like to come back sooner than later, so I brought Rose some dry clothes to wear."

"That was thoughtful. Thank you."

Ben entered the room just behind him, and Elizabeth's attention was stolen.

Ben handed her one of the steaming mugs of coffee and took a seat close by. He tickled Rose's bare feet, prompting a charming giggle from the little girl, and asked how they liked Little Falls.

Suddenly, Jude felt like an outsider and he was reminded once again that he didn't belong in a scene like this.

Chapter Nine

The heat continued to rise and the humidity intensified, but it didn't dim the enthusiasm of the patriotic revelers on Main Street. Jude walked beside Elizabeth and Rose, enjoying the excited shouts of children setting off firecrackers, the squeals of greased pigs as they evaded capture, and the laughter of friends and neighbors visiting over glasses of lemonade.

"Can I have some lemonade?" Rose asked Elizabeth.

"May I," said Elizabeth. "And no, you may not. We need to get back to help Martha as soon as possible."

Rose's bottom lip stuck out, but she didn't ask again and her attention was soon distracted by the squealing pigs.

Jude glanced toward the west. The heat shimmered off the dirt street in waves. If he wasn't mistaken, they were in for severe weather. Something needed to break the heat and humidity.

Elizabeth's gaze followed his. "Will the weather hinder anyone's plans?"

"Depends on what happens." If it started to storm, they would have a packed house, as people would need a place to get out of the rain. Hopefully it would rain before evening, so the ballroom wouldn't be suffocating with the heat and the humidity during the dance.

"Will people—?" Elizabeth paused midsentence as she stared across the street.

Rose glanced up at Elizabeth, who stopped walking and turned Rose to look the opposite way.

Jack Dew strolled down Main Street with two women on his arms. One looked quite pleased to be with Jack as she strutted along, enjoying the attention—but the other, the one named Gretchen whom Jude had met the night before, didn't make eye contact with anyone. She was thin and pale, and looked as if she had not slept or eaten well in months.

"What?" Rose asked, but Elizabeth kept her turned away as Jack paraded by.

If he had any question regarding how Elizabeth felt about prostitutes, he didn't now. He saw no compassion or understanding in her gaze. Only condemnation and contempt.

More than one mother did exactly what Elizabeth was doing and turned her children away. He didn't blame them. They had probably never spoken to a prostitute and asked how she had fallen into her profession. Most people believed it was a choice, yet so many women he spoke to had had no choice at all. Some were sold into prostitution, some were desperate to stay alive and others thought so little of themselves, they didn't know any other way.

Rose fussed and tried to turn, but Elizabeth held her tight. "Not yet. They'll be gone in a moment."

Gretchen looked up and her gaze fell on Elizabeth, and then on the other mothers, and her face became more ashen than before. Shame and embarrassment bent her shoulders. As she dropped her gaze, she noticed Jude. Recognition dawned in her eyes and for a heartbeat hope sprang forth. She paused and looked like she might approach him, but Jack yanked her to follow and she went along, the hope vanishing as they rounded the corner and disappeared from sight.

Elizabeth looked to Jude, questions in her eyes. "Do you know that young woman?"

Did he know her? Not really. But he couldn't lie, either. "I've seen her before."

"May I look now, Lizzie?" Rose asked.

Elizabeth let go of Rose's shoulders and the girl spun around, her eyes searching the street to see what she had missed.

"Who were those people?" Elizabeth asked.

"Jack Dew runs an establishment south of town." He glanced around to see who might be listening, but everyone was speaking in hushed tones.

"But why did they come downtown?" she whispered.

Jude hated to admit what Jack was doing, especially because he had been guilty of doing the same thing on more than one occasion in St. Louis. "He knew there would be a large crowd out today, so he was…advertising the women."

Elizabeth's eyebrows came together. "Truly?"

Guilt rose up in Jude's chest, but he pushed it down again. He knew he was forgiven, yet he hated the reminder of his former sins—especially when Elizabeth frowned with such disdain.

"Who was it?" Rose asked.

Elizabeth shook her head and prodded Rose to start walking again. "It was no one important."

He knew what she meant, yet he couldn't shake the feeling that if Elizabeth knew about his past, she'd say the same thing about him.

They walked back to the Northern. Several county commissioners and territorial legislators had gathered on the porch as they prepared to give their speeches. Jude greeted all of them and then he went into the hotel with Elizabeth and Rose.

"Mercy, but you gave us a scare," Martha said the moment she saw Rose in the kitchen.

Elizabeth took off her bonnet and hung it on the hook near the door. "She'll never do it again. Will you, Rose?"

Rose shook her head with wholehearted conviction.

Jude prayed she would stay in the hotel, just as she promised. He was afraid his heart couldn't handle another scare like today's.

The humidity was still holding that evening when Elizabeth looked at her reflection in her bedroom mirror. She wore her old ball gown, which she had altered as best as she could to look modern and stylish. It had been a couple of years since she'd worn it last, but under the fading light of evening, the rich purple silk looked just as beautiful as she recalled.

"Can I come to the ball, Lizzie?" Rose asked as she sat on the bed and watched Grace and Elizabeth dress.

"No, you may not." Elizabeth turned away from the mirror and picked up her long white gloves. "Mrs. Fadling will be here to sit with you tonight." The older Mrs. Fadling was a widow who lived with her son and daughter-in-law above the grocer's store. She had agreed to sit with Rose while the others celebrated the Fourth of July in the ballroom.

"I don't want to sit with Mrs. Fadling." Rose crossed her arms and frowned at Elizabeth.

"You are not old enough to come to a ball, Rose." Elizabeth pulled on her gloves. "You will stay up here with Mrs. Fadling and mind what she says, do you understand?"

A knock came at the door and Grace walked across the room to open it. Mrs. Fadling stood in the hallway holding a large knitting bag in hand.

"Hello," she said to Grace.

"Won't you please come in?" Elizabeth moved to the door to welcome her. "Rose, will you show Mrs. Fadling to the sitting room?"

Rose's face twisted in anger and she stomped to the sitting-room door.

Elizabeth gave her a stern look. "You be kind and respectful."

"She'll be just fine," Mrs. Fadling said. "We'll have a grand time, won't we?"

Rose opened the door and marched into the sitting room without answering Mrs. Fadling.

When the sitting room door closed behind them, Elizabeth turned to Grace. "Are you ready to dance?"

Grace lifted a bored shoulder. She had accepted an invitation from a young man named Mr. O'Conner who had asked to escort her this evening. Elizabeth had accepted Ben's invitation earlier at the Coopers'.

They left their room together and walked down the hall to the lobby. Ben and Mr. O'Conner stood at the bottom of the stairs and smiled eagerly when they appeared.

Elizabeth had a dance card dangling from her wrist and she was swarmed by men who wanted to be added to the list. She put Ben down for the first and last dances, as was customary for an escort, and soon filled all the other spaces—all but one.

"May I have the last waltz available?" Pierre LaForce asked Elizabeth.

She looked around the lobby, but could not see Jude. Would he ask her for a dance? If he did, she wanted to make sure she had one available for him. "I'm sorry, but it's reserved."

"For who?" Pierre puffed out his chest. "I will find him and wrestle him for the honor."

She smiled at his pompous statement and took the arm Ben offered. They walked into the ballroom, where members of the orchestra were tuning up their instruments. The room was full to capacity and hotter than she had imagined.

Men and women stood in small groups, talking and laughing, waiting for the dancing to get underway. There had to be at least two hundred people in attendance. Elizabeth recognized a few she had met already, but the majority were strangers to her. Jude was not among them.

"Hello, Miss Bell." Charlotte Cooper walked over to Elizabeth with a genuine smile on her pretty face. "How is Rose doing?"

"She's back to her old self," Elizabeth said. "Thank you, again, for your hospitality today."

"My pleasure. Any friend of Ben's is a friend of ours."

Ben's affection for Charlotte was evident in the kind smile he gave to her, and then he turned that same smile to Elizabeth.

Jude walked into the ballroom and scanned the crowd, his gaze landing on Elizabeth. He came directly to her side, as if she had been the person he was looking for.

He said hello to Charlotte and Ben, and then he turned to Elizabeth.

"I was attending to some business and couldn't get here until now," he said. "Am I too late for a dance?"

She didn't want to let her excitement show, so she picked up her dance card and looked at it for a moment. "I do have a waltz left, if you'd like that."

He gave a slight bow. "If it's all the lady has left, it's what I'll take."

The orchestra touched its strings, allowing the dancers to prepare for the first song. Elizabeth lifted the train of her ball gown and smiled up at Ben.

They left Jude on the side of the dance floor and joined the others in the first dance of the night. Though she tried to give Ben her full attention, she couldn't help noticing Jude from time to time mingling with their guests.

As the revelry intensified, and the ballroom grew hotter, Elizabeth danced with one partner after the other. In between songs, she visited the refreshment table with Ben and tried to quench her thirst with Martha's punch.

Grace was just as busy as Elizabeth, dancing with many of the men, but she didn't seem to settle on one in particular. She flitted from group to group, flirting outrageously. It troubled Elizabeth that she hadn't found a nice young man to spend more time with. Why didn't any of them seem to interest her?

Elizabeth sighed and looked down at her dance card. The next dance was the waltz with Jude. She looked around the ballroom and saw him speaking with Abram Cooper and another man she hadn't met. He must have sensed her gaze on him, because he looked her way and lifted his eyebrows, as if asking her a question.

She nodded and pointed at her dance card.

He excused himself from the gentlemen and made his way across the ballroom to her side. As he walked, she couldn't stop from admiring the clean cut of his suit and the confident way he moved. He was a handsome man, yet there was so much more to him than his looks. He was well respected in the community, he took in young women who needed training and a place to work, but above all that, he was kind. Truly kind.

The orchestra began the next song and Jude held out his arm. "Ready?"

"Are you?"

He grinned. "I've been looking forward to this dance all evening."

The other dancers were already twirling around the floor as Elizabeth put her hand on his shoulder and felt his rest on her waist.

She tried not to let herself dwell on how different his touch felt than that of the others. He would be her business partner before long and she needed to think of him that way.

Jude took a step, but then he paused and Elizabeth frowned. "Is something wrong?"

He tilted his chin toward the doors and Elizabeth followed his gaze. "It looks like we have an unexpected guest."

The crowd moved aside and Rose stood on the dance floor in her nightgown, a grin on her cherubic face.

"Lizzie!" Rose waved her hand as she ran around the other dancers and clung to Elizabeth's skirt.

Elizabeth looked down into her little face. "Where is Mrs. Fadling?"

Rose's wide-eyed stare took in the room. "She fell asleep."

Elizabeth sighed. "I told you to stay upstairs—"

"But it's no fun to stay in my room all night. The music sounds so pretty."

"I also told you it isn't safe for you to be wandering around the hotel alone."

Rose's face became crestfallen. "I just wanted to dance."

Elizabeth glanced at Jude and saw the compassion on his face.

"May I dance with her?" he asked Elizabeth quietly.

She studied him for a moment, her eyebrows furrowed. "You would do that?"

"It would be my pleasure."

"Please, Lizzie!" Rose tugged on her skirt.

She shouldn't let Rose get her way, but what was the harm in one dance, especially if Jude was willing? It would be a memory Rose would hold forever. "All right."

Jude smiled and bent at the waist. "May I have this dance, Miss Rose?"

Rose jumped up and down and nodded with enthusiasm.

Jude lifted her and she wrapped her arms around his neck. "My first dance!"

He grinned over Rose's shoulder at Elizabeth and then showed Rose how to hold his left hand with her right one. After she did as he instructed, he began to waltz.

Rose had never smiled so bright and Elizabeth couldn't take her eyes off the pair. She stood on the edge of the dance floor, her heart full. Rose had never known the love of their father, as Elizabeth had. She'd never sat on his lap, laid her head against his chest to hear the strong beat of his heart or twirled in a pretty dress for him to admire. Rose had missed all those things, but as she giggled in Jude's arms, she was able to taste a morsel of that experience.

Jude's eyes glowed as he watched Rose giggle. From time to time he would say something and she would laugh all over again. Around and around they went, and not once did Jude look away from Rose's delighted face. Others stopped to watch, their smiles on the mismatched pair.

When the song came to an end, Jude set her on her feet and bowed at the waist. Rose curtsied, just as Elizabeth had taught her, and then lifted her arms for Jude to pick her up again.

Elizabeth tried to conceal the depth of her emotions as they came back to her and she held out her arms to Rose. "It's time for bed."

Rose clung to him. "Can you put me to bed, Mr. Jude?"

Lightning lit up the windows and a crack of thunder boomed outside the hotel, causing many people to jump. Rose squeezed Jude tighter, her eyes growing large.

Soon rain was pounding against the siding.

"I'll take you, if Elizabeth comes," Jude said.

"Of course." Elizabeth lifted the train of her gown and led the way out of the ballroom.

The thunder continued to rumble, and each time it split the air, Rose squealed and hugged Jude tighter.

They walked up the stairs and down the long hallway, which lit up as the lightning streaked across the sky. Elizabeth went ahead of Jude and opened their bedroom door.

"Where is Mrs. Fadling?" Elizabeth asked Rose.

Rose yawned and pointed to the sitting room. "In there."

Jude followed Elizabeth into their bedroom and walked to the bed, where he lowered Rose.

Thunder filled the air once again and Rose refused to let go of Jude, though he didn't look like he minded being her protector.

"It's time for bed," Elizabeth said to her sister.

Rose shook her head. "I'm scared."

Jude gently pried Rose's arms off his neck and pulled the bedcovers back. "You have nothing to be afraid of. Climb into bed and I'll tell you a story."

Elizabeth stood by and watched as Rose got under the covers without a fuss.

Jude pulled them up to her chin and sat beside her. "Once upon a time, there was a little girl who was afraid of storms."

"That's me!" Rose said with glee.

Jude laughed and continued to tell Rose the story about the little girl and how she had to climb a mountain to capture the thunder and lightning and place them in a bottle. For years, the people in the valley endured a drought because there was no rain. Their crops did not grow, their animals could not drink and the people were starving and thirsty. The little girl realized her fear was causing everyone to suffer, so she went back to the mountain and released the thunder and lightning. Immediately, it began to rain again, but she was no longer afraid. She was excited that everyone would have water. She finally understood that the storm was not something to fear, but something to embrace because it meant life for all of them.

He told her the story in great detail, taking his time

and answering her questions as he went. Elizabeth sat in the rocking chair in the corner, content to listen to the storm and let the dancers continue on without her.

As Jude came to the end of the story, Rose's eyes closed and she was soon fast asleep.

"The end," Jude said softly as he slowly stood from the bed.

The storm had quieted to a gentle rain and the thunder had moved on.

Jude went to the window and opened it to allow a cool breeze to blow in.

Elizabeth closed her eyes and inhaled the fresh air. It felt wonderful against her warm skin. "Thank you," she said as she opened her eyes.

"Shall we go back to the dance?"

"After I wake Mrs. Fadling and ask her to sit with Rose."

"I'll wait in the hall."

Elizabeth stood and went into the sitting room, where Mrs. Fadling was asleep over her knitting needles. Elizabeth touched her shoulder. "Mrs. Fadling."

The woman opened her eyes, a bit confused.

"Rose is asleep in the bedroom. Would you mind sitting with her in there?"

"Oh, of course not." The woman stood and followed Elizabeth back into the room. "Enjoy the rest of your evening."

"I will." Elizabeth left the bedroom and closed the door.

Jude stood at the back of the hallway, his hands in his pockets, looking out the window. There was something heavy about his countenance.

"Is something wrong?"

He turned from the window. "I've never done anything like that in my life."

"What?"

"Put a child to bed."

She smiled. "You did a marvelous job."

He shook his head. "How do you do it?"

"What?"

"Say no to her."

Elizabeth laughed. "Believe me, it gets easier and easier the older she gets."

He joined in her laughter and then grew serious. "You're doing a wonderful job raising her. She's a sweet girl. Your parents would be proud."

His words pleased her. Raising a child was a thankless job, and knowing he had noticed her hard work meant a lot.

"Are you ready to return?" she asked.

"Not really." He smiled and offered his arm. "But I'll take you back so the others can enjoy a dance with you."

She had lost her opportunity to dance with him, but somehow she didn't mind. Listening to him tell Rose a story had been more enjoyable than any dance she'd ever experienced.

Chapter Ten

Four days later, Jude stood in the barn of the Northern Hotel, running the currycomb down Lady's flank. He'd just returned from Duluth and had ridden Lady hard to get back to Little Falls. He hated being away from the hotel for such a long period of time, especially with Hugh's threat still hanging over his head. He hoped the ladies hadn't had any difficulties while he was away.

Dust motes floated on the air and the smell of musty hay filled the barn. Two other horses stood in their stalls, twitching their tails and stomping their feet, mildly curious about Jude's activities.

He'd gone after Sally, but her employer must have caught on to her plan to leave, because when Jude arrived at Reed's brothel, she was nowhere to be found. He had spent two sleepless nights searching for her, but to no avail. If she'd been forced to a lumber camp, or moved farther west, he would never find her. The helplessness of it all made his stomach clench with anger and his fingers itch to let his emotions play out on the piano.

The midafternoon sky was overcast and a pall lay

over the land. Jude finished currying Lady and filled her bin with oats.

The barn door creaked and Jude looked up to find Elizabeth standing in the doorway. The sight of her made him forget all the trouble of the past few days in one heartbeat.

She came to a sudden stop, as if she'd run out to meet him, and color filled her cheeks. "Grace said she saw you ride up. I—I thought I'd check to see if it was you and if you needed anything."

She looked fresh and pure after countless hours of searching through brothels and taverns for Sally. It was good to see that she was safe and sound—and much prettier than he remembered.

He, on the other hand, was a disheveled mess. It had been days since he'd shaved, and his clothes were wrinkled and covered with trail dust. But he was happy to see her. Happier than he could let on—especially because she'd sought him out. "Hello, Elizabeth."

She studied him for a moment and then crossed the barn, concern deepening the lines in her brow. "Is everything all right?"

He started to gather his things, not wanting her to see his weary emotions. "Everything is fine."

She came closer. "What happened? Where did you go?"

Jude exited the stall, closing the gate behind him. "I had some business to attend to, but I'm done now." Hopefully she wouldn't ask any more questions, because he was afraid his raw emotions would encourage him to give away too much. He hung up the currycomb and saddle blanket, grabbed his travel bag and ducked out of the barn. "Is everything all right with the hotel?"

Elizabeth followed and he closed the door behind her. "Everything is fine."

They stood in the narrow alley as a dark cloud began to blot out the sunshine. Were they in for a storm? It didn't feel like rain was in the air.

"Was there something you needed?" he asked.

She shook her head.

He couldn't help but smile. "You just came out to welcome me home?"

She ducked her head. "I was actually eager to bring this list to you." She held up a piece of paper he hadn't noticed until now. "But I can see you're tired, so I'll wait to discuss it with you."

Despite his exhaustion and disappointment, something as mundane as a list was a welcome diversion. He tried not to smile. "I haven't even started on the other list. What is this one about?"

She put it behind her back. "It's nothing."

"What is it?"

She moved away, a smile on her lips. "It's really not that important."

He laughed. "Just tell me."

She took another step back, her cheeks filling with more color, a telltale sign that she was embarrassed. What could she have written that would embarrass her? "It's a list of gentlemen who have caught my eye."

Jude paused, his smile disappearing. "Caught your eye?"

"For Grace," she said quickly. "I've narrowed it down to five men."

Sweet relief washed over him, but he didn't want to take the time to analyze why he would be relieved that the list was only for Grace. "Only five?"

"Is there reason for more?" She smiled. "It only takes one, after all."

He sobered. "You're right—as long as it's the right one."

She looked down at the list and didn't meet his gaze. "Like I said, we can discuss it later. I just wanted your opinion. There have been so many men here this week, it would have been nice to have you here to help me weed them out."

The thought of all those men vying for her attention left a bad taste in his mouth and he suddenly wanted to see that list. Who had caught her eye? "Did Ben stop by?"

She shook her head. "I don't believe so."

What was Ben's problem? Didn't he realize he was racing against a ticking clock?

"What about Hugh Jones?"

"No. Thankfully."

The sky grew darker and Jude glanced up. "We should probably go inside. Looks like we're in for another storm."

Elizabeth looked up, as well, and frowned. "It's coming on fast. The sky was clear until about thirty minutes ago."

Jude walked to the end of the alley and Elizabeth followed. They stopped on Broadway and looked toward the west. A strange cloud filled the horizon. It didn't look like a normal storm cloud; it somehow shimmered and swarmed as it advanced and turned the sky a darker gray.

"I don't like the looks of it," Jude said.

From a distance, it appeared as if large drops of rain were falling from the sky.

"What in the world?" Elizabeth asked just as a locust fell near her foot. "Jude, look."

He studied the strange creature. It was large—much bigger than a normal grasshopper, with big eyes and long legs. The moment it landed, it started to march toward the east.

Elizabeth moved out of its way as another fell on her head. She squealed in surprise and flung it away.

More began to come down all around them. The sun was now completely hidden from view and the street was as dark as dusk. Hundreds of the locusts fell from the sky, their bodies hitting the roofs of buildings with little thuds. They advanced along the street and crawled up the legs of Jude's pants. He hit at them and swatted at his pants, but their feet clung to the fabric.

"What's happening?" she asked Jude above the noise of the whirring and humming.

"I don't know—but look." He pointed to her gown where a hole had been made by the little creatures. "They're eating everything in their path."

Thousands more fell around them, covering every square inch of ground.

"Quick," he said. "Let's get inside."

They raced down the alley toward the back door of the Northern as he brushed the locusts off his arms and shoulders. It was impossible to avoid the insects as they walked, and they crunched underfoot, making their path slippery and treacherous.

Jude rushed ahead and opened the back door. Elizabeth went inside, frantically trying to remove the horrible insects from her clothing and hair.

"They're pinching my skin," she said as she cried out in pain.

Jude slammed the door closed and dropped his travel bag. He went to her side, pulling dozens of insects off her. Then they removed the bugs that were clinging to him and crushed them under their feet.

The back hall was as dark as night and it was almost impossible to see each other.

"I've never seen anything like this," Elizabeth said, breathless. "Look at my gown. They've made holes everywhere. It's ruined."

His eyes adjusted to the darkness and he saw another locust on her shoulder. He gently pulled it off. "I think we got them all."

She didn't say anything for a moment, but then she looked down at her damaged gown. "If they're doing this to my clothing, I can't imagine what they're doing to the crops."

His heart started pounding even harder than it had been. "My corn." He grabbed the knob and yanked the door open.

She put her hand on his arm. "Corn?"

"My cornfield, remember? The corn pays for our winter mortgage." His words sounded harsher than he intended, but there was no time to waste explaining. He rushed outside, desperation in his movements.

"Wait!" She called to him and ran out the door.

"Get back inside, Elizabeth."

"I won't let you go alone."

He didn't have time to debate, but rushed into the barn, where burlap feed sacks sat in a pile near the wall. He picked them up and saw that she had followed him inside the barn. "Grab the can of kerosene and a box of matches. We'll try to smoke them out."

Elizabeth did as he said and ran to keep up with him as he headed toward his cornfield.

Elizabeth swatted at her head, trying to dislodge the locusts that clung to her hair. They swarmed around her in a storm of whirring and buzzing. She'd never seen anything like it in her life. It was like a plague right out of Egypt. Where had these insects come from and how would they get them to leave?

She ran down the street, her feet slipping and sliding on the horrid bugs as one crawled down her cheek and tried to get into her ear. She squealed and pulled the bug from her head.

Jude was gaining speed and she could barely see him in the whirl of locusts. She didn't know where he was headed, but if she lost him now, she'd never find him.

"Jude!" Elizabeth called to him. Her skirts were flying and her hair tumbled down her back in a tangled mess, but she hardly cared. If they could save his crop, she'd do whatever she could.

Jude stopped and took her hand, pulling her along the street.

"What do you plan to do?" she asked breathlessly.

"Build fires around the perimeter of my fields and try to smoke them out. We'll need to gather wood, too."

"I'll do whatever I can."

He pulled her over the ravine bridge and down a dirt road. The grasshoppers continued to fall from the sky and the munching noise threatened to drive her crazy.

They finally came to a field full of corn about knee-high. It was already infested with the grasshoppers. There had to be at least twenty of the insects to every square foot and they continued to come.

"Set down the kerosene and go gather wood wherever you can find it," he said to her.

Elizabeth did as he said, pulling bugs off her face and arms, and then rushing off to a wooded area on the edge of the field, where she began to gather sticks and piles of leaves.

She held as much as she could manage and brought it back to Jude. He quickly started a fire with the kerosene and matches, and when it was going strong, he set a couple flour sacks on it to start the smoke.

Elizabeth returned to the woods and brought back more sticks. He directed her to put her stacks of kindling farther down the field, then return for more.

She went back to the woods for countless loads and Jude built at least a dozen fires. Sweat dripped down her face and mixed with soot. She coughed and wheezed as smoke billowed out around the fields. For a time, she believed they were making a difference, but after two hours she returned and found Jude staring at a decimated field.

Elizabeth dropped another load of sticks and was about to return when he called for her to halt.

She crumpled to the ground, panting for air, pulling more of the horrible insects off her gown. Her chest rose and fell in a steady rhythm, but she couldn't sit for long. She stood and faced him. "Why are we stopping?"

"It's too late," he said. "There are too many."

Elizabeth walked over piles of grasshoppers to reach his side. "It's never too late."

"Look at the corn—there's nothing left." He bent over to catch his breath. "They've destroyed my crop in less than three hours."

Elizabeth ran her forearm over her sweating forehead, panting for air.

Jude watched her, his hair wild and covered in ash. He'd given up—she could see it in the weary lines of his shoulders.

"We can't give in, Jude. Not now."

He picked up a stalk of corn, eaten around the edges. "It's no use. We'll never win this battle."

She knelt on the ground and clasped her hands in her lap, then she lowered her head and took deep breaths. She looked around at the leafless trees and the barren ground. The land was dreary and bleak, the beauty gone. How long would she have to gaze upon the desolate earth?

Defeat hung about her and she wanted to weep. "I'm sorry. I wish we could have saved it."

He sat beside her and watched his field disappear under the hungry mouths of locusts, smoke rising up all around his crop.

"I don't think I can put into words what your efforts mean to me," he said. "I appreciate your help more than you'll ever know."

What else would she have done? She couldn't just sit back and let nature win without a fight. She put her hand on his arm. "Will we be able to make the winter payments?"

"We'll find a way." He stood and offered his hand. "Now that I know how hard you can work, I'm sure we'll find a way."

She accepted his offer to stand, but found no joy in his words. She'd worked hard because she thought she was making a difference. Now she knew her work had been in vain. Was that how it would be with trying to buy Jude's portion of the hotel? What good was her work when it felt like everything was conspiring against her efforts?

She followed Jude back toward the Northern. The streets were almost empty, except for the millions of grasshoppers piled up in corners of buildings and crawling over anything in their path. At least they had stopped falling from the sky.

They entered the hotel lobby and Elizabeth put her hands up to her hair, half expecting to find another bug there. Instead, she touched a snarled mess of curls.

Grace rushed down the hall, her skirts fanning out around her. “Elizabeth! What happened to you?” She touched Elizabeth’s gown, her eyes wide. “I didn’t know where you went. Rose woke up from her nap and no one went up to get her. She finally came down the steps bawling.”

Elizabeth’s heart constricted at the news. She’d put Rose down for a nap moments before meeting Jude in the barn and had told her not to leave the room alone. After the incident at the river, she had not let Rose leave her sight. “I forgot.”

“I took her to the kitchen and Martha is giving her cookies.” She shook her head. “What is happening out there and why do you two look like you’ve been through an inferno?”

“I feel like we’ve been through worse.” Elizabeth looked outside where the world was crawling with bugs and couldn’t hide her despair. “This place is a nightmare.”

“We tried smoking the locusts out of the cornfields.” Jude sighed. “It was no use.”

“You must be exhausted,” Elizabeth said to him. “I’ll

have someone draw a bath for you and then you should eat and go to bed."

"You're in just as much need of a bath." He touched her stained sleeve.

She looked down at her black hands and ruined gown, trying not to cry. She had so few dresses to begin with.

"I don't think anyone is coming out for supper tonight," Grace said. "I'll have Martha and Violet warm up enough water for both of you to bathe and then you can eat." She wrinkled her nose. "We should throw away your clothing, too. There's no use trying to save it."

Elizabeth didn't debate as Grace disappeared down the hall.

With a sigh, Elizabeth crumpled to the stairs in a mass of soiled calico and buried her face in her hands. "What am I doing here?"

Jude sat beside her. "It will be okay. I've been through a lot worse and lived to tell about it."

"You were right." She played with the ruined cuff of her dress. "I don't think I can survive until winter."

"You're exhausted. Tomorrow things will look better."

She wanted to laugh. If the locusts continued to eat everything in their path, who knew what tomorrow would look like?

Was she strong enough to endure the hardships of frontier living or owning her own business? If she continued to lie around and bemoan the setbacks, then maybe she wasn't.

She took a deep breath, inhaling the heavy scent of smoke that lingered on their clothes, and squared her shoulders. "I suppose it doesn't pay to dwell on what we can't change. We need to turn our attention and energy onto what we can do—like make enough money to get us through the winter."

"Your tenacity astounds me." He shook his head. "We're barely through one crisis and you're ready to tackle the next."

What choice did she have? If she gave up now, she'd have nothing.

Chapter Eleven

A week later, Elizabeth stepped out of the Little Falls Company Store just after breakfast. She'd gone under the pretense of purchasing calico to make a dress, but she'd also used the opportunity to speak to Abram Cooper about work.

Unfortunately, the Little Falls Company, like so many other businesses in Little Falls, was struggling to make ends meet. The national depression, outlaw activities and locust invasion had affected the local economy and no one had money to hire her. She'd offered her bookkeeping services to half a dozen companies, and even asked if they had other jobs for her, but there was nothing. At this rate, she'd never make enough money to own the Northern Hotel.

Elizabeth trudged along the boardwalk, frustrated at her own limitations. It didn't help that the landscape was as barren as winter under the hot July sun. Leafless branches clawed at the blue sky as dust billowed up around a passing wagon. Sweat gathered under her bonnet and disappointment weighed down her shoulders.

Ever since the Day of the Locust, as she'd come to call

it, business had slowed at the hotel and their income had continued its downward slide. More break-ins and vandalism had occurred around town and new construction had dwindled. Everywhere she looked, hopelessness invaded. It was evident in the half-constructed buildings, desolate gardens and empty stares of people passing by.

The glimmer off the Mississippi was the one bright spot in an otherwise dismal day. Ducks played in the shallow waters along the banks and a fish jumped near the middle, causing a cascade of ripples.

She longed to go to the water's edge and lose herself in its beauty, but work awaited her back at the Northern. Violet had come down with a cold and Martha had insisted the maid rest for the day. Elizabeth had promised to help Martha with the noonday meal preparations as soon as she returned.

The Little Falls Company Store was only two blocks behind the Northern, so Elizabeth made it back in short order. She approached from the rear of the hotel along the narrow alley.

Shouts from within the barn made her halt. If she wasn't mistaken, someone was yelling in German.

Before she could get into the hotel, the barn door opened and an older man with a ruddy complexion stormed out. She recognized him as one of their guests. He was a peddler who had tried selling her his wares yesterday. According to Martha, the man stopped by every three months on his circuit around the territory. Martha had bought a pretty brooch from him and Jude had bought a pair of leather gloves. He had other goods in his cart—clothing, shoes, patterns, household items and even a sewing machine.

He had eaten in the dining room the night before and

slept in one of their rooms. She was surprised he hadn't left town yet.

"You!" The man pointed at Elizabeth, his German accent thick. "How do you explain such things?"

Elizabeth blinked. "Me?"

"Someone broke into the barn and my goods was stolen."

Elizabeth expected to see that the barn door latch was broken, or the boards kicked in, but everything appeared in working order.

"I'm sorry."

He spoke in German, his words coming fast and furious.

"I'll get Mr. Allen." Elizabeth hiked up her skirts and rushed into the hotel. She peeked into the kitchen, but Jude wasn't there.

Martha looked up, her eyes wide with surprise at Elizabeth's sudden appearance.

"Where is Jude?"

"He's probably in his room, lovey. He's working on some correspondence to the territorial legislature. He's asking for assistance to help local farmers after the locusts." She wiped her hands on her stained apron. "Is something wrong?"

"The German peddler claims someone broke into the barn and took some valuable items."

Most women would look shocked or even concerned, but Martha's eyes narrowed and she put her hands on her hips. "And I know who's to blame. Those ruffians are cowards, that's what they are, and that sheriff, too."

Elizabeth left Martha stewing in the kitchen to race up the back stairs and down the long hallway to the front room where Jude slept. She knocked on the door, out of breath, and waited.

She heard the scraping of a chair and then the door opened. Jude's eyebrows went up. "Elizabeth."

Today he looked much like he had the last time she'd come to his room. His suit coat was tossed over his rumpled bed, his shirtsleeves were rolled up and his top button was open. Even his hair, which was usually in perfect order, dipped down over his forehead in a most becoming way. "Mr. Ackermann claims someone broke into the barn and robbed his cart. He's out there right now."

Jude didn't hesitate but grabbed his coat and followed her out of his room and down the hall. As he walked he unrolled his shirtsleeves and ran his hands through his hair.

They took the back stairs and exited the hotel into the alley. Mr. Ackermann was inside the barn spewing German words and shouting unintelligible English.

Jude entered the barn ahead of Elizabeth.

"What happened?" he asked.

Mr. Ackermann turned to Jude, his face redder than before. "I pay extra for my cart in barn to keep safe." He pointed wildly at a window facing west. It had been pushed through and lay broken on the floor. "This is disaster."

Jude walked over to the window, his shoes crunching the glass beneath his feet. He ran his hand along the opening where the window had once sat. With a sigh, he turned back to Mr. Ackermann. "What was stolen?"

Mr. Ackermann went to his cart and threw back the oiled tarp. "Jewelry, tools, clothing." He rattled off other items and Jude listened carefully, casting a look at Elizabeth while the man rummaged around his things.

"I'm very sorry this happened," Jude said to Mr. Ackermann. "Next time you come through, your room is on the house."

The short man threw the tarp back over his cart. "We must speak to sheriff."

"I'm afraid the sheriff won't do anything."

"I go and see." Mr. Ackermann walked around Elizabeth and out the barn door.

Jude sighed and started to pick up the broken glass.

Elizabeth grabbed an empty bucket and hurried to his side. She bent to help him.

"This was the work of Hugh Jones," Jude said.

"How can you be sure?"

Jude was quiet for a moment. "I went to Dew's place last week and told him to stay away." He tossed some bigger pieces of glass into the bucket. "Apparently this is his form of retaliation."

"You went to Dew's place?" Was that why the prostitute had recognized him on the Fourth of July? She had heard enough about the saloon and brothel to know it wasn't a safe or respectable place to go.

"I had to go where I knew I'd find him." He picked up another piece of glass and dropped it into the bucket with a quick jerk of his hand. Within seconds, his finger dripped with blood.

Elizabeth let go of the glass she was holding and knelt in the dirt by his side. "Are you hurt?"

"It's nothing. Just a little cut."

She took his hand and examined the wound. His hand was large and calloused with work, but it looked strong and capable—just like him. "You'll need a bandage."

He didn't say anything and she glanced up to find him watching her. The warm look in his eyes took her by surprise and unsettled her in ways she didn't understand. She'd served countless men in the general store in Rockford and met countless more after moving to Little Falls. Many of them looked at her the same way, but none made her heart respond like Jude did.

She should walk away, but she couldn't. He had done so much for her family she wanted to do something for him.

The blood dripped from his finger and landed on the dirt in dark spots.

"Come," she said. "I'll ask Martha for a bandage."

He stood and offered his good hand to her. She took it and allowed him to help her to her feet.

No one had made her feel this way since James. She'd missed this sense of awareness and the flutter in her midsection, but what good had come from it before? Her heart had been broken and her dreams destroyed. She had no business entertaining such notions now—especially if they were going to become business partners in January. She must keep her thoughts in line with her plans.

Every muscle in Jude's body was taut as Elizabeth stood before him. The attraction he felt toward her had been growing steadily since the day they met, but he could no longer stuff it inside and pretend he wasn't fully aware of her every move.

The touch of her hand had been more shocking than the shard of glass that had sliced his skin. If he wasn't careful, he'd fall in love with this woman, and that was the last thing he needed. If she ever learned the truth about him, she'd run as far and as fast as she was able—and she'd take his heart if he wasn't careful.

He walked over to the door, needing some space, and held it open for her to leave the barn. She passed by, close enough for him to smell rose water and ink. "Martha keeps the bandages in the kitchen," he said, hoping his voice didn't betray his feelings.

Elizabeth walked across the alley and opened the back door of the hotel. He followed her into the dark hall, all thoughts of Mr. Ackermann and Hugh Jones pushed away for the moment.

They entered the kitchen and for once Martha was not in her usual spot near the stove.

Jude pointed to a cupboard along the back wall. "The bandages are over there," he said. "On the top shelf."

She went to the cupboard and stood on tiptoe to remove the box of bandages. He loved the gentle grace and elegant confidence she exuded in everything she did. When she turned, he was still watching her and the look in her eyes suggested that she was feeling something, too.

The idea that she might be attracted to him made it all the more difficult to push his feelings aside.

She grabbed a clean rag and dipped it into the warm water Martha kept on top of the stove, then she nodded toward the worktable. "Have a seat."

He did as she requested and pulled a stool out from the table.

She took a deep breath and seemed to gain some sort of resolve before walking across the room to him. She reached out to take his hand and he noticed the slightest tremble in her fingers.

The moment her skin touched his, his feelings only intensified. Thankfully she put the cloth to his wound, sending a sharp sting up his arm, which pulled his thoughts out of danger.

As she worked on his finger, he relished the warmth of her care. It had been years since someone tended to him. When he was a boy, he had taken care of his own needs for the most part. Whether big or small, he was often forced to scrounge for the things he needed. As an adult, he was just as self-sufficient. Whenever he needed help, Martha had to practically force him to allow her to care for him. Since he was rarely sick, and usually cautious, he needed little attention.

Yet now, with Elizabeth's soft fingers wrapped around his injured hand, he wondered if he could ever refuse her help.

She looked from his hand to his face, but didn't say a word. The silence was thick with tension as she ministered to his wound. She dabbed at the blood again and the action stung even worse. He had to catch his breath before he flinched.

"It's deeper than I first thought," she said. "I wonder if you'll need stitches."

He looked down at the wound. It was deep, but he'd never been stitched in his life. "I'll be fine. Just tie the bandage tight and I'll be as good as new."

She didn't object, but did as he said, tying the strip of cloth snug around his finger. When she finished, she ran her gentle fingers over his hand, as if petting him or comforting him.

The sensation almost undid his resolve to keep his distance, so he stood and picked up the box of bandages to put away. "Thank you," he said a bit more gruffly than he'd intended. "I can't remember the last time someone bound up my wounds."

"You're welcome." She stood and dropped the stained rag into a bag Martha kept in the kitchen for soiled cloths and walked over to the pitcher and bowl to clean her hands. "I spent a great deal of time in my mama's kitchen getting bandaged up." She smiled as she wiped her hands on a towel, her gaze wandering off for a moment.

"Since I was the oldest, and Papa didn't have any boys, I always believed he was disappointed in me. I tried to do all the things I saw the boys doing, like foot races, playing ball and climbing trees." She rested against the cupboard and met Jude's gaze. "I wasn't very big or strong, so I was often hurt trying to keep up. Eventually, I think my mama caught on and she must have told Papa, because one evening he took me on his lap and told me how happy he was that God had made me a girl. He said I was smart and strong, and good at things boys couldn't do." She tilted her head and the lines around her mouth softened. "From that day forward, I decided I would stop trying to be like the boys and, instead, make him proud of all the things I could do that they couldn't."

She painted such a warm and beautiful picture of her childhood. Jude yearned for memories like hers. What would it be like to know his father and be told he was perfect just the way he was? Instead, he'd been reminded time and again that he had been a mistake, a child born of sin, a fatherless boy who was not wanted by the woman who bore him and probably unknown by the father who sired him.

How different their lives were.

Jude looked down at the bandage, his chest constricting with the weight of emotions and the reminder that he wasn't worthy to have feelings for her.

"I imagine you were a busy boy," Elizabeth continued, moving away from the cupboard. "I'm sure your mother kept busy bandaging up your scrapes, too."

He wasn't ready to tell her about his childhood—would probably never be ready. Instead of answering, he simply smiled and moved to the door. "I should finish cleaning up the mess in the barn and order a new window."

"I'll help."

He loved the idea of being close and working alongside her, but the more he was with her the more he wanted to be with her. It had become harder to resist the growing affection he felt and he needed to keep his distance to prevent it from going further. "I can finish by myself." He grabbed the broom and left the kitchen before she could volunteer again.

He strode out of the hotel and took a deep breath, purposely relaxing his muscles. He rolled his shoulders and tried to shake off his pent-up emotions—yet nothing he did seemed to lessen the feelings Elizabeth's touch had created.

Jude walked into the barn and found Mr. Ackermann hitching his horse up to the cart. "The sheriff would not come." The peddler's accent was thicker than before, his congenial personality long gone. Jude had known him for two years and had always found him to be kind and agreeable. He'd never seen this side of him.

"Last time I come," Mr. Ackermann said. "I lose goods, too." He crossed his arms and stared at Jude. "You are stealing from me?"

"Why would I break my own window to steal from you?"

"To make it look like break-in."

"I have no need to steal."

"Then your man?" He must mean Pascal.

"No." Jude also crossed his arms. "I know who stole from you, but you won't get your things back. They are men who have been causing trouble all over town and the sheriff refuses to help."

Mr. Ackermann took a step closer and pointed at Jude. "Then you do something. You start vigilance committee. You and others watch the streets." He stared at Jude, his jaw set. "I won't come back until you do."

The peddler wouldn't come back, nor would others. Already, Little Falls had gained a poor reputation for its lawlessness. They had petitioned the territorial legislature to remove Sheriff Pugh from office, but they had been denied since he was an elected official. Until he was gone, the trouble would continue. If they didn't do something about the gang, the Northern would lose more business and Jude would lose money. He needed every penny he made to rescue women and keep the hotel doors open.

"It's a good suggestion," Jude said. "I'll call a meeting this evening."

Mr. Ackermann nodded, apparently satisfied. "I go now." He took hold of the horse's bridle and led it out of the barn, his cart rattling behind.

"Remember," Mr. Ackermann said. "I won't come back until you do something."

"You have my word."

Mr. Ackermann nodded and moved down the alley.

Hugh's gang would be dealt with, even if it meant more retaliation.

Chapter Twelve

Jude stood by the fireplace in the sitting room of the Northern Hotel surrounded by eight men he would trust with his life—which was what he might end up doing. The evening sun had slipped beyond the horizon, taking with it the last trace of daylight. Jude struck a match and lit the lamp in the corner.

"I like Jude's suggestion," Abram Cooper said from his chair near the door. As the founder of Little Falls, he was highly respected and commanded attention wherever he went. "We'll need to gather several more men and rotate nightly shifts."

"Are you willing to volunteer?" Judge Barnum asked. His gray whiskers and balding head should be a sign of wisdom, but his red cheeks and watery eyes hinted at his penchant for alcohol. "I don't trust Hugh's men. They have no respect for authority and no regard for humanity. I wouldn't put it past them to shoot one of you in the back if they had a hankering."

"What do you suggest, judge?" Timothy Hubbard stood on the other side of the fireplace. He and Abram owned the Little Falls Company and they had more to lose than anyone in the room. "We can't sit idle while they destroy everything we've worked for. I personally know of two gentlemen who had looked at moving their businesses to Little Falls, but chose to go elsewhere because of this lawlessness."

"We must take matters into our own hands," Jude said. "I'll be the first to volunteer." He'd been in his fair share of dangerous situations. This one was no different. "If people are scared to come to Little Falls, I lose customers."

"I'll be the second," Abram said. "If the sheriff won't do his job, we'll do it for him."

"What do you think, reverend?" Judge Barnum turned to Ben, who sat quietly. He hadn't said a word since he walked in, listening to each man's opinion.

"I would never advocate violence," Ben said evenly. "However, I don't support passivity, either. We must fight for justice, no matter the cost."

"So you think a vigilance committee is necessary?" Judge Barnum asked.

Ben nodded slowly. "I do." He looked at Jude. "And I'll also volunteer."

"So will I," Dr. Jodan said.

"And I," said Roald Hall.

"You have my cooperation," Timothy added.

Jude looked at Judge Barnum. "You know the outlaws better than most of us, so I understand your concern. But we need to do something before it's too late."

The judge sighed and ran his wrinkled hand down his forehead. "I wish you Godspeed and great success, but I'm too old and too tired to fight."

No one in the room debated him.

"I have no power to grant you," the judge continued.

"You are taking the law into your own hands and I won't try to stop you. If the legislature refuses to remove Sheriff Pugh from office, then it's every man for himself." He grabbed his cane and rose from the sofa. "I think I'll mosey on home. You young men carry on."

"Good night, judge," Abram said.

The others echoed Abram's farewell and the judge left the room.

Timothy took the judge's spot on the sofa. "Now all we need to do is gather about a dozen more men and create a schedule, allowing for two men to patrol the town each night."

Pascal appeared at the door and nodded at Jude, indicating he had some news for him. It wasn't like Pascal to interrupt a meeting, so Jude knew it must be important.

"If you'll excuse me," he said. "Have another cup of coffee and one of Martha's cookies. She has more where these came from."

The others helped themselves to the refreshments and continued to talk as Jude left the sitting room.

Pascal waited patiently near the counter, but when Jude entered the lobby, he nodded his chin toward the corner.

Jude turned and found a young man standing there. He crushed his hat in his hands and after meeting Jude's gaze, he lowered his eyes, his countenance filled with apprehension.

"May I help you?" Jude asked.

The man looked around the lobby like a skittish animal. "Is there somewhere we could speak in private?"

Jude led him to a small parlor off the ballroom. He lit a lantern and closed the door.

The young man swallowed, his Adam's apple bobbing several times. Under the light of the lantern, Jude saw the man's right eye was swollen and bruised. "I—I heard you could help."

Jude crossed his arms. "It depends. What do you need help with?"

The man leaned in, his eyes desperate. "I need help… for my friend."

"What's your friend's name?"

His skin looked pale and waxy. "Her name's Maggie Ray and she's in danger."

The name sounded vaguely familiar and an alarm went off in Jude's mind. He'd seen enough men like this to know he had come on behalf of a prostitute he loved.

"Where does she live?"

"In Crow Wing…a-at the brothel, sir."

Jude had to step carefully. He was always leery of traps set by brothel owners trying to discover if he was the one responsible for helping their prostitutes escape. The man looked truly upset, but he could never be sure.

"You gotta help her, mister. She's being held against her will." His voice shook with fear. "I went to see her tonight and asked her to marry me, but One-Eyed Pete won't let her go. When she said she was leaving, he hit her so hard, she passed out." He swiped at his cheeks with the back of his sleeve. "I tried to get her, but Pete hit me, too, and then he kicked me out and wouldn't let me back in." His voice broke and he twisted his hat back and forth. "I'm afraid he'll hurt her real bad if we don't do something."

"How'd you hear about me?"

The young man wiped his cheeks again. "One of the other ladies told me about you. Said I should come to the Northern and get you."

Crow Wing was only twenty miles north on the river and Jude hated to bring a woman to the Northern from somewhere so close. Too many people would talk. But he had little choice. There was no time to find someone else to get her. If what he said was true, she had probably been beaten into submission by now. "Why don't you ride on home and I'll see what can be done about your friend."

"Will you help her?" The pain and desperation in the man's voice was so raw, Jude suddenly pictured Elizabeth in his mind's eye. If she was hurting and afraid, he'd do everything in his power to help her. This man was no different.

"What's your name?"

"John Sloan."

"And where do you live?"

"Near Belle Prairie."

Jude put his hand on John's shoulder. "I'll do what I can and I'll get word to you, either way."

John nodded and shoved his hat back on his head. "Thank you, sir. I'm going to marry Maggie and take care of her. She'll never have to step foot in a brothel again. You just gotta get her out of there."

Jude nodded, praying he could help. "Go home now."

Jude followed John out of the parlor and into the lobby.

Elizabeth was standing at the counter speaking with Pascal. She handed him the ledger, which they kept under the counter, and looked up when Jude entered.

John opened the door, his eyes full of tears. "I'm in your debt."

After John closed the door, Elizabeth turned her curious gaze to Jude. "What was that about?"

"It's too complicated to explain."

Jude couldn't leave now, not with the meeting still running in the sitting room. But he could have Pascal get his things ready for him. At least then he could leave as soon as the meeting ended.

But Elizabeth stood there, her blue eyes watching him closely.

Pascal waited for a signal, which Jude gave with a quick nod, and then he turned his attention to Elizabeth. "Is there something you need?"

She shook her head. "No."

For some reason, he wished she had said yes, because then he wouldn't need to return to the meeting right away but might have a few more moments with her.

Pascal sat poised for action. He would need to saddle Jude's horse and put a few things in his saddlebags, including Jude's pistol.

"Actually, there is something you could do," Jude said. "Would you mind taking over behind the desk for Pascal? He has a few things he needs to take care of."

Elizabeth glanced at Pascal and then back at Jude. He could tell she wanted to ask about Pascal's business, but since she was a lady, she'd probably refrain. "Of course."

"Good."

Pascal moved away from the counter and immediately walked toward the back of the hotel. After so many years with Jude, he knew what was needed.

"How is the meeting?" Elizabeth asked.

"It's going well."

"Will you be forming a vigilance committee?"

"Yes."

She paused for a moment, her eyes searching his face. "Will it be safe?"

He wouldn't lie to her. "Probably not."

She looked down at the counter and moved something from one spot to another. "Will you try to be safe?"

Was she worried about him? The thought made him smile. "Of course I'll try to be safe." If a vigilance committee worried her, what would she think if she learned he was about to enter a brothel to try to rescue a woman?

She dropped her gaze again. "I'll pray for you."

Martha had said the same thing to Jude countless times—but, for some reason, it felt like an entirely different matter to have Elizabeth's prayers covering him. "Thank you." He hated to leave her, but he needed to get back to the meeting and hurry things along so he could get to Crow Wing.

He walked away, but turned to look at her one more time.

She was watching him and her cheeks filled with color at being caught.

What was happening between them? Whatever it was, it must stop before one of them was hurt…or disillusioned.

Elizabeth smiled politely at the two men standing on the other side of the counter, though she didn't want to encourage them.

"Ah, Miss Elizabeth." The one named Hank put his hand over his heart. His curly blond hair made him look younger than he probably was. He was cute, to be sure, but he couldn't be a day over seventeen. "Why won't you marry me? I know I ain't got much more than the clothes on my back, but what more do two people in love need?"

"A house, a little furniture, maybe a meal once in a while." Elizabeth had grown used to men like Hank.

Almost every day she turned down one marriage proposal or another. “As much as it breaks my heart, I can’t marry you.”

“What about me?” the one named Alphonse asked. He was tall and gangly with jet-black hair and eyes to match. “I got me a little money saved up to buy a cabin and a piece of land. I could provide real nice for you.” He looked at her with such longing, Elizabeth truly felt bad.

“I appreciate the offers, gentlemen, but I’m staying right here with my sisters.”

Hank slapped Alphonse on the shoulder. “That’s it. Let’s go ask Miss Grace again.”

“Grace is in the dining room,” Elizabeth said, only too happy to send them on their way. Grace didn’t seem to mind the attention or the marriage proposals. She’d received even more than Elizabeth, and hadn’t turned anyone down yet. Instead, she pretended to consider each one. It remained to be seen if she’d accept any she’d received.

Elizabeth still had the list of men she considered suitable for Grace. Ben and Roald were on the list, though Grace had shown no interest in either one. The other three were men who had respectable jobs, attended church and appeared to be gentlemanly in all respects. Grace never once turned her attention to any of them.

Hank and Alphonse left the lobby and passed Pascal in the hall as he walked toward the front counter.

“I’m all done, Miss Elizabeth,” Pascal said. “I can take my spot again.”

“We had one guest register.” Elizabeth pointed to the large book they kept on the counter for their guests to sign in. “I put him in room eighteen.”

Pascal nodded and resumed his seat on the stool.

The sitting room door opened and Jude led the way out of the meeting, deep in conversation with Abram Cooper.

Ben walked out behind them, his gaze meeting Elizabeth's. His eyes filled with delight at seeing her and he crossed the lobby. "Hello, Elizabeth. I've been hoping to get a chance to speak with you." He stood before her with his hat in his hands, a gentleman in every way. It endeared him to her all the more. "Do you have a moment?"

"If you're done in the sitting room, we can meet in there."

"I'd like that."

Jude stood by the front door and said goodbye to all the others as they left. He barely glanced at Elizabeth and Ben as he turned toward Pascal. "Are my things ready to go?"

"Are you leaving?" Elizabeth asked.

Jude looked back at her. "I am."

"It's late. Will you be back tonight?"

He paused. "I'm not sure. I hope so."

"A routine run?" Ben asked.

"Yes. Up to Crow Wing."

Ben studied him for a moment. "Do you need help?"

Help? Elizabeth looked between both men. Why would Jude need help?

Jude shook his head. "Thanks, but I don't need help." He turned to Pascal. "Are my things ready to go?"

"Everything's waiting for you in the barn."

Jude nodded once and grabbed his hat. He tipped his head at Ben and Elizabeth, and strode down the hallway out of sight.

Ben watched him for a moment and then opened the door into the sitting room.

Elizabeth walked in, her thoughts jumbled. Was Ben aware of Jude's mysterious activities? Would Ben know what the note meant that she had put in her trunk? If Ben knew what Jude did, and he seemed to approve, was it all that bad?

Ben followed Elizabeth into the sitting room and motioned to one of the chairs. "Would you like to sit?"

She took the chair across from the sofa and he sat facing her.

He clasped his hands together and looked everywhere but at her.

Was he nervous? Why?

Unless...was he going to be like all the others and speak of love and marriage? She would much rather spare him from disappointment.

"Ben—"

"Elizabeth—"

They both paused and he smiled. "Go ahead," he said.

His brown eyes sparkled with pleasure at seeing her, yet there was no heat or hunger in his gaze, not like the others who had asked to speak to her. What if he wasn't going to talk of love and marriage? Would she embarrass herself if she brought it up?

"No, you go." She sat up straighter and braced herself for whatever he had to say.

He nodded. "I'm not practiced at these sorts of things, but Jude encouraged me, so I thought I'd give it a go."

"What sort of thing did you have in mind?"

"I admire you, Elizabeth, and I would like to get to know you better. Would you allow me the honor of calling on you?"

It wasn't a marriage proposal, thankfully, but it was still more than she was willing to grant.

She moved to the edge of her seat, hoping to turn him down without hurting his pride. Nerves bubbled in her stomach, because despite the fact that she had refused dozens of men, she liked and respected Ben more than all the others. She couldn't agree to a courtship, but she hoped to preserve their friendship—and maybe she could encourage him to court Grace.

"I'm honored by your request and flattered that you would want to get to know me better. I'd like the same thing."

He unclasped his hands, his face shining, so she continued quickly.

"However, I would like to get to know you as a friend and nothing more. It bears no reflection on you, but I'm simply not interested in a romantic relationship. I want to focus on the hotel and raise my sister, nothing more."

Ben offered a disappointed smile, but he didn't look defeated. "Thank you for your honesty."

"I would like to be friends, though." She smiled and hoped she conveyed the truth behind her words.

"Of course."

"And…" She was even more nervous now than before. "May I make a suggestion?"

"Anything."

"My sister is a lovely woman…" She wanted to tell him that Grace would be honored if he asked her to call, yet she couldn't make such a statement in all honesty. She had no idea what Grace wanted and that was part of the problem.

"She is a lovely woman." He smiled and stood. "I won't take up more of your time."

She also stood and watched him move toward the door.

"Ben." She said his name softly.

He stopped and looked back at her.

"I truly meant what I said. I'd like to be friends."

Ben put his hat on and nodded at Elizabeth. "I would, too."

She followed him out of the sitting room and into the lobby.

"Goodbye, Elizabeth." He opened the door and stepped out onto the porch.

"Goodbye." The door closed and she stood in the lobby alone with Pascal.

She felt bad about Ben and she hoped he would take the hint to call on Grace…but at the moment her thoughts returned to Jude and his mysterious whereabouts. "Pascal, where did Mr. Jude go?"

Pascal looked up from whatever he was working on. "Mr. Jude likes to keep his business to himself."

"Yet you know where he went."

"I do, because Mr. Jude trusts me and I help him when I can."

"He can trust me," she said with a smile. "You can, too."

"You'll have to ask him."

Elizabeth sighed. It was beyond time to ask Jude some questions. As soon as he returned, she'd do just that.

Chapter Thirteen

Elizabeth stood at the window facing the back of the hotel and looked out at the stormy night. Rain pounded against the side of the building and lightning flashed across the sky. A crack of thunder tore through the air and reverberated through her chest. She watched as Jude pulled the barn door closed and splashed through the puddles to the back door.

It was after three in the morning and she had not been able to sleep. But it wasn't the storm that had kept her awake. It was concern for Jude. She had wrapped a robe around her body and come to the window to watch the western sky. That's when she'd spotted Jude plodding down the alley on his horse. What errand had required his immediate attention and why in the middle of the night?

She stood for several minutes, watching the storm, expecting to hear him trudge up the back stairs to go to his room. She was ready to confront him, ask him to be honest. After all, if they were going to be partners, she needed to know if his personal affairs would hurt or hinder their business. The note in her trunk demanded answers once and for all.

After ten minutes, Elizabeth grew impatient. The wind continued to rattle the windowpanes and the rain slashed against the siding in wave after wave.

A soft noise rose above the sounds of the storm—one she would never have expected at such a late hour.

The piano.

Not wanting to see Pascal, who sat at the front counter, Elizabeth took the back stairs and made her way along the dark hallway on the main level. The sound grew louder as she walked past the dining room and toward the parlor off the ballroom. She'd only been in there once or twice and had glanced at the piano, but thought nothing of it.

With a trembling hand, she turned the knob and pushed open the door just enough to look inside.

Jude sat on the piano bench, his wet hair falling over his forehead and his white shirt clinging to his skin. His suit coat was flung over the back of a chair nearby as he played the most beautiful rendition of "Amazing Grace" she'd ever heard. His eyes were closed and his hands moved with amazing speed and dexterity across the keys. Every inch of his body was engaged in the song and he swayed with the movement of the melody.

A flash of lightning lit the room and then died down, allowing the light from the fireplace to flicker over his handsome face once again. Rain pattered against the window, matching the steady tempo of her heartbeat.

On and on the song went. His face was filled with such pain and heartache, yet there was an overwhelming sense of joy and hope radiating from his fingertips.

Amazing grace how sweet the sound.

That saved a wretch like me.

I once was lost but now I'm found.

Was blind but now I see.

The last note echoed in the room and he slowly opened his eyes, pulling his hands away from the piano keys.

Their gazes met as another flash of lightning filled the room and faded away.

She hated to break the still moment with words, but she couldn't hold back her praise. "That was beautiful."

His thoughts were imperceptible as he stood and walked around the piano. "Did I wake you?"

She wanted to enter the room, but her hair was unbound and she wore a nightgown, though she was modestly covered with her robe. No. She should stay where she was. "I couldn't sleep."

"Why not?"

She had told herself that she couldn't sleep because she was angry with him for keeping a secret from her. But truth be told, she couldn't sleep because she needed to know he was safe. Yet she couldn't tell him the truth. If she did, he might suspect that she cared for him more than she ought—and that would not be good for their working relationship.

The fire crackled and popped, sending smoke spiraling up the chimney.

"The storm..." Her words died off as she met his handsome gaze. She couldn't lie to him. "And I was worried about you."

His eyes softened at her admission.

She couldn't allow her thoughts—or his—to wander down the wrong path. "Where did you learn to play like that?"

Jude ran his hand along the piano, but instead of joy,

something unpleasant passed over his countenance. "I taught myself."

She blinked several times, surprise washing over her. "That's incredible."

"It was necessary."

"Necessary?" She tilted her head. "What do you mean?"

Jude sighed. "I need to tell you something, Elizabeth. Would you like to sit with me for a moment?"

He indicated the two sofas in front of the fireplace.

She shouldn't enter a room with him at such a late hour, with no chaperone—but she knew in her heart of hearts that Jude was trustworthy. She walked across the room slowly, her nightgown billowing out around her legs as she took a seat on the sofa.

He sat across from her, studying her. He didn't speak for a moment, but then he leaned forward and clasped his hands. With another sigh, he dropped his gaze. "I prayed about telling you the truth all the way back from Crow Wing. I told God I didn't want to say anything, because I didn't want to risk losing your respect. But He kept prompting me, so I told Him I would only tell you if I had a moment alone with you. Since we have so few of those, I didn't think I'd have to tell you for a long time." He stopped and looked up at her. "But I'm sensing this moment was orchestrated by Him and I need to be obedient and tell you."

Elizabeth swallowed the nerves climbing up her throat. What could he say that would make her lose respect for him? She tried to keep her face clear from any thoughts or emotions that would give away her trepidation.

Jude stood and walked to the fireplace. He took the

poker and repositioned the logs. Sparks jumped in the air and coals cascaded down the pile. He placed another log on the fire.

"I won't try to make this sound any better than it is." He took a deep breath and then faced her. "I was born in a brothel. My mother was a prostitute and I never knew my father."

Elizabeth held her breath for a split second and then her lips parted and the air escaped on a gasp. She stared at him, unsure how to respond.

"I learned how to play the piano at the age of ten because I was afraid the brothel owner would kick me out when I was old enough to work on my own. He needed a piano player to entertain his customers while they drank and gambled, so I became the best piano player around. I wanted to be irreplaceable. I did it so I could stay close to my mother and help her if she needed me."

He looked back at the fire and pushed one of the logs with his boot. "I wanted to earn enough money to buy a home for us and remove her from the life she hated." He was quiet for a moment. "She died when I was twelve. I kept playing the piano, because I had no other skills. No schooling. Nothing I could rely on to make a way for myself."

Elizabeth stood, her heart racing at the revelation. She didn't know how to feel or what to think. She wanted to be repulsed, but she couldn't bring herself to feel that way about a boy who'd had no choice about where he was born or who his parents were. She pictured herself at the age of twelve, her mother and father keeping her safely ensconced in a loving home. He'd never known such care and comfort.

She wanted to reach out and offer it to him now, but

he looked into the flames, his pain and loneliness making the lines of his body sag, and she sensed he wasn't finished speaking.

"I needed you to know, because I don't want to try and keep it hidden anymore." He finally looked at her and she could see sadness in his eyes. "If we're going to be business partners, then we need to be honest with one another."

She needed him to know she understood—as well as she could at the moment. It would take time to process this information, but how could she lose respect for a man who had pulled himself out of the mire of his childhood and made something of his life? Her heart broke for him as a child. She couldn't imagine what it was like to grow up the way he had.

Elizabeth faced him, not dropping her gaze, and hoped she could convey the renewed respect she felt for him. "I'm proud of you for what you've become, Jude. You have more courage and class than any man I've ever met. I couldn't lose respect for you. If anything, I have more respect, knowing where you've come from and where you are now."

Hope flickered in his gaze—but just as quickly it died away and he focused on the fireplace once again. "That's not all, Elizabeth. My childhood is only part of my story. There's so much more to share—so many things I'm ashamed of."

His voice was so low—so filled with regret—she wrapped her arms around her waist and braced herself.

Jude's emotions were raw tonight, his disappointment and guilt so thick, he didn't care if he told her everything and she rejected him for good. What did he risk in telling her the truth now? He could never ask for her to love him, so why should he be afraid if she knew? The only thing he risked was her displeasure at bringing ex-prostitutes into the hotel, but he was tired of trying to hide his work, tired of forcing Violet to keep quiet about her past and the others to keep the information hidden. Eventually she'd learn the truth, why not get it over with and be free?

She studied his face. Her blue eyes were so tender and pure, so full of trust and innocence. There had never been another woman who had looked at him the way Elizabeth did now. Even after learning the truth about his parents. If that had been all—if it was that simple—maybe there would be a way for them to move forward. He could pull her into his arms and allow her compassion to heal his wounds. But it wasn't that simple. There was more to his story—things she wouldn't understand—and he had to tell her. He sensed God wanted her to know the whole truth, not just part of it.

Jude's clothing was wet and clammy against his skin, and his thoughts were dark and stormy. The heat from the fireplace offered warmth to his body, but it couldn't penetrate to his conscience.

He hadn't made it to Maggie Ray in time. She'd died moments before he arrived.

Jude hated to think about the note he'd have to send to the young man named John. He didn't doubt that John really loved Maggie, and if he had been given the chance that he would have married her. But now he would have to mourn his loss and plan her funeral.

Jude should have immediately gone to her, instead of finishing the meeting. Maybe he could have gotten her to a doctor and saved her life. He'd never know. But just like when his mother died, Jude had been too late. His mother had been beaten, too, but Jude had been afraid to go for a doctor. When he finally brought one the next morning, she was already gone. The doctor said if he had been summoned the night before, Jude's mother would have lived. He'd blamed himself from that day forward, and the only thing that brought him comfort was playing the piano.

Music was the one constant in his life. It was the one thing besides Christ that he could trust and rely on. It would never change, hurt him or demand anything in return for the gift it gave.

"What else is there to tell me?" Elizabeth sat on the sofa again, her voice uncertain.

He risked everything by telling her, but he couldn't shake the feeling that he needed to get the truth out in the open. It was the only way he could face her.

"When the brothel owner died, I used all my earnings to buy his business."

Her eyes grew wide, but she didn't say anything.

"I operated the brothel for over five years."

Her lips parted and her face filled with shock. "You profited off the innocence of women?"

There was no way to make it sound any better than it was. "Yes. And I live with the guilt every day of my life."

He sat on the sofa beside her, desperate for her to know the rest. "I never went to school. I had no skills. It was all I knew. I had no other options."

"There are always other options." Her eyebrows came together.

"One of the reasons I bought the brothel was to take care of the women who worked there. As strange as it may sound, they were like family to me. The only family I ever had. I truly thought I was helping them."

Elizabeth looked away from him and it broke his heart to know that she would never look at him the same way—yet, what choice did he have? His past was just as much a part of him as his present.

"Martha came to work for us as a cook. She was unlike anyone I'd ever met. She taught me how to read using the Bible and I slowly began to understand the Gospel of Christ. I learned there is truth and forgiveness available to us all."

She still wouldn't look at him, so he went on quickly.

"As soon as I learned the truth, I burned down the brothel and found jobs for the ladies who worked there. Martha and I came north and…" He stopped. This was the part he didn't want to tell because this was the part she had control over. If she made it to January she would be his business partner, just as he promised, and she could tell him to stop his work immediately. He'd struggled with this reality all night—yet, Martha was right. God didn't make mistakes. Somehow this was all part of His divine plan.

Elizabeth finally looked at him. Disillusionment and anger in her eyes.

"I came north to start a hotel so I could rescue women out of the bonds of prostitution. Martha came to help. After I rescue them I bring them here and Martha teaches them. Then I find them other work—and some get married."

"Violet?" Her eyes grew wide again. "Violet is an ex—" She stopped before she said the word.

"Yes. Though I don't see her as anything but a child of God who has been given a second chance."

Elizabeth stood and paced to the fireplace. She spun and her hair fell like a curtain around her shoulders. She had to be the most beautiful woman he'd ever met—yet she was out of his reach. More now than before.

She wrapped her arms around her waist. "Did my father know?"

"Yes."

"And he allowed you to do something so…so…" She let the words trail away, yet he could easily fill in the blank.

"He didn't help me, but he didn't refuse me, either." Jude stood, but he didn't move toward her, afraid she might bolt from the room. "We were a good team. He managed the books and the finances and I operated the hotel. The women I rescued were assets to the business. They were eager to learn and none were afraid of hard work."

"Do others know?"

"Ben knows, but he's the only one. Our customers don't know, though I think some of them suspect. But out here, normal society rules don't apply as much. People are more willing to overlook things."

She didn't seem to hear him. "What self-respecting woman would choose such a life?"

"Most don't. It's forced upon them."

"Everyone has a choice."

"Not everyone."

"I had a choice!" She said the words so quickly and with such force, Jude was speechless.

Elizabeth turned away and looked at the fireplace, her shoulders tight and her body shaking.

Had she been propositioned?

The thought sent anger pulsing through his veins.

He went to her and turned her by the shoulders. "Who would ask you to do something like that?"

"It doesn't matter." She looked up at him with fury in her eyes. "What matters is that I said no."

"Not everyone has that luxury."

She pulled away from him and walked around the back of the sofa to get to the door.

Lightning filled the room once again, lasting for several heartbeats and then dying away.

"I want Violet to leave as soon as possible," she said without looking at him. "And I don't want you to bring any more women into this hotel. Grace and I will see to all the work."

With that, she left the room.

Jude leaned against the wall as a crack of thunder reverberated through the hotel. Shame and disappointment crowded his thoughts. Why couldn't he be like other men? Why couldn't he have a past he was proud of? And, most important, why did he have to tell her everything?

"Was that what You wanted, God?" He looked out the window, wishing he could see the God he spoke to. "Was she supposed to get angry and upset? Am I supposed to stop bringing women into this hotel?" He prayed he had done the right thing and that somehow God would make things right with Elizabeth.

Chapter Fourteen

Elizabeth opened her eyes the next morning and found a mop of blond curls cuddled up beside her. Elizabeth wrapped her arms around her sister, pulling her tight as all the memories from the previous evening returned.

Anger and shame flooded her at the way she had responded to Jude. Her own fear of what had almost happened to her after Papa left had made her feel humiliated and self-righteous. Last night she had been defending her own choices and actions, instead of listening to Jude, and it had caused her to speak without thinking.

The dawn had not yet broken and the sky still boasted its early morning stars. She had come back to the room around four o'clock—only an hour ago. Her eyes felt gritty and her head pounded—but it was her broken emotions that hurt the most.

She'd admitted her greatest secret to Jude. After their father had left, and she was desperate for a way to provide for her sisters, she'd almost accepted a man's invitation to be his mistress. In exchange, he'd promised to keep her and her sisters comfortable, well fed and housed. It was easy to refuse at first, but after weeks of not finding work, and practically starving, she had almost caved. She would have done anything to take care of her sisters, but when she went to the man's office to tell him yes, she couldn't bring herself to knock on his door. Instead, she had gone down the street and stopped at Brown's General Store. There, she had found a job and been spared from the deplorable life she'd almost accepted, though Mr. Brown's advances hadn't been easy to deal with, either.

"Lizzie?" Rose turned, her face half-hidden behind her curls. Big brown eyes blinked up at her. "I'm hungry."

Elizabeth kissed the tip of her cute nose and closed her eyes, the lure of sleep and the reality of what awaited causing her to burrow deeper into the covers. "Just a few more minutes."

Rose giggled and pulled out of Elizabeth's embrace. She bounced on her knees. "I can smell Martha's bacon!"

What was the use in putting off the inevitable? Elizabeth climbed out of bed and realized she still wore her robe from the night before.

Grace rolled over and moaned. "It's too early to wake up."

"Another day is calling," Elizabeth said as she pulled her hair back. "Rose, where is my blue ribbon?"

Rose shrugged as she continued to bounce on the bed. "Maybe the kitten took it."

"Kitten?" Elizabeth opened the lid of her trunk to pull out her extra hair ribbon. "What kitten?"

"The one Mr. Jude gave me."

Elizabeth turned her full attention on her sister. "He gave you a kitten?"

"Yes. He found it in the alley without its mama yesterday. He said he and Martha would take care of it, but I could play with it."

Elizabeth looked at Grace. "Did you know about this kitten?"

Grace sat up and yawned. "Yes. I thought everyone knew about Edgar."

"Edgar? Is that the name of the kitten? How do I not know about this new pet?"

Rose stopped bouncing and shrugged again.

"You've been busy," Grace said, as she sat up and leaned against the headboard.

She had been busy, but too busy to hear about the nuances of life? She let her hair go and walked over to the bed, where she sat next to Rose and pulled her into her arms. "Could I meet Edgar?"

Rose smiled and nodded. "He's sleeping in a box in the kitchen."

"It wouldn't hurt for you to spend a little more time with her." Grace pushed aside the covers and climbed out of bed.

Rose blinked up at Elizabeth, her sweet, trusting gaze filled with unconditional love. "Could we go on a picnic by the river?"

Elizabeth ran her hand over Rose's curls, trying to tame them. "I'd love to go on a picnic, but today is laundry day and I promised Martha I would take down the drapes in all the rooms so we could wash them."

Rose's countenance fell.

"But I could use some help." Elizabeth touched her nose. "Would you like that?"

"Could Edgar help, too?"

"I don't think it would be smart to bring Edgar around

drapes *or* a tub of hot water. We can play with him for a little while before we get started."

Rose nodded and began to bounce again.

Elizabeth stood and went to her trunk. The letter she'd buried there made so much more sense now. It was probably a note from someone who was helping Jude rescue another soiled dove.

The thought at once repelled her and humbled her. Jude had been a brothel owner. He had taken advantage of an immoral situation and profited from the sins of others. Yet he had found redemption and forgiveness for his sins. Christ had died to cleanse him of his unrighteousness. God had offered mercy. How could she offer anything less?

If nothing else, she admired him for telling her the truth. He could have kept it hidden, but he had chosen to be honest at the risk of her scorn, which was exactly what she had given him.

Elizabeth dressed in an old gown, one she wasn't afraid to get dirty, and braided her hair in a simple coronet around her head. She put on an apron and laced up her boots, the whole time dreading her encounter with Jude. Now that she knew about his past, would she look at him differently? Would she treat Violet any different?

Rose tried to dress herself, but Elizabeth had to button up the back of her dress and help her with her boots. She brushed Rose's curls and put them in two braids then tied a small apron around her waist.

"Shall we go down to breakfast?" Elizabeth asked Rose.

Rose clapped. "Yes!"

"Grace?" Elizabeth looked over her shoulder. Grace had been dawdling and was still in her nightgown.

"I'll be down later. I have a bit of a headache this morning."

Grace didn't get sick often. She was too stubborn to be kept down, but she did look a bit pale this morning.

"Let me know if you need anything."

"I'll be fine."

Elizabeth took Rose's hand and they left their room.

The morning went by quickly and Elizabeth stayed busy helping Martha with the laundry. Rose was a fun distraction from the work and loved introducing Elizabeth to the kitten. In between loads of laundry, they took breaks to play with Edgar, who was much smaller and cuter than Elizabeth had anticipated.

Jude was nowhere to be found. Even Martha didn't know where he had gone.

Violet was still under the weather, and Martha had told her to remain in bed for a second day. Elizabeth was thankful she didn't need to face her quite yet.

When they had finished the laundry and it was drying on the clothesline in the yard next to the barn, they began supper preparations.

"What can I do to help?" Elizabeth asked.

"I put a few chickens in to roast earlier," Martha said, closing the oven door. "They're coming along nicely. You and Rose can peel potatoes."

"All right." Elizabeth pulled a stool out for Rose and helped her climb up to the worktable, then she took the potatoes and a large bowl and sat beside her.

Martha left the kitchen and went into the cellar for milk and eggs. When she came back, she set them on the cupboard. "I just saw Jude enter the barn."

Elizabeth gripped the paring knife. She would finally have to face him. Would he be cold and angry?

Would he ignore her and pretend nothing had happened the night before?

She had the overwhelming desire to flee from the kitchen, but she needed to face him eventually.

After a few minutes, he entered the back door and came into the kitchen.

Elizabeth glanced up and caught his eye for a brief moment before he looked at Rose.

"How's Edgar today?"

"She's ever so funny." Rose giggled. "She chases Lizzie's hair ribbon around and around."

"She?" Jude asked, bending down to pet the kitty that lay in the box near the door.

"Martha said she's a girl." Rose jumped off her stool and knelt beside Jude. "She purrs."

"If she's a girl, do you think she should be called Edgar?"

"Yes."

Jude smiled at Rose and pet the furry white kitten a few more times before he stood and faced Martha. "How is Violet feeling?"

"She'll be as good as new by tomorrow." Martha mixed up biscuits while she spoke to Jude. "She probably could have come back to work today, but the lamb needs a bit o' rest."

Jude took off his hat and clutched it in his hands. He still didn't meet Elizabeth's eye.

"I went to St. Cloud today and found a job for her."

Elizabeth stopped peeling her potato.

Martha also stopped her work. "Do you think she's ready?"

"I think she'll do fine. If she's willing, she'll be working at the *St. Cloud Visiter*."

Martha's eyebrows rose like twin peaks. "Isn't that the paper owned by Mrs. Swisshelm? I've read some of her editorials about Sylvanus Lowry and his swindling of the Winnebago Indians. She's not afraid to speak her mind."

"And she's not afraid to take on a young woman with Violet's past." He finally looked at Elizabeth, his gaze hooded. "I was honest with her about Violet and she's happy to continue her training."

Martha glanced between Jude and Elizabeth. "Did you…?"

Jude looked away from Elizabeth. "I told Elizabeth everything last night."

Martha nodded slowly, her keen gaze assessing the situation. "Do you think Violet will want to go?"

"I'll ask her this evening, but I don't see why not."

"It's probably for the best," Martha said, going back to her biscuit dough.

"I have some correspondence to see to." Jude pet Edgar one more time and patted Rose's head, then he pushed through the swinging door and disappeared.

Elizabeth let out the breath she'd been holding and looked down at her potato. She started to peel once again, though her thoughts were not on supper anymore.

Martha didn't say anything for a few moments, but then she wiped her hands on her apron and grabbed her roller.

"So now you know everything," Martha said.

"I do."

"And what are you thinking?"

Elizabeth glanced at Rose, who sat preoccupied with the kitten.

"I'm not sure what I'm thinking."

"Are you disappointed in Jude?"

Was she? She hated to think of what he used to be, but she couldn't fault him for what he had become. "No."

"Did you ask him to send Violet on her way?"

Elizabeth stopped peeling, shame and guilt lying heavy on her conscience. "I did."

Martha nodded. "I thought so." There was no censure in her voice, just understanding. "I think she'll be happy in St. Cloud. Maybe she'll gain a bit more confidence under Mrs. Swisshelm's lead."

Elizabeth's shoulders stooped. "I feel awful. I reacted without thinking and I probably hurt Jude and Violet in the process."

"Probably." Again, her voice held no blame. "But it will all work out, you'll see." She patted Elizabeth's hand. "Now don't fret, lovey. Sometimes we make mistakes, but we get second chances every day. Everything will be just fine."

Elizabeth wished she had Martha's confidence.

A week later, Jude rode home after dropping Violet off in St. Cloud, about thirty miles south of Little Falls. She had seemed eager to start working for Mrs. Swisshelm and be done with cleaning rooms. Jude asked that she write from time to time so they knew how she was doing. Some of his favorite letters were from the women he'd helped liberate.

The Wood's Trail spread out before Jude with the Mississippi River to his left and a wooded thicket to his right, the leaves gone from the trees after the locust invasion. Humidity hung in the air and mosquitos buzzed around his head. His mood was sour and his thoughts jumbled.

He and Elizabeth had barely spoken since she learned about his past. They had kept a cool distance between them, speaking only when necessary. He was relieved that she finally knew the truth—yet he missed her. His heart still beat faster when she entered a room and he looked for her when he hadn't seen her in a while. Some nights he couldn't sleep, knowing she was only a few doors down the hallway, yet unreachable.

Abram's sawmill came into view, and activity in the millpond reminded Jude of the day he'd rescued Rose from the log. Over the past few weeks, he had come to enjoy the little girl more and more. Every morning they played with Edgar in the kitchen while Martha and Elizabeth cooked breakfast. In the evenings, he had taught her how to play checkers and she taught him games like Hot and Cold, Who Has the Penny and others he'd never played as a child. He found it hard to say no to her, but more than that, he loved seeing life through her innocent eyes.

Jude rode up Main Street and took a left on Broadway. He drove to the middle of the block and pulled the wagon into the alley behind the Northern Hotel. The thought of seeing Elizabeth again and yet not being able to fully enjoy her presence made him want to turn around and find somewhere else to go. But he had a pile of correspondence to see to. His request for assistance from the territorial legislature had been approved and they had asked for a representative to come to St. Paul to purchase the seeds and grain being granted to the Little Falls residents. Jude had been named the Little Falls representative. The letter he needed to write would let the legislature know when he planned to go to St. Paul.

Jude unhitched the wagon and rubbed down his horses, then he went into the kitchen.

"Mr. Jude!" Rose had been crouching by Edgar's box, but she jumped up when he entered the kitchen. "You're back in time."

"In time for what?" He picked up Edgar and ran his hand over the soft fur. The kitten purred in response.

"For my picnic." She raced over to the worktable, where Martha stood filling a basket with food.

"You're going on a picnic?"

"Yes. Lizzie said she has time today." Rose's eyes sparkled with anticipation. "Will you come, too?"

Go on a picnic with Elizabeth? The thought was at once appealing and disconcerting.

"Who else is going?"

"Just you and me and Lizzie!" Rose's braids swung as she turned in a circle.

How would he say no to her? He hated to see her upset, yet he couldn't spend that much time with Elizabeth.

"Oh, go on with you, Jude," Martha said as she wrapped a sandwich in a clean cloth. "It's just a wee bit of a request." She winked. "And I've put in some of my dried-apple pie that you love."

Elizabeth entered the kitchen as she finished tying the bonnet ribbon under her chin. She wore a pretty new dress that fit her snugly at the waist and had belled sleeves. Her cheeks were pink and her eyes shining. "Are you ready?" she asked Rose, pausing when she spotted Jude.

He nodded once, wishing his senses didn't become so alive when he saw her.

"Mr. Jude is coming!" Rose jumped up and down and clapped.

Elizabeth looked at Jude, her eyes growing a bit wider. "You're coming?"

Rose took his hand and tugged him to the door. "Grab the basket, Lizzie."

Elizabeth didn't move for a moment. Was she wondering how she could get out of being with him?

"I'll grab the basket," Jude said.

Martha closed it tight and nudged it toward him. "Have fun, lovey."

"Come, Lizzie." Rose pulled on Jude's hand once again and led him to the door.

"We'll be back as soon as possible to help with supper preparations," Elizabeth told Martha. "Grace is at the front counter and I changed the linen in room number eleven."

"Go on." Martha pushed Elizabeth out of the kitchen. "We'll be just fine without you for a couple hours."

The three of them walked out the back door and into the alley.

Elizabeth faced forward, hiding her features behind the brim of her bonnet.

"Where are we going?" Jude asked Rose.

"To the river." Rose took one of Jude's hands and one of Elizabeth's and pulled them toward the north.

The river was only two blocks away and they soon came to the banks. Grass had begun to grow again and a slew of wildflowers had popped up along the edge of the water. Pink and purple blossoms nodded on the breeze. A mama duck must have sensed their approach, because she led her ducklings away from the banks out into the open water.

"Look," Rose said, pointing to the ducks. Her giggle was infectious and Jude smiled.

Elizabeth stood facing the river. The gentle wind rippled the skirt of her gown and tossed her brown tendrils of hair against her cheeks. From this angle, he could see the reflection of the river in the blue of her eyes.

"I'll lay out our picnic," she offered.

"And I'll pick flowers to enjoy while we eat." Rose skipped toward the patch of flowers.

"Don't go too far," Elizabeth warned. "And stay away from the water's edge."

"I will." Rose wandered off a little way and Jude set the basket on the ground.

Elizabeth opened it and pulled out a cloth, which she laid over the grass.

Jude knelt beside her and pulled each item out of the basket to hand to her.

They worked in silence for a few minutes, each tense with words unspoken. He didn't know what to say. He'd told her the truth and she'd responded exactly how he thought she would.

"I'm sorry, Jude." She sat back on her heels, her gaze searching his. "I'm sorry for the way I behaved the night you told me about your…past. And I'm sorry about Violet, too."

Her words were so heartfelt and so laced with regret, he paused for a moment and just stared at her.

"I hope—" She stopped and took a deep breath. "I hope we can still be friends. I do admire you for what you've done for Violet and the others. It just took some getting used to."

"Do you mean that?"

"I behaved poorly, but my pride was in the way and that's why it took so long to apologize."

"I'm sorry, too."

"For what?"

"For keeping it from you."

"But I know why you did. You were afraid I'd tell you to stop."

"And now?" He waited for her to answer, afraid of what she'd say.

"Now I understand why you do what you do."

"You don't have a problem if another woman needs a place to live and work?"

She looked off toward the river and glanced in Rose's direction. It was clear she was struggling with her answer. Finally she met his gaze, though her eyes weren't filled with the conviction and assurance he had hoped. "It's your hotel, so do what you think is best."

"If you're still here after January, what then?"

"It will still be your hotel—at least part of it—and you can do as you'd like."

He wanted to pull her into his arms and tell her how much he appreciated her cooperation, but instead, he sat where he was and smiled. "Thank you."

She nodded and rearranged the plates on the blanket, though they didn't need to be rearranged.

Dare he say what he hoped? "I'd like us to be friends, too, Elizabeth."

Her gaze came up to meet his and this time there was reassurance in her eyes. "Good."

Rose ran back to the blanket, her hands full of wildflowers, and chatted away about the river and the butterflies and all the waterfowl playing along the banks.

Jude and Elizabeth listened and laughed, brimming

with the cautious expectation of forgiveness and the joy of a child.

Was this what it felt like to be part of a loving family?

He inhaled a sweet breath of fresh air, thankful for a new beginning with Elizabeth and a chance to experience family—even if it wasn't his family and it couldn't last forever.

Chapter Fifteen

A moonless night hung around Jude and Ben like a dark shroud. It was their first shift on the vigilance committee and they were both aware of the stories the others had shared about their run-ins with Hugh's gang. Two men had gone out on watch every night, and every night they went home reporting vandalism, theft and violence.

Jude and Ben rode their horses at a slow canter going up and down each street and alley. It had to be well past two o'clock, but all was still and quiet. There had not been any disturbance from the gang, only a group of teenage boys who had been smoking behind the livery stable. They'd rebuked the rascals and sent them home, but that had been the extent of their work for the evening.

A long night stretched ahead and Jude was determined to use his time to talk some sense into Ben about Elizabeth. His friend knew him well enough that he didn't have to make small talk. "Are you going to get serious about Elizabeth?"

Ben looked around the alley, appearing to be in no hurry to answer. "I tried. She wasn't interested."

"When will you get a little backbone where women are concerned?"

"Backbone?" Ben turned to Jude. "It has nothing to do with backbone. I'm honoring her wishes and keeping a respectable distance."

Jude snorted. "If I was interested in her, and I saw she had even the slightest interest in me, I'd pursue her."

"You don't think she has the slightest interest in you?"

"Of course not. How could she be interested in a man like me?"

"And what kind of man is that?"

A noise came from behind the bank and both men pulled up on their reins to stop their mounts. Jude held his breath as he listened for another sound.

A cat jumped off a barrel and raced down the opposite end of the alley.

Jude let out his breath and noticed Ben sat more loosely on his horse.

They continued down the alley and finally Ben said, "Are you going to answer my question?"

Jude looked over the shadows, his eyes alert and his ears attuned to every noise. "I told Elizabeth about my past. All of it."

"So?"

"So, how could I expect a woman like Elizabeth to be interested in a man like me?"

Ben pulled on his reins again, drawing his horse to a stop. "The way I see it, we all have things in our pasts we're not proud of."

Jude stopped Lady and faced Ben.

"We all need Christ's forgiveness," Ben continued, "or He would have never come. You're no different than me, or any other man for that matter."

"You aren't the child of a prostitute."

"No, I'm not. My father was a French fur trader with a wife and family in Montreal. My mother was the daughter of an Indian guide who worked with my father along the Mississippi. My father loved my mother, but after she died, he went back to his family in Montreal and he brought me to live with a missionary at Pokegama. I've never seen him since and I suspect he's never told his family about me."

Jude frowned. He'd never heard Ben's story before.

"So how are we any different?" Ben asked. "Both of us are from ill-begotten relationships."

"But you didn't perpetuate your father's sin by owning a brothel."

"No, I didn't, but I struggled for many years with being abandoned by my father and I rebelled against the missionary's message. I did things I'm not proud of in that time, just as you did. But by the grace of God, I was forgiven and set free from my past. The same as you. What the enemy intended for evil, God has used for good."

Jude had lived with the idea that he wasn't good enough to ever enjoy the love of a wife and family. He'd been called to walk alone…or had he? Could Ben's words be true? Was he worthy of finding love and happiness, despite his parentage and despite his sinful past? Part of him wanted to cling to Ben's words—and the other part mocked him for hoping.

They nudged their horses into motion again and left the alley.

Broadway was dark and deserted at this hour. The sky stretched over them like a canopy filled with the twinkling stars of summer. They rode alongside the Northern, where a single lantern shone from the front window, letting the late passerby know the hotel was open.

A movement down the dark alley behind the Northern caught Jude's eye. He reached out and put his hand on Ben's shoulder to stop him.

Jude dismounted and handed Lady's reins to Ben. He edged along the back of the Northern, his hand hovering over his pistol, and noticed two people near the barn.

They were caught up in a passionate embrace. The woman's back was toward Jude and for a sickening heartbeat he thought it was Elizabeth—but then he recognized the silhouette of Grace.

The man pulled away. "Well, lookee here," said Hugh Jones. "The great and mighty vigilance committee found us, Grace."

Grace looked over her shoulder, keeping her head down, as if she didn't want Jude to see her.

"Get inside the hotel, Grace." Jude's voice held no room for argument.

She began to move away, but Hugh took hold of her arm. "You don't have to do what he says, sweetheart. You're a grown woman with a mind of your own."

Jude planted his feet, his hand still in place over his gun. He would defend Grace's honor, if need be.

It was hard to read her features in the darkness, but by the way she held her body Jude could tell she was uncertain which way to go.

"You'll hurt your sisters even more if you don't get inside immediately." Jude's voice was even. "If nothing else, think about your reputation."

"What good's a reputation?" Hugh asked her. "They're for boring people who don't want to live a little."

Grace straightened her shoulders. "I'll go back inside,

but not because you've told me to, Jude." She glanced up at Hugh. "I've already had all the fun I can tonight."

Hugh kissed her, long and hard.

Jude took a step toward them, but Grace broke away and walked toward the hotel.

Hugh stared at Jude until the hotel door closed behind Grace. "I ought to skin you alive for busting that up."

"Get out of here, Jones, and don't come back. Next time you step foot on my property, or you come near Grace, you'll be looking down the end of my pistol." Jude's body shook with the force of his anger. "Grace deserves better than you."

"Is that right?" Hugh spoke through clenched teeth. "If you try to stop me you'll regret the day you made this threat. I aim to see who I want, when I want. I won't let no self-righteous killjoy tell me otherwise."

"Get out of here," Jude said.

Hugh made a slow move toward his horse, which stood tethered to the clothesline in the barnyard. With unhurried movements he untied the horse and mounted. Though he moved with deliberate care, his body was tight with hatred.

He spurred his horse and trampled through the yard, connecting with the alley and then making his way north.

Ben stood at the opposite end of the alley. He was in a position to help, if needed, but he had stayed back, no doubt to protect Grace's self-respect—if she had any left.

It had been so long since Grace had mentioned Hugh, Jude had hoped she'd forgotten about the scoundrel. He hated to think what Elizabeth would feel when she found out.

Jude joined Ben and mounted his horse. He took the reins and put his spurs to Lady's flanks.

Ben didn't say anything for a time and neither did Jude. They took Broadway until they reached the river and then took a left onto Wood Street.

Finally, Jude broke the silence. "Did you hear all that?"

"I did."

"What should I do?"

"Talk some sense into Grace."

"Do you think it will help?"

Ben sighed. "Unfortunately, some people insist on making mistakes before they gain wisdom. I have a feeling Miss Grace is one of those types of people."

"I still need to try."

"Never give up trying," Ben said. "And, for what it's worth, I don't think Hugh is going to honor your demands."

Dread knotted in Jude's gut. How far would Hugh go to prove his point with Jude?

"The gang is becoming more desperate," Ben continued. "With the economy as bleak as it is, many have lost hope of making an honest living. They're drowning their sorrows in alcohol and making poor choices. I wish I knew how to reach them with the message of Christ's hope."

Jude wished he could look at the situation like Ben—but his fear was so tightly wrapped up in the threat Hugh had just issued and his concern for Grace, he had no desire to offer them hope. He only wanted to see justice served—and his makeshift family protected.

Elizabeth sat behind the front counter with the ledger open before her, but her focus was not on her work.

Bright sunshine poured through the lobby windows beckoning her outside, if for no other reason than to be free of her sister's icy glares. Though it was Grace who had been caught dallying with Hugh Jones, Grace treated Elizabeth like she was the guilty party. No matter how much Elizabeth tried to talk to her sister about the incident two weeks ago, Grace refused to give her any details.

"There you are, lovey." Martha entered the lobby, her ever-drooping bun slightly askew and her dress wrinkled.

"Is Rose asleep?" Martha asked.

"She's taking her afternoon nap."

"Good, then you can do me a favor." Martha came behind the counter, tugging Elizabeth to her feet. "I'll take your spot here and you can bring Jude some refreshments."

Jude and Pascal were splitting wood in the barnyard. They had been at it for days, laying in the supply they would need for the coming winter. Whenever Elizabeth passed a window facing the back of the hotel, she would pause and watch Jude work. He had been wearing a pair of denim trousers and a plaid shirt rolled up at the sleeves last time she looked. His hair was tousled and his skin glistened with perspiration. It had taken all her willpower to look away.

"Why can't you bring him refreshments?" Elizabeth asked as Martha shooed her out from behind the counter.

"I've been on my feet all day." Martha took a seat on the stool. "I could use a bit of a break."

Martha rarely took breaks, but who was Elizabeth to contradict her?

"There's cool water and fresh baked molasses cookies

in the kitchen." Martha crossed her arms, a self-satisfied smile on her face.

Elizabeth glanced at Martha as she walked down the hallway. The older woman just smiled and waved.

The refreshments were waiting on a tray in the kitchen, just as Martha promised. Balancing the tray, Elizabeth left the back of the hotel. The sun felt wonderful on her shoulders and the fresh air invigorated her mood.

Jude had his back to Elizabeth as he set a log on end and then brought the ax down with a mighty swing. Two halves of the log fell away from the blade and he picked up one, leveled it, and swung his ax again. He tossed each piece onto a growing pile to his left.

Over and over again he swung the ax, his muscles rippling under his shirt. He wiped his brow with the back of his sleeve and kept working.

She wished she could watch him all day—but she'd be mortified if he caught her staring.

He swung the ax one more time and she used the slight lull to speak. "Care for a break?"

Jude lowered the ax to his side and turned to face her, his eyes lighting with pleasure. "I'd love a break," he said with teasing in his voice. "Are you here to take over?"

"I could never compete with your skill or speed." She held up the tray. "So I brought refreshments to give you the strength you need to finish."

He swung the ax and it stuck into a log nearby. "Sounds like a good compromise."

Since their truce near the river, they had enjoyed a simple camaraderie, even if there was still distance between them. They maintained a professional relationship, never speaking of personal issues. When the situation with Grace arose, he had spoken to her plainly and then let her deal with her sister. He had not overstepped his boundaries, but treated her and Grace with respect for their privacy.

"Did you make the cookies?" he asked.

She set the tray on an upturned log. "Martha made them."

He was clearly pleased with the news. "I love her molasses cookies, but let me wash up a bit first."

He went to a water barrel near the barn and rinsed his hands.

It was strange seeing him in work clothes. Usually he was in a well-pressed suit with his hair neatly combed. It was harder to think of him in a purely professional manner when he didn't look the part.

"Where's Pascal?" Elizabeth asked. "Martha has two glasses on the tray. I assumed he'd be out here."

Jude looked over his shoulder. "Martha sent him off on an errand to the general store."

"How long ago?"

"Maybe five or ten minutes."

So Martha had planned for her and Jude to be alone. She would need to tell Martha that there was no use playing matchmaker. Her thoughts about marriage had not changed. She would focus on raising Rose and finding Grace a husband—though her sister was not cooperating.

Jude came back and took the glass of water. Elizabeth watched him drink it in one fluid motion. He arched his head back until he'd swallowed the last drop, and then he set down the glass, looking up at her as she still watched him. "That hit the spot."

"The ball is on Friday," she said quickly, trying to divert her thoughts.

He chuckled. "Yes, I know."

"Do you think there will be any trouble from Hugh's gang?"

The lines deepened around Jude's mouth and his countenance became grim. "There's always trouble with them."

They were both quiet for a moment. "Grace and I will wash the windows in the ballroom tomorrow and Martha has extra coffee beans stocked up. Is there anything else we need to plan?"

He took a cookie and examined at it as he spoke. "Do you have an escort to the ball?"

For some reason, the question made her uncomfortable, even though it shouldn't. "Ben asked if he could be my escort."

"Ben?" He looked at once irritated and surprised.

Her defenses rose. "Is there something wrong with Ben escorting me?"

He shook his head. "No. I'm just a little surprised that you said yes, given your stance on marriage."

"What does the ball have to do with my stance on marriage? Ben is a good friend. I respect and admire him. Nothing more."

He nodded, though his eyes were still troubled. "And Grace?"

Elizabeth sighed. "Grace hasn't accepted anyone's invitation, though she's had plenty." She hated to think that Grace would go unescorted. Yes, they lived and worked at the hotel, but it didn't seem right for a lady to go to a ball without a proper partner.

A thought came to her. "Would you escort her?"

"Me?" Jude shook his head. "I was planning to man the front desk."

"But couldn't Pascal do that?" Elizabeth asked. "It would mean a lot to me if you came."

He studied her, his brown eyes full of so many questions. "You'd like me to come?"

"For Grace," she said quickly.

A twinkle returned to his eye. "If I come, would I finally have the honor of a dance with you?"

The unexpected thought of being in his arms sent pleasure racing through her midsection. Ever since their last dance had been interrupted she'd hoped to get another chance. But how would she manage to keep him at a safe distance if she was in his arms?

"You did make me a promise," he said.

"What promise?"

"That we could be friends, and friends are known to dance together on occasion." He crossed his arms triumphantly.

Friends did dance together and remained friends. Perhaps she and Jude could dance together, after all. "Are you any good at dancing?"

A slow grin spread across his handsome face. "I guess you'll have to wait and see—or ask Rose."

His happiness pleased her more than it should.

"I need to get back inside." Just the thought of dancing with him again was enough to make her cheeks warm.

Elizabeth picked up the tray and he quickly grabbed another cookie before she turned away.

She was halfway across the alley when he called to her. "Elizabeth."

She turned. "Yes?"

"I might want two dances." He winked and picked up his ax, whistling as he went back to work.

Heat filled her cheeks as she watched him for a moment, enjoying the sweet pleasure of his friendship. She forced herself to return to the hotel and deposit the tray in the kitchen. When she returned to the lobby she found Martha on the stool, her back against the wall and her chin bent toward her chest. Soft snores filled the air around her.

"Martha." Elizabeth tapped her shoulder. "I'm back."

Martha blinked her eyes open. "What?"

"I'm back."

"You just left."

"No." Elizabeth giggled. "You fell asleep."

"I did no such thing." Martha stood and stretched her neck. A sheepish smile tilted her lips. "That's why I don't sit down during the day, lovey. I fall asleep too easily."

"You work harder than anyone in this hotel. A break once in a while is a good thing."

"We all work hard." Martha paused and assessed her. "Did you and Jude have a nice time?"

Elizabeth sighed. "I know what you're trying to do, but it won't work."

"And why not?"

"I have no interest in love or marriage."

"Oh, don't you, now? I've seen the way your eyes follow Jude. If I didn't know better, I'd think you're falling in love."

Love? It couldn't be love. "I have a deep respect for Jude and all that he does, but I don't love him. And even if I fancied myself in love, I have no interest in marriage."

"And why not? You're young and pretty. You have a

whole life ahead of you to enjoy in the arms of a good husband."

"I have a sister to raise and a hotel to buy." She readjusted the ledger, lining up the book with the edge of the counter. "A husband would complicate matters. And, besides, what man would want me with all the troubles I have?"

"Who doesn't have trouble, I ask? If a man loves you, he'll want to help shoulder your burden."

Elizabeth shook her head. "I thought a man loved me once." Her voice was laced with bitterness. "But as soon as I said I'd marry him, he demanded that I leave my sisters behind to follow him. I could never risk giving away my heart again, just to have it pulled from my chest by a man who has far too much power over my emotions." She met Martha's gaze. "I won't sacrifice my sisters for a man I love."

"Maybe the man you loved before didn't have the character qualities you need in a husband, and maybe God was sparing you from future pain by having him leave."

Elizabeth had never contemplated that James's betrayal was really a way to protect her.

"Before you give away your heart again," Martha continued, "learn his true intentions and ask him how he feels about your sisters. Find out what he hopes to gain by marriage and what he expects from you. If you know up front, there won't be any heartache later."

Could it be that simple? Was there hope that she could find someone who would love her and accept her just as she was? Had she already met him?

"Just as important," Martha cautioned, "is knowing

what you expect from him. Don't walk into marriage expecting to change him after you say 'I do.'"

Unease climbed up Elizabeth's spine when she thought of Jude's dangerous work with soiled doves. How long did he plan to continue? If she did give her heart to him, and if he did accept her as she was, could she live with the danger inherent in his calling? The thought of waiting up through the night, wondering if he'd return home, and then helping care for a fallen woman if he did was more than she could imagine.

Before she would even consider letting her heart go, she must know what his future plans included.

Chapter Sixteen

For the rest of that day and the next, Jude found little ways to seek out Elizabeth. In the past he had discussed the details of a ball with Martha, but now he went over everything from dance cards to orchestra music with Elizabeth. He even asked her where she thought they should position the ferns in the ballroom. Each time he appeared at her side with another obscure issue, he was rewarded with her patient smile, though he sensed something troubled her every time she looked his way.

Now, evening had fallen and Elizabeth was putting Rose to bed.

Jude sat on the front porch of the Northern, needing some time to clear his thoughts and seek God's wisdom. He longed to speak to Elizabeth about the things stirring in his heart, but fear of rejection held him back. He'd lived for so long with the idea that he was unlovable, it was hard to wrap his mind around the idea that he could be loved—and by a woman as sweet and beautiful as Elizabeth Bell.

He sensed she liked him and he couldn't deny the attraction they had for each other, but there was something that made both of them hesitate. He knew what it was for him, but he didn't know what troubled her, and that was the thing he needed to talk over with God.

He rocked his chair as he watched the town go to sleep. Abram and Nathan Richardson were on duty this evening and they had already ridden past the Northern once. They had stopped briefly to speak to Jude and give him the latest report on the gang's activities. Apparently, there had been a fight at Dew's place the night before and some of the gang had been hurt. The two vigilantes had brought the injured to Dr. Jodan and he had patched them up as well as he could.

Jude prayed for Abram and Nathan as they patrolled the streets and for Little Falls as a whole. After two years of incredible growth, all construction had come to a halt. Jude wondered if it meant the end for their town—or if it was just a lull until the economy picked up again. It was hard to tell, but he knew one thing: if the gang didn't break up soon, they would lose more business.

A rider approached from the south and it was apparent his destination was the Northern. As he drew up to the edge of the porch, Jude rose.

Ben sat atop his horse, his shoulders tight and his back rigid. "There's been some trouble." He dismounted and tied his reins to the hitching post.

"What kind of trouble?"

Ben walked up the steps and joined Jude on the porch. "One of the women at Dew's place was hurt bad last night and it took until now to get word to me."

"What's her name?"

"Gretchen. One of the other ladies snuck away and came to me. She said you told Gretchen that if she ever needed help to find me." He spoke more quietly. "From what I surmise, Gretchen was the impetus behind the fight last night. Two men were arguing over her and then others got involved. She was hurt during the fight, but it wasn't until after everyone left that Dew took out his anger on her. He blamed her for inciting the men and causing all the damage to his place."

"How bad is she?"

"She's bad, but according to the lady who came to me, her wounds aren't life threatening. She wants out and said you could help."

"I can help—but it will be hard to get in and out without being spotted. Everyone knows who I am."

"And if they link you to her disappearance, it will mean serious repercussions for you and the hotel." Ben's voice was grave. "Not to mention everyone who lives here."

For the first time in his life, Jude had more people to worry about than himself. Yes, he'd always been concerned for Martha's safety, but she had willingly worked alongside him to help. She knew the dangers and had said yes. Elizabeth, Grace and especially Rose were innocent in the whole matter and would have the most to lose if something went wrong.

Jude paced across the porch as a gust of wind whipped around the side of the Northern. The western horizon was dark with impending storm clouds.

"If we get her out of there," Jude said, "we'll have to find somewhere else to take her. She can't stay at the Northern."

"Which means we'll need the help of a female."

Jude paused in his pacing. "Why is that?"

"Doesn't Martha usually take care of their needs once you bring them here? We'll need the expertise of a woman to help Gretchen, too. According to the lady who visited, Mr. Dew won't let anyone in to see Gretchen. She'll need help cleaning up when we get her out."

"Maybe Martha will come."

"That's what I was thinking." Ben sat on one of the rockers and leaned forward, his elbows on his knees. "I think we should use the ball as a distraction tomorrow evening. While you are hosting the ball, I'll go to Dew's place and sneak her out. I'll hide her in my barn and then I'll come back. After that, you can bring Martha to tend to her."

A lot could go wrong with their plan, but it was the best they could do for now.

The front door opened and Elizabeth paused on the threshold. Her body was silhouetted by the light seeping out of the lobby.

Ben stood and Jude stopped his pacing.

Elizabeth looked from one to the other. "Hello, Ben."

"Hello, Elizabeth."

"Was I interrupting something?" she asked.

"No." The light from inside illuminated Ben's face, revealing the deep admiration he held for her. "We were just finishing."

"Do you need something?" Jude asked her quickly.

Before she could answer, Ben spoke. "I should go." He offered a slight bow to Elizabeth. "I'll see you tomorrow evening."

"I'm looking forward to it."

Ben mounted his horse and rode south toward the parsonage.

Jude hated how he felt when he witnessed Elizabeth and Ben together. It was clear they liked each other. If given the chance, would their mutual respect turn to something more? It's what he'd originally wanted…but was it what he still wanted?

At least, for now, he had her full attention.

He indicated the rocking chairs. "Would you like to join me?"

She closed the door and stepped onto the porch. With the elegance he had come to anticipate, she lowered herself onto the rocking chair and began to move it back and forth.

Jude also sat, but his movements felt choppy and out of rhythm. Though he'd spent his entire life around women, with Elizabeth he felt like he had no experience to draw upon. Everything with her felt new and uncertain.

"Tomorrow at this time the hotel will be full to capacity," she said.

"And I'll finally get a chance to dance with you."

Soft light seeped out the windows of the hotel, making rectangles on the porch and the street. It allowed him to see the smile of anticipation on her face, though there was a catch in her gaze.

The steady click of their rocking chairs filled the night air and competed with the sounds of crickets and frogs from the river. The wind continued to blow and a soft patter of rain started to fall on the porch roof. It danced upon the dusty street and dripped off the eaves.

Elizabeth took a deep breath. "I—" She paused and then said, "This place is beginning to grow on me." He sensed it wasn't what she had started to say, but he'd give her time and space to pull her thoughts together.

"It has a way of doing that." He recalled her fear during the Indians' dance and her despair after the locust invasion. He was certain that she'd pack up and leave after each incident, but she had stayed, revealing her commitment and dedication to the hotel and her sisters. "If you can claim that this place is growing on you, even after an Indian dance, a locust invasion and a gang of desperadoes, then I was wrong." He looked deep into her eyes, wanting her to believe him. "You *are* meant for frontier life."

"Even though I'm a single woman?"

"Probably even more so because you're single." He stopped rocking his chair. "You've had to learn how to be strong and courageous on your own, without relying on a man's help. I admire you for that, Elizabeth, more than I could ever say. You've shown strength of character at every turn. Your sisters should be proud of you."

She also stopped rocking and looked down at her hands. "I don't have the strength of character you give me credit for." Her voice was filled with regret. "I'm weak and easily discouraged. I've done things I'm not proud of and my faith falters at every turn."

He wanted her to know that what she said wasn't true, but she wouldn't look at him, so he reached out and placed his hand over hers. Her skin was warm and soft.

She looked up and met his gaze. Longing flickered in her eyes and for a moment hope flared in his chest.

But then she stood and walked to the porch steps, keeping her back to him. "I can't lie. I heard some of what you and Ben were discussing."

Jude stood, as well. "I was going to tell you."

She nodded, but still did not look at him. "It sounds dangerous."

"It's very dangerous."

She finally looked at him, her eyes beseeching. "Can someone else do it? Why does it have to be you?"

Her words tore at him. "Who else would do it?"

"Ben."

"Ben is helping, but he can only do so much. This is my calling—not Ben's. He just helps when I need him."

She clasped her hands together. "How long do you plan to continue this work?"

They stood for a few moments, neither one saying a word. A heaviness fell over him, because he knew what she was getting at. She might agree to let him use the hotel to help women, but if given the choice, would she let him continue rescuing them? He'd wanted to share his heart with her, but now he feared what it would cost him.

Resolve strengthened his spine. "I plan to keep helping women as long as I can. I made a promise to God and I aim to keep up my end of the agreement." He wouldn't apologize for his decision or back down from his commitment.

She nodded slowly, though her shoulders drooped. "I needed to know where you stand—and now I do." She unclasped her hands and walked across the porch to the door. "Good night, Jude." She slipped inside and disappeared.

Jude sank to the rocker as deep melancholy engulfed him. He had been foolish to hope.

The next evening, Elizabeth pulled on her long white gloves and wished she could muster more excitement for the ball. She wore her purple gown again and had her hair in ringlets, but she didn't feel like putting on a smile and entertaining a room full of men.

"Lizzie, may I come?" Rose asked, as she sat on the floor and played with Edgar.

"You've already asked at least a dozen times," Grace

said, securing a hair comb above her curls. "What has Elizabeth said?"

Rose's bottom lip slipped out into a pout. "No."

Elizabeth placed her dance card onto her wrist. Ben would arrive any minute and she didn't want to keep him waiting. She went to Rose and put her gloved hand under her sister's chin. "You've already been to one too many balls, young lady." She bent down and kissed her nose. "Someday you'll be all grown and you'll go to as many balls as you'd like."

Rose clamped her mouth shut tight and frowned. "It takes too long to grow up."

"Miss Nellie is here to sit with you tonight," Elizabeth said. "Be a good girl and mind your manners."

Nellie Carlisle was a teenage girl Elizabeth had met at church. She had agreed to come and spend the evening with Rose and promised not to fall asleep, like Mrs. Fadling had done last time. Nellie was in the sitting room waiting for Rose.

"Go on now," Elizabeth said, touching her curls once again to make sure the pins were secure. "Tomorrow we'll do something fun, just the two of us."

Rose grasped Edgar close to her chest and stood. She stomped her way to the door and made sure Elizabeth saw her frown.

Elizabeth tried to hide her smile, knowing it would only anger Rose more. Instead, she frowned, too, and looked as stern as possible. "No more of that, Miss Rose Bell."

The little girl opened the door to the sitting room and Elizabeth saw Nellie waiting for her on the sofa before the door closed behind Rose.

Elizabeth allowed herself to smile and then turned to Grace. "Are you ready?"

Grace nodded and stood. She wore a beautiful gown of blue-and-white-striped silk. Her dark hair, so like Elizabeth's, was also in ringlets.

"You look very pretty," Elizabeth said. "I hope you enjoy your time with Jude this evening."

Grace picked up her gloves and shawl. "I'm only permitting him to be my escort because Hugh isn't allowed on the property."

Elizabeth tried not to let her sister's words frustrate her. "Hugh isn't good for you, Grace. He doesn't have your best interest at heart. How do you picture your life in ten or fifteen years? Do you plan to be married and have children? Why would you continue to see Hugh if he's not the man you picture yourself with in the future?"

Grace put her hands on her hips. "Who says I don't picture a future with Hugh?"

"What kind of a future could he provide? He doesn't have a job or even a home. Will he be a good provider? Someone you can trust and rely on?"

"Like our father?" Grace said the word with venom. "Why try so hard to find a good man when none can be trusted? I might as well have a little fun while I'm young."

"Grace." Elizabeth took a step toward her sister. "How could you think like that? Papa did what he did out of grief."

"Who's to say the 'good' man I marry wouldn't behave poorly out of grief or melancholy or whatever life throws at him?" Grace pulled on her gloves and didn't look Elizabeth in the eyes. "You keep looking for that elusive man and I'll focus on the one who hasn't made any false promises to me."

Grace strode across the room and walked out before Elizabeth could find her voice. How could her sister think that way? Maybe, now that Elizabeth understood why Grace had been making such poor choices, she could talk some sense into her.

Elizabeth left their room to find Grace, but she was already on her way down the front stairs before Elizabeth could reach her.

Jude's door opened and he stepped out, adjusting his cravat. Elizabeth almost ran into him, but he put out his hands to stop her.

He looked striking in his evening coat, just as he had the night they'd met. Slowly, he lowered his hands from her arms, his eyes filled with admiration. "You look stunning."

She tried to smile, but her lips trembled and her stomach filled with butterflies. Here before her stood a man who was more dependable than any other. She knew he would always make the right choices under dire circumstances. Hadn't he proven that by making the most out of his life? Instead of running from his past, he'd embraced it and used his experiences to help others. Not only that, he was kind, handsome and funny. He was nothing like her father or James or anyone else she'd ever known.

Why, oh, why did he have to continue his dangerous work? It would be easy to fall in love with him if she didn't have to be concerned about his safety every time he went away. She had enough to worry about with her sisters.

Elizabeth didn't want to think about anything unpleasant tonight, so she tried to mask her whirling emotions by reaching up and fixing his cravat. "You look pretty dapper yourself."

He put his hands over hers. "Is everything all right?"

She shook her head, but couldn't find the words to tell him what troubled her.

The hallway lighting was dim with only a lantern on the end and a scant amount of daylight left in the sky outside the single window. Noise from downstairs indicated their guests had begun to arrive. The sound of an orchestra tuning up was a prelude to all the wonderful dancing to be had—including the dances they would share.

His brown eyes searched her face. "What's wrong, Lizzie?"

The use of her pet name made her want to melt into his arms. She had tried to keep their relationship on a professional level, but she longed to share her hopes and fears with him, to rest in his arms and let him help. He was the kind of man who could not only shoulder her burdens, but offer her wisdom and advice, too. "It's Grace," she whispered. "I finally understand why she's been acting the way she has and I'm frightened she may do something foolish before I can talk sense into her."

"Would you like me to try?"

She shook her head, thankful to have someone on her side, but knowing it would do no good. "I need to speak to her, but I'll have to wait until after the ball. I don't believe our conversation will be easy or over quickly."

Jude lowered their hands, and Elizabeth held her breath as he looked into her eyes.

"After tonight," Jude said while he rubbed his thumbs over the top of her hands, "I was hoping we could find some time to speak, too."

She dropped her gaze. It was too painful to see the

hope in his eyes when she knew she couldn't offer him her heart—not if he continued his work. "Jude—"

He reached up and put his finger against her lips. The gesture stilled her mouth but sent her pulse skittering. His touch was gentle, yet it felt like fire against her skin.

"Don't say anything yet," he said softly, looking at her lips. "Let's enjoy this evening and then we'll find the right words later."

It took all her willpower not to sigh with pleasure—instead, she nodded and swallowed, afraid she couldn't find the words right now even if she tried.

He lowered his hands, a tender smile on his lips, but so much more danced in his eyes. His look was full of longing and it made her want to believe that they could overcome anything—yet she knew it would only be a matter of time before his mission work came between them.

"Shall we go downstairs?" He held out his elbow and she was thankful her legs worked properly as she stepped to his side and wrapped her hand around his arm.

They descended the stairs together and found Ben waiting in the lobby.

His face brightened at her arrival and he quickly came to her side.

Jude slipped away, without another word, and went to Grace, who stood by the door greeting all the men and women who were arriving.

"Your cheeks are the most becoming shade of pink right now," Ben said with a smile.

Elizabeth put her hand up to her cheek, hoping he didn't suspect why she was blushing.

"Are you ready to dance?" Ben asked.

She nodded, still unsure if she could speak properly.

Chapter Seventeen

The ballroom had never felt more intimate or looked as amazing as it did when Jude watched Elizabeth. She twirled around the dance floor in Pierre LaForce's arms. Her cheeks were pink, her eyes were shining and her curls were bouncing to the lively tune. Jude was counting down the songs until it was his turn to hold her close, but until then, he would simply take pleasure in watching her.

He had danced the opening song with Grace, and Elizabeth had danced with Ben. Afterward, Ben had slipped out of the ballroom. Jude expected him back at any moment to let him know if Gretchen had been brought to safety. Jude tried to act nonchalant, but his insides were knotted up with concern for his friend's safety and all he had left to do tonight.

Jude scanned the ballroom for a sign of Martha. She usually wandered in and out, looking over the refreshment table and tapping her toes at the music. It had been a while since he'd seen her, so he left the ballroom to see if she needed help. He walked down the long hall, through the dining room and into the kitchen.

Martha sat on a stool near the worktable, her head resting in her hand.

"Martha?" Jude squatted before her. "Are you not feeling well?"

"Oh, go on with you." She tried to shoo him away, but he could see she was fighting pain just by the look in her eyes. "I'm fine."

He stood and put his hand on her forehead. "You're running a fever."

"What do you know about fevers?" she asked, trying to stand.

She swayed and then sat on the stool again.

"You're sick. You should be in bed."

Martha sighed and rubbed her temples. "I'm afraid I've caught something, to be sure. But I have no time for lying around in bed."

"I insist." Jude helped her to her feet and put his arm around her waist. "You're going to bed and I'm going to have Dr. Jodan come and take a look at you."

He expected her to refuse his offer, but she went along without further protest, her soft moans indicating she was in more pain than she'd let on.

"Where does it hurt?"

"Mostly my head, but my body is full of some aches and pains, too."

He walked her up the back stairs and then they took the steps up to the attic room. There were three single beds, but only Martha's was being used. Now that Violet had gone to St. Cloud, Martha was the only person sleeping on the third floor.

Jude helped her to her bed and she sat down.

"I'll go and get Dr. Jodan. He's in the ballroom."

Martha nodded and lay down without another word.

Jude left the attic, intent on finding the doctor, realizing he would have no help with Gretchen now. Jude and Ben would have to see to her needs…or he'd have to ask another woman. The only one he knew well enough to ask was Elizabeth.

He easily found Dr. Jodan, who was more than willing to check on Martha, and then he turned his attention on Elizabeth.

How would he convince her to help?

Ben walked into the ballroom, his face grim and his mouth set in a firm line.

He walked straight to Jude. "Can we speak in private?"

Jude nodded and led him to the parlor off the ballroom, where he kept his piano. They entered the room and Jude turned to Ben. "Did you get her?"

Ben nodded, but he didn't look pleased. "I found her in pretty bad shape. She's been lying on her own for days without help. She's still in the bloody clothes Dew left her in. Her cuts haven't been attended to and her clothes are torn and soiled." Ben swallowed and shook his head. "I've never seen anything like it."

Jude wished he could say the same, but he'd witnessed more abuse than anyone should ever have to see.

"We'll need Martha to bring her some clean clothes and toiletry items," Ben continued. "She has nothing."

"Martha's not well. She's in bed and Dr. Jodan is seeing to her now."

Ben's face filled with concern. "Who will help?"

Jude paced across the room, hating to ask the one person he wished to keep out of this mess. "Our only option is Elizabeth."

Ben shook his head. "It's too dangerous."

"Then who?" Jude lifted his hands. "No one else knows about this girl. Elizabeth is the only person I can think of. I'm supposed to dance with her soon and I'll ask her." He paused. "Is Gretchen in your barn? Did anyone see you with her?"

"Yes, she's in my barn and I don't think anyone saw."

"Good. We don't have much time before someone notices she's gone and comes looking for her. If Elizabeth agrees to help, I'll have her gather some things and then take her to your barn. I'll come back here, make an appearance so people don't suspect, and then take my wagon back to your place, where I'll pick up Gretchen and head to St. Cloud. You can come and get Elizabeth and bring her back to the ball."

"It sounds complicated."

"It usually is."

Ben nodded. "I'll head back to the ball with you. It's important that as many people as possible see us so Dew doesn't link us to Gretchen's disappearance."

"I agree."

They left the parlor and returned to the ballroom. Elizabeth stood on the side of the dance floor, her eyes searching the crowd until her gaze landed on him.

Jude strode across the dance floor as the orchestra began a waltz and the other dancers started to spin around the room. All thoughts left Jude as he stood before Elizabeth and looked into her beautiful face.

"May I have this dance?" he asked.

She curtsied and offered her hand. "You may."

He led her onto the floor and turned to face her. She looked up expectantly and deep affection stirred within his chest. He slipped his right hand around her tiny waist and loved when she rested her hand on his shoulder.

Their other hands clasped and he took the first step. She followed, matching him step for step, their graceful bodies moving in perfect rhythm. Not once did he take his eyes off her face or pay any attention to the other dancers. In this moment, it was only the two of them and nothing else mattered.

They swayed and twirled around the floor, and with each step they took he drew closer to her, wrapping his arm around her waist a little tighter.

"You're a marvelous dancer," she said, almost breathless.

"You doubted me?"

She smiled and the light glimmered in her eyes.

The dance would end all too soon, so he needed to make his request while he still had the chance.

"Ben returned."

For the first time since he'd approached her, she tore her gaze from his and scanned the room.

"He was able to get the young lady to his barn," he said quietly.

"Now it's your turn to see her to safety elsewhere?"

He nodded. "But there's been a little trouble."

Concern deepened the creases between her eyes. "What kind of trouble?"

"Martha was going to come with and see to Gretchen's needs. She's been beaten badly and needs some help tending to her wounds. Her clothes were destroyed and she has nothing." He paused, watching the emotions flicker across her face. "But Martha's sick. She's come down with some malady. Dr. Jodan is seeing to her now."

"Martha is ill?" Elizabeth's eyes opened wider.

"Yes. She's in bed and the doctor is taking care of her."

"Who will help the…the…"

"Gretchen?"

"Yes."

"I don't have anyone to help her now that Martha is sick." He took a deep breath as they continued to twirl around the room. "I was wondering if you'd be willing to help."

"Me?" Her steps faltered, but she quickly regained her stride. She shook her head. "I don't think I could."

"Why not? Neither Ben nor I can help her. There's no one else who knows about her but you."

Elizabeth looked away from his beseeching eyes. "I shouldn't leave the ball."

"Now is the perfect time. Everyone is dancing and having fun. They won't notice if you're gone for an hour."

She bit her bottom lip, but still did not look at him.

"Please, Elizabeth. I know what I'm asking is hard—but I wouldn't ask if I didn't think you could do this. Gretchen needs help and if we don't give it to her, no one will."

She finally looked at him. "I'll help you this time." She swallowed. "But please don't ask again."

If it was all she could give, it was all he'd ask. "Thank you. You're saving a woman's life, Elizabeth. She'll be forever grateful, and so will I."

She didn't respond, but continued dancing. When the song ended, she pulled away from him. "I'll go put some things together in a bag."

"Use the back stairs," he whispered. "I'll meet you there in five minutes."

He watched her walk away, her head held high, as others turned to look, too.

Jude found Ben where he'd left him by the parlor door. "Elizabeth agreed to help. She's gathering some things now. I'll meet her by the back stairs in five minutes and bring her to your barn. I should be back here in less than twenty minutes."

Ben nodded. "I tucked Gretchen in the back of the barn, behind a stack of hay."

Jude left the ballroom and waited for Elizabeth at the bottom of the back stairs. True to her word, she arrived in less than five minutes with a small bundle. She had put on her cloak and bonnet, and silently passed by him as she walked out the back door and into the dark alley.

Nerves overtook Jude as he thought about the danger he was putting her in. He wished there was some other way, but right now they needed to get Gretchen to safety as soon as possible. He'd have Elizabeth back to the ballroom in less than an hour and then he'd never ask her to help again.

Elizabeth stepped into the inky darkness of night, hating the shudder that raced down her spine. Why had she agreed to help Jude? How would she respond to the soiled dove when she saw her? Her only experience with women like her was in Rockford as a child. Whenever one of them appeared on the street, Mama had turned Elizabeth's head in a different direction and shielded her from seeing the women up close, just as Elizabeth had done with Rose. After she learned the truth about Violet, she'd had to fight the urge to look away every time the girl had entered a room. How could Elizabeth help this woman if she struggled to look at her or talk to her?

She followed Jude down the dark alley. Ben's home

was just south of the church, only a block away from the Northern.

"Thank you," Jude said quietly.

Elizabeth was silent for a few moments, still upset that he had asked her to do this thing, but understanding why he had. There was no one else to help. "You're welcome."

The stars hung overhead in a brilliant array and the moon lent a soft light for her to see his troubled features. He had been just as uncertain about asking her as she had about accepting. How could she stay mad at him when he was doing the right thing?

It didn't take long for them to reach Ben's barn. Right before they left the alley to approach the small structure, Jude reached out and took her hand, pulling her to a stop.

She held her breath as he stood like a statue. Was he listening for something? Had he heard a noise?

"Is everything all right?" she whispered.

He nodded and then his gaze found hers. "I was just listening to see if we'd been followed or spotted." He spoke so quietly, she could hardly make out his words.

Jude continued to stand there and she didn't move a muscle. Abram and Charlotte's house and barn were visible at the bottom of the hill behind Ben's home. The Mississippi River sparkled in the light of the moon and crickets filled the air with a natural symphony.

His grip tightened around her hand and she looked up to find him watching her. A part of her longed for him to pull her into his arms and reassure her that all would be fine, that she would return to the ball soon, that he would come back safe from escorting the lady to St. Cloud and that he would finally agree to stop this dangerous work.

He looked at her with such trepidation she couldn't help but whisper, "Are you sure everything is all right?"

"Be careful," he said. "As soon as I leave, bar the door and don't let anyone in until Ben or I return."

She nodded.

Without warning, he drew her into his arms and held her tight.

Elizabeth inhaled a sharp breath and then gave in to the yearning she'd felt before. She wrapped her arms around him and nestled into his solid body.

He pulled her closer and she loved the way her body formed to his. She inhaled his scent and felt the warmth from his embrace all the way to her toes.

He set his cheek upon her hair and ran his hands up the length of her back. The sensation made her sigh. She wanted to linger there all night, and the longer he held her, the more she wanted to stay.

"Be safe," she whispered as she pulled away.

"You, too."

Jude led her across the small yard and they walked through the door leading into Ben's barn.

A horse stood on one side, quietly munching on hay, but nothing else moved in the dark interior. Another shudder ran up Elizabeth's spine and she clutched the bundle of clothes and food she'd brought for the lady.

Jude closed the door and walked across the barn to a pile of hay in the corner. He motioned for her to follow, so she picked her way across the space, trying to ignore the musty, foul smells of the barn.

"Gretchen?" Jude whispered.

Again, silence.

"It's me, Jude Allen." He squatted behind the hay and Elizabeth could only see his head in the meager light.

"I've brought someone to help you." He looked at Elizabeth and nodded for her to approach.

"Miss Bell has brought clean clothes," Jude whispered. "I'll leave her here with you, and when I come back I'll have a wagon to bring you to St. Cloud. There's a woman there who has agreed to take you in until we can find a more suitable place for you to live and work."

"I want to get as far away as possible," said the woman Elizabeth could not see. Her voice was surprisingly cultured and refined, though it was bitter and laced with pain.

Elizabeth rounded the corner of the hay pile and choked on a gasp that threatened to release. The woman lying in the hay was so badly beaten that her eyes were almost swollen shut and her cheeks were bruised. A cut above her eye had bled and scabbed over, leaving a mess in her eyebrow and down the side of her face. Her hair was tangled and her dress—what was left of it—was torn in several places. She clutched it around her body as she stared at Elizabeth.

What monster would do such a thing to a woman?

Jude watched Elizabeth closely and she knew she needed to mask her response, so she forced a smile.

"This is Miss Elizabeth Bell," Jude said softly to the lady. "Elizabeth, this is Miss Gretchen."

"Abbot." Gretchen tried to rise up on her elbows, but she fell back to the hay with a groan and pressed her lips together, not looking at Elizabeth. "My name is Gretchen Abbot."

"It's nice to meet you, Miss Abbot."

Jude offered Elizabeth the slightest smile and then he stood. "I'll leave you women to tend to things. I'll return in about a half an hour." He went to the door and looked back at Elizabeth. "Remember, bar this door and don't let anyone in but Ben or me."

Elizabeth walked toward him and he grabbed a board that looked about the right size to block the door shut.

He handed it to her, his eyes searching hers, then he leaned down and placed a kiss on her cheek. "Thank you," he whispered. "I know how much I'm asking of you."

Her cheek tingled where he'd kissed her and she placed her hand there.

Jude opened the door and walked out.

Elizabeth placed the board in the slots on either side of the door and tugged it to make sure it was firm.

A lone window faced the alley and Elizabeth watched Jude pass by. He strode with purpose back the way they'd come. In no time at all, he'd return to get Gretchen, so she needed to make sure the lady was ready to go.

Elizabeth walked back to the straw pile and took a deep breath. When she rounded the corner she found Gretchen lying exactly as they'd left her.

"I have a clean gown and some undergarments," Elizabeth said. "They're not much, so I apologize."

Gretchen didn't say anything as she looked at Elizabeth.

"I'll try to help you up so we can remove your other things first." She knelt beside the lady and slipped her arm under Gretchen's back. There was nothing to the woman but skin and bones.

Gretchen moaned as Elizabeth helped her sit up. It was dark in the barn, but Elizabeth was able to work with efficiency. Gretchen was little help, since it hurt for her to move. Elizabeth suspected that a couple of ribs and perhaps her collarbone were broken from the way she responded to different movements.

The barn was too quiet. Elizabeth could hear herself breathing above Gretchen's labored moans.

"You'll need to see a doctor as soon as you get to St. Cloud," Elizabeth said, hoping to fill the space with her words. "I don't know where Mr. Allen will take you, but they'll see to your needs."

Gretchen began to cry and Elizabeth suspected it had nothing to do with her physical pain.

As she helped Gretchen slip into the clean undergarments and then the dress, the young lady's cries turned to sobs. They racked her body as Elizabeth buttoned up the back. She worked as gently as she could, trying to adjust the dress to fit the smaller woman. When the dress was on, she helped Gretchen lie down again and started on the stockings and boots.

Gretchen turned her face away from Elizabeth, her body trembling.

Tears began to form in the back of Elizabeth's eyes as she pulled a hair ribbon from the bundle and knelt by Gretchen's head. She helped her sit up once again and allowed Gretchen to lean against her as she pulled the woman's thick hair together and combed it with her fingers. There was little more she could do without soap and water, but she wanted to make Gretchen feel as normal as possible, so she braided the woman's hair and tied it off with the prctty blue ribbon.

For a long time, Gretchen's head lay in Elizabeth's lap and she continued to cry as Elizabeth stroked her hair.

What could she say to this woman that would make everything better? How could she offer hope in this moment of darkness? What did Elizabeth know of such suffering?

As she sat there quietly, allowing Gretchen to cry, she realized that there was nothing to say, after all. Maybe it was enough just to offer her strength and compassion, to be a friend when the young lady had no one else in the world.

Chapter Eighteen

Jude let himself into the back of the Northern and readjusted his cravat to make sure he looked presentable for the ballroom. He needed to make an appearance, check on Martha and then hitch up the wagon and get back to Elizabeth and Gretchen.

He strode down the hall and entered the ballroom, his thoughts on Elizabeth and the embrace they had shared. He had kissed her cheek before he left, wanting to offer so much more.

The ballroom looked the same as before, with the orchestra playing and the dancers swirling around the floor. Grace was in the arms of Alphonse, smiling and laughing at whatever the young man was saying.

"Jude." Ben approached, concern lining his face. "Is everything going as planned?"

Jude nodded, though he tried to keep his face and voice calm, in case someone was watching. "I think I'll make my way around the room and say hello to a few people." He spotted Dr. Jodan as he entered the ballroom. "I'll start with the doctor."

Jude walked to Dr. Jodan and caught his eye. "How is Martha doing?"

Dr. Jodan was a kind man with a big mustache and thinning hair. He smiled jovially. "She's resting now, and she'll probably be in bed for a few days, but she'll be fine."

Jude breathed easier at the news. "Thank you."

"My pleasure." Mr. Jodan lifted a glass of lemonade off the table. "Thank you for another fun evening."

Jude shook the man's hand and made his way around the room. Abram and Charlotte Cooper were in attendance, as were other friends and neighbors.

When fifteen minutes had passed, Jude stepped out of the ballroom and into the lobby, where Pascal was standing behind the counter. "How is everything out here?" Jude asked.

"Good. All the rooms are full."

Jude had told Pascal about his plans, so he knew what to expect. "I'll be leaving—"

A shot rang out, followed by the sound of shattering glass and shouting.

"Murder! Murder!" A woman ran out of the sitting room and into the lobby. "Someone's trying to murder me!" She pushed her way into the ballroom and continued to scream.

Pandemonium ensued as the orchestra stopped playing and people began to panic.

Jude ran into the sitting room and found one of the windows had been broken.

"Over there, Allen." Timothy Hubbard pointed to the opposite wall. "The bullet went into the wall just a few inches above the Indian agent's head."

Two agents had stopped by the hotel that night when

they heard about the ball. They stood in the room with the other men now.

"I saw Hugh Jones standing outside the window moments after the bullet entered," Timothy said. "He sauntered down the street with his gun still smoking."

Ben entered the room, followed close by Abram and a few other vigilante members.

"This nonsense has got to stop," Jude said. "Someone could have been killed."

They all began to speak at once, but Ben raised his hands to quiet them. "Gentlemen, please. We won't get anything accomplished this way."

"Why don't you go for the sheriff?" one of the agents asked.

"No use," Timothy said.

"Those men need to get out of this town tonight," Abram continued. "We can't afford for them to stay a moment longer."

A teenage boy named Tucker skidded to a stop in the room, his eyes wild with fear. He was the young man Judge Barnum had taken in the year before. Tucker lived with the old bachelor in a shanty near the ravine. "Come quick," Tucker cried out in his high-pitched voice. "The judge has been hurt."

Jude put his hand on the boy's shoulder. "Slow down, Tucker. What happened?"

"A group of men came to our shanty and demanded that Judge Barnum come out and get his punishment. They was yelling all sorts of things and said the judge had seen his last day." Tucker took in a deep breath. "But when the judge refused to open his door, they tore down one of the walls and pulled him out. He told me to run for help."

"There's no time to lose," Abram said. "We must go now. Who's with me?"

The thought of Elizabeth and Gretchen alone in Ben's barn sent alarm through Jude. The women would be worried when he didn't come back right away. There was no telling how the war against Hugh's gang would play out and how long it would last. If he tried to move them now, they might be seen. It was probably safer for them to stay in the barn for now.

"I'm in," Timothy said.

"And me," Ben added.

Jude took a deep breath. "I'll go."

Several men were pulling pistols out of their boots and holsters.

"It's time to take back Little Falls," Abram said.

The men surged out of the sitting room, their wives, mothers and daughters looking on. Several of the men stopped to speak to their loved ones, while Ben turned to look at Jude. "What about Elizabeth and Gretchen?"

"They'll be fine for a little while longer," Jude said. "Right now Judge Barnum needs us."

Already, some of the men were on their way outside. Jude wished he had time to tell Martha what was happening. He looked around the crowd for Grace and spotted her near the front counter with Pascal.

Jude strode across the lobby. "Pascal, stay with the ladies and let Martha know what's happening." He hated to speak so plainly in front of Grace, but there was no use sparing her. "Hugh's gang has broken into the judge's shanty and Hugh shot a bullet into the sitting room. We're going out to bring them all to justice, once and for all."

Grace lifted her chin. "Where's Hugh?"

"I don't know, but I'm going to find him."

She looked over his shoulder, toward the windows facing Main Street, and watched all the men going out to confront Hugh's gang.

"Grace, listen to me." Jude took her shoulders and forced her gaze to lock with his. "Elizabeth isn't here." He whispered for her ears alone. "She's in Ben's barn with a prostitute we helped escape tonight."

Grace's eyes grew wide.

He looked at Pascal. "If anything happens to Ben and I, that's where you can find them. I will try to get to them myself as soon as possible. For now, just stay here and wait for me to get word to you."

Pascal nodded, his face grave.

Jude looked back at Grace. "Go to Rose and make sure she's all right. Do you understand?"

Grace nodded dumbly, but he could tell her thoughts were not on what he had just said.

"Are you coming, Jude?" Ben asked.

Jude left the lobby with the others and stepped out into the darkness.

Two dozen men were spreading out in all different directions. Some were heading toward the ravine and the judge's home, some were going toward Dew's place, and others were sneaking into alleys.

"Let's go see if the judge needs help," Ben said.

Jude slipped his pistol out of his holster. He wanted to be ready in case he needed it.

They walked up Broadway toward the judge's place. Every movement made him jerk to attention. Each time, it was one of the vigilantes and he lowered his gun.

They crossed the ravine bridge and came to Judge

Barnum's shanty. The wall was torn down, just as Tucker had said, but there was no one around.

Jude went inside, but it was empty.

"They had to have taken him somewhere," Abram said.

The sound of running met their ears and they turned to find Nathan Richardson approaching. "Someone found Judge Barnum," he said. "He was crawling to the Northern when Hugh's gang overtook him for the second time. They pulled him into an alley and beat him some more. He's barely alive. They brought him to the hotel and Dr. Jodan is examining him."

"If the judge dies," Abram said, "those men will hang. I want everyone to spread out. Go in pairs and find each gang member and bring them in to the jail. Nathan, I want you and Roald to go to the jail and relieve the sheriff. Keep an eye on the prisoners we bring in."

Jude and Ben left the shanty, but instead of crossing the bridge, they went under the wooden structure and into the ravine.

Jude's pulse pounded in his ears and his breathing was shallow.

The slightest sound brought his attention around and he peered into the shadows under the bridge.

Moonlight glittered off the cold steel of a pistol raised and pointed at them.

Ben must have seen it a split second before Jude, because he'd already raised his pistol, and before Jude could take aim, Ben pulled his trigger. At the same moment, a blast of fire came from the enemy's pistol. A flying bullet rushed past Jude's head as they dove behind a pile of discarded wood.

A sharp cry came from under the bridge.

Ben lay breathing hard beside Jude. “I hope I didn’t kill him.”

They could hear the man groaning in pain.

“Should we check on him?” Ben asked as he peeked over the pile of wood.

“He could still use his weapon on us,” Jude replied. “We need to wait here.”

The man under the bridge came out from hiding and he threw his gun far away. “Help me,” he cried out. “I need help.”

Ben and Jude stayed where they were. There was no telling if he was still dangerous or if there were others in hiding. “Come this way,” Jude called.

The man came toward them, holding his side. Blood covered his hands. It was Hugh Jones, the menace behind the havoc in Little Falls. Just looking at the man filled Jude with fury.

“I need help. I’m bleeding.” Hugh stumbled and almost fell.

“We need to help him,” Ben whispered.

Jude called out to Hugh, “Are you alone?”

“Yes.” Hugh’s voice was ragged. “I need help.”

“Come closer, if you can,” Ben ordered him.

Hugh took three more steps and fell into the dry creek bed.

Ben groaned beside Jude. “I shot him, now I’m going to have to perform his funeral.” He stood and moved toward Hugh.

Jude also stood and scanned the dark space under the bridge. There had to be more of them down here. Hugh wasn’t a man to do things alone. He always had someone by his side.

Jude kept the hammer cocked and watched carefully.

Ben made it to Hugh's side and started to roll the big man over. Suddenly, Hugh pulled a knife from his boot. In one swift movement he raised it and thrust it toward Ben.

Jude didn't hesitate. He took aim at the blade and pulled the trigger. The bullet connected with Hugh's hand and the knife flew from his fingers before it touched Ben's flesh. Hugh screamed in agony and rolled on the ground.

Ben stumbled to Jude's side, out of breath. "There was no blood on his clothing, just his hands. He wasn't the man I shot. There must be someone else under the bridge."

"Let's deal with Hugh and then we can search for the other man."

Hugh rose to his feet and staggered backward.

Jude raised his pistol. "Don't move."

Hugh took off at a dead run. Jude fired, but the bullet hit a wooden post with a thud.

Jude scrambled to his feet and ran after him, but when he arrived at the post, Hugh was gone. Jude leaned heavily against the bridge, drawing in one deep breath after another.

"Are you okay?" Ben asked.

"Yes. And you?"

Ben knelt beside a man gasping for air. "I'm all right, but we need to get this man back to Dr. Jodan."

"And I need to get to Elizabeth and Gretchen."

The Little Falls War had only just begun, but Jude couldn't risk leaving Elizabeth and Gretchen alone for a moment longer—not when Hugh Jones was still on the loose.

* * *

Elizabeth peered out the window one more time, her arms wrapped around her waist for warmth. The evening had turned cold and she had given her cloak to Gretchen, who was sleeping on the pile of hay in the corner. She hadn't moved since Elizabeth gave her a biscuit to eat over an hour ago.

Where was Jude?

Another group of men moved through the alley and, like last time, Elizabeth ducked so they wouldn't see her in Ben's barn. She had no idea why there were so many men prowling about tonight. She'd seen at least a dozen going up and down the alley, their pistols raised, searching in the shadows. Were they looking for Gretchen? Maybe that was why Jude had stayed away. He needed to wait until all was clear before he came to the barn to fetch them.

Fear clawed up her spine and tightened her throat. She had no weapon to protect them—nothing to prevent someone from taking Gretchen and doing her harm, if they were found.

She waited until the men were out of sight and then she walked over to the door again to make sure it was secure.

A rustling in the corner indicated that Gretchen was awake. "Miss Bell?" Her weak voice trembled. "Are you still here?"

Elizabeth walked across the barn. "I'm here."

"How long has it been since Mr. Allen left?"

"It's hard to tell. At least two hours."

Gretchen's whole body trembled. "He's not coming back."

Elizabeth knelt in the hay beside her. "He'll come

back. I don't know what's taking him so long, but I know there has to be a good reason."

"I should have known," Gretchen said in a dejected tone.

"Don't talk like that," Elizabeth countered. "I've never met a more trustworthy man." She thought about all that Jude had done for her and her sisters. His honesty in telling her the truth about his mission work, even when he didn't have to, his patience for Rose—all of the things she had grown to appreciate about him.

"I've never met a man I could trust, except my papa," Gretchen said. "I wouldn't know one if I met him."

"I'm sorry."

Gretchen looked at Elizabeth, the lids of her eyes puffy and discolored. "I know what you must think of me."

An uncomfortable lump grew in Elizabeth's throat. She wanted to deny Gretchen's claim, but couldn't.

"I didn't want to become like this." A single tear slipped out of Gretchen's eye. "I grew up in a good home in New York, with a mother and father I loved. I had a little brother, too." More tears appeared and she didn't seem to have the energy to wipe them away. "My parents died of typhoid fever when I was fifteen. They were gone within days of each other. It was just my brother and me. He was ten at the time." She paused and took several deep breaths. "My only living relative was my father's brother. He arrived from St. Paul to collect us. I was eager to come to Minnesota Territory, since the memories in New York were too difficult to bear."

Gretchen's whole body shook, but whether it was from the cold or the memories, Elizabeth couldn't tell.

"Within a week of arriving, my uncle told my brother

that he'd found a home for him with people who needed a son. I was devastated and I tried to fight. I even tried to run away with my brother, but my uncle caught us and locked me up. He sent my brother away and I never knew where he went, or who took him. I later learned they had paid my uncle."

Elizabeth put her hands over her mouth as she listened. She thought of Rose and what it would feel like to have her stolen away, never to see her again. "How awful."

Gretchen looked away from Elizabeth. "The night my brother was taken, my uncle visited me for the first time." She swallowed several times before going on. "When he grew tired of me, he sold me."

Bile rose in Elizabeth's stomach as she tried to process Gretchen's words.

"Eventually, I was sold to Mr. Dew and brought here." Gretchen tried to pull herself off the hay, her eyes desperately searching Elizabeth's. "None of this was my choice. I need you to understand. I wouldn't choose this life, but every time I've tried to escape, I'm pulled back under." She wept now. "Can your Mr. Allen save me?"

Tears covered Elizabeth's cheeks, too, and she reached out to make Gretchen lie down again. "If anyone can help, it's Jude." She wanted to believe he could save her—just like he had Violet and the others—but could she make a guarantee to Gretchen? "If he can't," Elizabeth said, "I will."

Gretchen stared at Elizabeth, despair and hope mingling in her eyes. "What will become of me? What kind of a future does a woman like me have?"

"Gretchen." Elizabeth took her hand and looked her earnestly in the face. "Do you know Jesus?"

More tears fell down Gretchen's cheeks. "I thought I did. My parents taught me that He loves me and cares for me—but I called out to Him for help and He didn't deliver me. How can I believe in a God who doesn't listen?"

"I understand completely. But I'm here to tell you that He did hear you and He does listen. He brought you to Little Falls so Jude could help you. I believe that with all my heart. You have every right to a good and promising future. Maybe, even now, there is a woman crying out to be rescued and God is waiting to use you to help that woman. He hears her cries and He needs soldiers to go to battle for Him."

The truth of the statement made Elizabeth hang her head. Wasn't that what Jude was doing? He was going to battle for women like Gretchen who had no other hope of rescue. Yes, it was dangerous, and no, he couldn't guarantee his safety—but he was doing something more honorable than anything she'd ever known before.

Gretchen studied Elizabeth as she slowly nodded.

"It might not ease the pain you've endured," Elizabeth said gently. "But I hope it gives you hope for your future."

Gretchen relaxed into the hay and closed her eyes.

Elizabeth came off her knees and sat with her back to the barn wall, thinking through all the things Gretchen had just told her.

If not for the grace of God, Elizabeth might have walked the same road as Gretchen. There was no telling how her life might have looked if things had not happened in the sequence they had. Who was she to judge Gretchen or any other woman cast into such depravity? She didn't know their stories. How many mamas had sheltered their little girls from looking at Gretchen—

Elizabeth included? What must that have felt like? Gretchen had been forced into her shame and others had perpetuated it. Guilt and remorse filled Elizabeth's chest as she let the tears fall for Gretchen and all the others like her.

How could she not help Jude? Now that she knew there were others who needed rescuing, how could she sit back and knowingly let them suffer?

She sat there for a long time thinking and praying.

Eventually, she stood and went to the window. As she looked out, a man appeared out of the shadows. Elizabeth stepped away from the window and pressed herself against the wall, praying he hadn't noticed.

"Who's in there?" the man called.

Elizabeth's heart ricocheted in her chest and she held her breath.

"Gretchen? Is that you hiding in there?"

Elizabeth closed her eyes, hoping and praying the man would move on.

The door began to shake and Gretchen started to whimper in the corner.

Elizabeth rushed to her side. "Don't worry. I barred the door."

"That won't stop him," she said in a dreadful voice.

"Is it Mr. Dew?"

Gretchen's sobs were the only answer.

"Come out of there!" the man bellowed. "I'll get you out one way or another—and I'll kill the man who took you from me."

Elizabeth began to pray. She tried to block out the man's curses and threats as she took Gretchen's hand in hers. "Pray with me."

Mr. Dew banged into the door over and over again, but it didn't budge.

The horse became skittish and pulled at his tether.

Finally, the noises stopped and Elizabeth held her breath again. Had he given up?

"Where is Mr. Allen?" Gretchen asked in a frantic voice.

The window shattered and Elizabeth screamed.

"I'll get you out of there if it's the last thing I do," Mr. Dew said.

Elizabeth looked around, but the only weapon she could see was a pitchfork. It was resting against the wall, across the barn. She leaped off the ground and raced over the dirt floor. Out of the corner of her eye she saw a large man climbing through the window, his curses filling the night air.

"What do you think you're doing?" He stumbled into the barn and reached for her as he fell.

She screamed again and lunged for the pitchfork, but he caught her ankle and she fell to the ground with a hard thud.

For a moment, the impact disoriented her, but the feel of his meaty palms against her ankle, and then her calf, brought her to her right mind and she began to kick as hard as she could with her other leg.

She landed her heel in his face. He groaned and let go of her ankle. She used the opportunity to scramble for the pitchfork, but he was faster. He stood and grasped her around the waist. Her finger grazed the handle of the pitchfork, causing it to fall to the ground.

She kicked and screamed, but he pinned her arms to her sides and pulled her tight to his body.

"Where is she?" he asked over her screaming.

"I won't tell you," Elizabeth said.

"Leave her alone," Gretchen cried from the corner. "You don't want her, you want me."

Mr. Dew spun around and Elizabeth felt like a rag doll in his hold. He dragged her across the barn and threw her into the hay beside Gretchen.

He stood above them, his eyes glittering with anger and triumph. "So it was this little twit who stole you?" He put his hand up to his mouth and wiped away the blood. "Didn't like to be at my place?" He crouched next to Gretchen and grabbed her face in his hands.

She cried out in pain, but he hauled her up by the chin and shook her. "Where'd you think you were going? You're mine and I'll keep you until I can't get any more work out of you."

"Leave her alone!" Elizabeth yelled and lunged for him. "You're hurting her."

Mr. Dew lifted his right hand and hit Elizabeth's chest with such force she fell to the ground again. He dropped Gretchen like a sack of meal and she landed against the hay with a thud. She didn't move and Elizabeth feared she had been rendered unconscious.

"Who are you?" he asked as he stepped over Gretchen.

Elizabeth was sprawled in the hay and she tried to get to her feet, but he pushed her shoulders down and crushed her with his weight. "You're prettier than Gretchen. I could make some quick cash off of you, too."

Panic swept through Elizabeth as she tried to push the brute off her.

"Actually," he said, his hot breath on her face. "I think I know just the man who'd buy you tonight." He grasped her arms and hauled her to her feet. She kicked and screamed, clawing at him with her nails, but he didn't seem to notice as he dragged her across the barn again. He shoved the pitchfork out of the way and lifted the bar off the door.

"No!" she yelled, but he continued out into the dark night.

Elizabeth didn't know where he would take her, or what would become of her, but all she could think about was how she had failed Grace, Rose and Jude.

Chapter Nineteen

Jude stood in the lobby of the Northern Hotel as he answered yet another question from another worried wife. “Yes, I saw Leo with my own eyes. He’s still safe and he’ll probably be back to get you in no time,” he assured the woman.

“Mr. Jude.” Pascal lumbered over. “Mrs. Atkins says she needs the doctor. She twisted her ankle when she heard the gunshot earlier and it’s not feeling any better.”

“Dr. Jodan is seeing to Judge Barnum in the parlor off the ballroom,” Jude said. “I’ll go tell him Mrs. Atkins is in need of attention.”

“Yes, sir.”

Jude had not meant to stop back inside the hotel before going after Elizabeth and Gretchen, but he’d needed to get his other pistol. When he was spotted, he’d been cornered by one person after the next. Pandemonium had ensued at the hotel and Pascal hadn’t been able to contain it. No one wanted to leave the safety of the ballroom to go home, so people had stayed, huddled in groups. He assured everyone they could remain until daybreak, which wasn’t too far off.

Jude went down the hall to the parlor, where Judge Barnum had been taken. He knocked lightly on the door and waited for Dr. Jodan to tell him to come in.

"Mrs. Atkins is in need of assistance when you have a moment."

Dr. Jodan nodded. "Judge Barnum is stable for now. I'll go see about Mrs. Atkins."

Jude left the room and saw this as his opportunity to finally leave. He couldn't wait another moment. If he stayed, someone else would need something.

He'd sent Ben to hitch up the wagon a half an hour ago, and he'd expected him to be ready by now, but Ben hadn't come back into the hotel to tell him all was set.

Jude slipped out the back door as he lifted his pistol out of the holster. The gang was still on the loose and he didn't want to risk being caught unarmed.

Lantern light glowed from the barn as Jude pushed open the door. Ben sat on an upturned bucket holding his face in his hands.

"What happened?"

Ben looked up and his face was sporting a puffy eye and a cut on his cheek. "One of Hugh's men came in here and tried taking off with your horses." He offered a wobbly smile. "I have a few bruises, but he had more. He left when he realized he couldn't beat me."

"Are you all right? Do you need to see Dr. Jodan?"

"I'm fine." He stood. "Just a little shaken. It's been a while since I've been punched." He moved his jaw back and forth a few times. "I don't think it's a good idea to try to move Gretchen tonight. There are too many people on the streets. I don't think we'd make it out of town alive at this point."

Jude nodded, though he hated to take any more

chances. They needed to move Gretchen as soon as possible.

"We'll have to try again tomorrow night, but she can't stay in your barn," Jude said. "We'll need to bring her to the Northern until we can transport her elsewhere."

They left the Northern's barn and walked out of the alley. Jude's senses were alert to any sound or movement, yet he could see nothing that looked out of place. They crossed Broadway and entered the alley behind Ben's house.

A faint scream filled the air and Jude's hair stood up on his neck. "That was a woman."

Both men took off at a run. Blood pumped through Jude's veins at an alarming rate as they neared Ben's barn.

"I'll go around the front and you go around the back," Jude whispered to Ben.

Ben didn't comment as he left Jude's side and went around the barn.

The screaming intensified as Jude rounded the corner.

A large man was hauling a woman out of Ben's barn—and Jude's heart dropped as he realized it was Elizabeth.

Jude raised his pistol and pointed it at the man he now recognized as Dew. "Let her go!"

Dew stopped and Elizabeth tried to pull out of his grasp, but he had her pinned tight. "I should have known you were in on this," Dew said as he scowled at Jude.

Jude couldn't think straight as he watched Elizabeth struggle. "Let her go now!" he said to the larger man.

"You took my woman, so I'm taking yours." His voice was full of menace. "You can make this hard or easy, Allen."

Jude took a step forward, but Dew pulled a pistol out of his holster. "Don't come any closer or she's dead."

Jude halted. Panic threatened to overwhelm him, but then he caught a glimpse of Ben peeking around the corner. Jude took a deep breath, needing all his wits about him as he dealt with Dew. "This has nothing to do with her," he said. "This is between you and me."

Dew pulled Elizabeth tighter and buried his face in her hair, taking a long, deep sniff. "I like this one better."

Anger and revulsion swelled in Jude's chest as he watched Elizabeth gag.

Ben used that moment to jump out of hiding and knock Dew off balance. Dew's gun flew across the yard and Elizabeth stumbled out of his grasp.

Jude ran to her and gathered her into his arms before she fell.

Ben pinned Dew to the ground and pointed a pistol at him.

"Elizabeth." Jude breathed her name as he held her close. "Are you all right?" It had been hours since he'd left her in the barn. How long had Dew been there? Had the damage already been done?

She trembled from head to foot as she clung to him. "I-I'm all right."

He pulled back enough to look her in the face. "Did he hurt you?"

She shook her head. "No, not really." Tears streaked her face. "Nothing that won't heal."

He looked her over and saw that her beautiful gown was stained with dirt and a shoulder had been torn. He didn't want to ask the question that burned in his mind, but he must. "Did he…misuse you?"

She swallowed and let out a shaky breath, but she looked him directly in the eyes. “No. I’m all right.”

Jude pulled her close again, thanking God that she’d been spared.

It could have been so much worse. She could have been kidnapped and he might never have seen her again. He’d placed her in danger and he wouldn’t have been able to live with himself if something had happened to her.

“Is Gretchen all right?”

She nodded. “I think she passed out earlier, but she should be okay.”

It was a relief to know that both women were safe. He didn’t want to let Elizabeth go, but Ben needed help.

He picked up Dew’s gun and walked over to where Ben still had the man pinned to the ground. “You’ll be spending time in jail for attempted kidnapping and slavery,” Jude said to the brothel owner.

Jude found rope and they tied Dew’s hands behind his back, then Jude went into the barn and lifted Gretchen into his arms. The young lady was still unconscious, so he carried her into the alley where Ben still pointed a gun at Dew.

“You won’t get away with this,” Dew said. “I’ll have revenge.”

“By the end of tonight there will be many men sitting in jail with you,” Jude said. “And the citizens of Little Falls will finally have the justice we’ve been seeking.”

“You won’t be able to do any business in town after tonight,” Ben added.

Jude held Gretchen as Elizabeth walked beside him. Ben pointed the gun at Dew, who walked ahead of them.

They went to the Northern first, and Jude took Gretchen up the back stairs to Elizabeth’s room.

"Rose must be asleep in the sitting room," she said as Jude laid Gretchen on the empty bed.

"I'll get Dr. Jodan," Jude said.

"Go help Ben with Mr. Dew. I'll take care of things here."

He stopped for a moment and met her gaze. "I'm sorry things turned out this way."

"So am I."

He exited the room leaving many words unspoken and found Ben in the alley with Dew. The eastern sky held the first blush of morning as they walked their prisoner to the sheriff's office.

Roald Hill and Nathan Richardson were sitting in the office keeping watch on the three men the others had brought in during the long night. Sheriff Pugh cowered in the corner as Jude and Ben delivered Mr. Dew and told them what his crime had been.

"Watch Sheriff Pugh closely," Jude told Nathan.

"Don't worry," Nathan said as he held up a shotgun. "He's not moving from that spot until morning."

Jude and Ben left the sheriff's office and stepped onto the boardwalk.

Abram and Timothy approached from the south. "Any progress?" Abram asked.

"We brought in Dew," Jude answered. "He attempted to abduct Elizabeth Bell."

Abram's mouth parted in shock. "That's despicable."

Jude's gut still twisted at the memory. It had been his fault and he couldn't shake the reminder that she had suffered because of him.

"We're taking over at the sheriff's office," Abram said, "and I'm advising everyone to go home and get a few hours of sleep. The rest of Hugh's gang hightailed it to the west and are either long gone or hiding out somewhere. We'll meet back here around ten o'clock this morning and discuss our next steps."

"I'm advocating that a posse go after them to see what can be done," Timothy added.

"Dr. Jodan feels Judge Barnum will live," Jude told them. "And as far as I know, there were no murders."

"What are you saying?" Abram asked.

"I'm saying that since it will be almost impossible to get them to pay for all they've done, the best we can hope for is to force them to leave town and never come back."

"I agree with Jude," Ben added. "If any of them are ever seen in town again, they'll be arrested and brought to St. Paul to face a harder sentence."

Timothy sighed. "You're probably right. I have no desire to see any of them hang for their transgressions. I just want them gone."

Abram rubbed his beard as he considered their thoughts. "I think it's a good solution."

"Except for Dew," Jude said. "I learned that he had purchased at least one of his prostitutes and was holding her against her will."

Timothy crossed his arms. "That's a hanging offense."

"Exactly." Jude nodded toward the Northern, down the street. "Not to mention attempting to abduct Elizabeth."

"He'll definitely be brought to St. Paul." Abram indicated the Northern. "Why don't you get on back to the hotel and deal with everyone there? Tell Charlotte I'm safe. We've got it from here."

"I'll do that and I'll be back for the vigilante meeting," Jude assured him. "Count on me to ride with the posse."

The men shook hands and then they parted ways.

"I'll come with you to the Northern," Ben said to Jude. "I have a feeling there will be a lot of people who would like some prayer right about now."

Jude offered a tired smile. "You're a good man, Ben."

"So are you. I'm proud of what you're doing for Gretchen and the others."

"Yes, but at what cost? I put Elizabeth in jeopardy tonight. I can never do that again."

Ben didn't comment as they made their way across the street.

What could the reverend say? Jude had been wrong to involve Elizabeth. His was a solitary calling. He'd always known it to be true, but he'd hoped otherwise. Now he knew without a doubt in his mind that he could never have Elizabeth. He would never endanger her again.

The cost was too high.

As soon as Jude left, Elizabeth changed into a new gown, one that wasn't stained or torn. The last thing she wanted was to run into someone and explain why she looked like such a fright. They would want to know where she'd been and what had happened. She still shook from the whole ordeal with Mr. Dew, but after being mistreated the way she'd been, she felt more convinced that she was called to help women like Gretchen. No one should be treated the way she had been treated, least of all a defenseless woman with no one to protect her.

She left her room and found Pascal in the lobby with dozens of other people. As discreetly as possible, she asked him to find Dr. Jodan and send him up to her room, then she went into the kitchen and got a pitcher of water for Gretchen.

As she walked up the back stairs to her room, she

prayed for Gretchen and all the women like her. Hearing Gretchen's story had opened Elizabeth's eyes to the reality of prostitution. Her estimation of Jude, and what he did to help them, rose higher and higher with each step she took.

Elizabeth went back into the bedroom and found Gretchen still lying unconscious. Instead of troubling her, Elizabeth opened the door to the sitting room to tell Grace she had returned.

The sitting room lamp was extinguished, but the faint hint of daylight offered enough light to see into the room. Rose lay on the sofa, curled up in a ball, her feet tucked under her nightgown. Edgar was beside her, nestled snug against Rose.

Grace was not in the room.

Could she be helping with the others? Surely very few people had slept in the hotel last night.

Not wanting to disturb Rose, Elizabeth turned to go back to her room, but a white envelope on the secretary caught her eye. She walked across the room as dread mounted.

The envelope was addressed to Elizabeth.

With unsteady hands, she opened the flap and pulled out a single piece of paper. The words were scribbled quickly, but she was able to make them out.

Dear Elizabeth,
I've gone away with Hugh. We will make a new life for ourselves out west. I'll write again when I know where we end up.

Don't fret, Lizzie. I'm a grown woman and I know what I'm doing.

Love, Grace

"No." Elizabeth shook her head as she crumpled to the floor. What had her sister done? This was the very thing Elizabeth had tried to avoid by bringing Grace to Little Falls. Once word got out that Grace had run away with Hugh Jones, her sister's reputation would be ruined forever. No matter how far Elizabeth went to track her down, the damage would be done.

Tears stung the back of Elizabeth's eyes, tears of sadness, anger and frustration. How could her sister be so foolish to throw her life away, especially for someone like Hugh? Grace had sacrificed her family for the love of a man—exactly what Elizabeth had sworn she'd never do. She'd never imagined her sister would be the one to give it all up.

Yet, wasn't that what Elizabeth had done tonight? In her heart, she knew she'd only agreed to help Jude because of her love for him. And she'd sacrificed her sisters because of it. Grace would still be at the hotel if she'd been there to talk some sense into her. None of this would have happened if she'd only stayed and fulfilled her promise to Mama to take care of her sisters.

Great sobs rose in Elizabeth's chest until she felt she would be choked by them. Her sister's chance at happiness was forever gone. The grief she felt over that knowledge was as great as she felt when Mama had died.

She curled up on the floor and let the tears overwhelm her. Her emotions were already so frayed she couldn't stop them if she tried.

"Lizzie?" Rose sat up, her sleepy brown eyes filled with fear. "Why are you crying?"

Elizabeth rose on shaky legs and went to the sofa. She pulled her sister onto her lap and held her tight, feeling as if Rose was the only anchor in her tumultuous world.

How could she hold on to Rose's innocence? Why was the world such a cruel and wretched place?

"What's wrong?" Rose asked.

Elizabeth would need to pull herself together for Rose and for Gretchen. Dr. Jodan would be in soon to see her and he'd need to know everything she knew to help the young woman.

She wiped at her face to remove the tears and took a deep breath to steady her emotions. "Everything will be all right. Don't worry."

Rose looked up at Elizabeth, her lips puckered in sadness.

"When was the last time you saw Grace?" Elizabeth asked.

Rose lifted her shoulders. "I don't know."

"Did she come in here last night?"

"Nellie put on my nightgown."

"Did Nellie talk to Grace?" Elizabeth tried to be patient as she asked her questions, but she needed to know everything.

Rose nodded. "Grace told Nellie she could leave and then she packed her bag. She told me to sleep on the sofa. I said I wanted Edgar." She nodded decisively. "Grace said go ahead."

"And then what?"

Rose shrugged again. "I went to the sofa."

"Do you remember Grace writing a note?"

Rose shook her head.

"Do you remember anything else?"

The little girl screwed up her face as if she was thinking hard. "I remember Edgar tried to scratch me."

"But nothing else about Grace?"

"No." Rose frowned. "Where is Grace?"

Elizabeth didn't want to tell her—at least not yet. "I don't know right now. But hopefully I'll know more soon."

"Miss Bell?" Dr. Jodan spoke on the other side of the sitting room door. "Are you available?"

"Yes." Elizabeth set Rose on the sofa and said, "I'll be back soon to help you get dressed. For now, I want you to stay here and play with Edgar. All right?"

"I'm hungry."

"I'll bring you downstairs for something to eat soon." Elizabeth showed the doctor into her bedroom, conscious of how she might look to him with her tear-stained cheeks, and closed the door softly behind them.

"Mr. Doucette told me a little about this lady," Dr. Jodan said as he studied Elizabeth's face. "It seems you were both in a bit of trouble lately."

"It's a long story," Elizabeth said. "But I'm fine. Gretchen is the one who needs attendance."

"I can see that." Dr. Jodan opened his medical bag and pulled out his stethoscope. "I need to know everything from the beginning to the end." He looked at her over the rim of his glasses. "And don't leave anything out. Even if you're embarrassed or it seems unimportant, tell me everything. It might be exactly what I need to treat her correctly." His eyes and voice were gentle as he spoke. "Whatever you say will be held in the strictest confidence."

Elizabeth nodded, hoping she could recall all that Gretchen had told her—even as her thoughts were far away with Grace.

Remorse hit her all over again. Why had she left

with Jude? Her place was with her family. She'd always known that. Now she would have to live with the reminder of her mistake every day of her life.

Chapter Twenty

Jude walked into the Northern and was immediately greeted by a few dozen people who all looked up with wide eyes.

"It's safe to go home now," he told everyone. "Hugh's gang was seen riding west out of town and the sun is almost up."

The relief on their faces put a smile on Jude's. "You'll be happy to know that we've arrested four men and the fifth is under guard here, being attended to by Dr. Jodan for a gunshot wound to the leg." He glanced at Ben, who'd entered just behind him, but he could see by the look on Ben's face that he didn't want to take credit for the shooting—at least, not yet.

Jude spoke to a few people briefly as he made his way over to Pascal, who stood in his customary place behind the front counter.

"Did Dr. Jodan go up to see Gretchen?"

"He's with her and Miss Elizabeth now."

"Good." Jude was anxious to hear how they were both doing. "I'll head up there."

Jude maneuvered between people as they gathered

their loved ones and left the hotel. He climbed the stairs and met Dr. Jodan as he came down the hall.

"How is Gretchen?"

"She'll live." Dr. Jodan's face was grave. "But she has a long way to go. I'll come in and check on her periodically, but it could be several weeks before she's out of bed."

With the threat of Dew out of the way, Gretchen could stay for as long as she'd like. "Thank you, doctor."

Dr. Jodan patted Jude's shoulder as he moved past him in the hall. "As for Miss Bell—she's been through quite an ordeal. See that she gets some rest."

"I will."

Jude walked the rest of the way down the hall and knocked softly on Elizabeth's bedroom door.

The door creaked open after a moment and Elizabeth stood on the other side. Her face was red and streaked with tears. Jude wanted desperately to take her into his arms and apologize all over again for causing her such pain.

"Is everything all right?" he asked, instead.

She opened the door a little wider and stepped out into the hallway. The pink morning sky filled the window just behind her with a soft glow.

Elizabeth bit her bottom lip as a tear trailed down her cheek. "Everything is not all right."

Dread knotted in his gut. Had she lied to him about Dew? Had he misused her in a way that she was now feeling the need to confess? He took her by the shoulders. "What is it?"

"It's Grace. She left with Hugh last night. I—" She broke off with a sob and stepped into his arms.

He held her close, wishing he could do more to comfort her. “How do you know?”

“She left a note.”

“What did it say? Maybe there is a clue to help us locate her.”

“She said they’re going west to start over and not to worry, because she’s a grown woman and she knows what she’s doing.” Elizabeth pulled away and put a little distance between them.

He hated how it felt when she left his embrace, but it was for the best. Yet the thought of never holding her again was almost more than he could bear. “I’ll be meeting with the others in a couple hours and we plan to put a posse together and ride after Hugh’s gang.” He lowered his voice, wanting to reassure her. “I’ll do whatever I can to find her for you, Lizzie.”

She studied him for a moment, her eyes filled with doubt and hope and a range of other emotions too painful for him to identify. “I’ve made a decision. You were right all along. Little Falls is no place for me.”

“Elizabeth—”

“If the offer still stands for transportation costs, I’d like to take my sisters back to Rockford.”

He shook his head, desperate to change her mind. “You have a home here. You don’t need to leave.”

“It’s the only way to preserve Grace’s reputation and save her from the shame and embarrassment of her actions.”

“There has to be another way. I’ll get her back to you without the others knowing.”

“It’s no use. People will talk.”

He wanted to reach out to her again, but refrained.

"Don't make any rash decisions. I'll find her and we'll work it all out."

"I should clean up and then get downstairs to start breakfast." She put her hand on the doorknob, but he reached out to stop her.

"Get some rest first. Everything will look better after you've had some sleep."

She shook her head. "I won't rest until I know Grace is safe."

He let go of her hand and took a step back. "I'll see to that myself."

She slipped into her room and closed the door, leaving Jude alone in the hall. The thought of never seeing her again was too much to think about right now—but wouldn't it be better for both of them? Having her so close, without having her completely, was driving him mad. He needed to focus on rescuing Grace and then he'd worry about what he would say to Elizabeth.

He went to his room and changed out of his evening clothes into denim pants and a cotton shirt. He'd be riding with the posse and he needed to be ready.

Four hours later, he sat in his saddle waiting outside the sheriff's office. He'd been the first to arrive, too anxious to rest and wanting to get to Grace as soon as possible.

Ben appeared down the street on his mare and trotted toward Jude. As soon as he came to a stop, Jude told him what he'd dreaded saying for the past few hours. "Grace left with Hugh."

Ben closed his eyes and rubbed his face with his hands. "Why would she do something so foolish?"

"Who knows?" Jude made sure no one was close enough to hear. "She left a note and said they would make a life for themselves out west, but Elizabeth wants me to find her. If we can bring her back without anyone knowing, maybe we could save her reputation."

"That is, if she hasn't done something even more foolish than simply leave with him."

Jude hated to think of the repercussions. "I don't know how we'll get her back here without the others in the posse knowing."

"*If* we find her," Ben said, "it would be impossible for them to not see her."

Jude hated that Ben was right—but they still needed to try.

"You had a chance to speak to Elizabeth, then?" Ben asked.

"For a few minutes." He could still feel her in his arms.

"When this is all done, will you propose to her?"

Jude tried to hide his disappointment. "No."

"Why not?" Ben's horse sidestepped and he had to pull on the reins. "I saw how you two embraced after we rescued her last night. I thought you'd propose right there."

Jude looked off to the north, hoping for a sign of one of the other vigilantes so he could stop having this conversation with Ben.

"Why are you scared?" Ben asked.

"I'm not scared."

"I can see fear written all over your face."

Jude repositioned himself in the saddle. "Haven't we already had this conversation? I'm not the right man for her. I could never ask her to marry me, because my life is too dangerous. I can't give up my rescue work, and even if she agreed to let me continue, I would never put her through what she endured last night again." He felt his shoulders slump, so he purposely straightened them.

"What if she feels called to continue rescue work, too?"

"Why would she?" Especially if she went back to Rockford.

"I saw the way she worried over Gretchen last night. It's obvious she realizes how important this work is. Maybe she'll continue, even if she's not married to you."

"That's ridiculous."

"And wouldn't it be better if you're there to protect her?"

Jude shook his head. "You have no idea what she's thinking."

"And neither do you." Ben's voice became serious. "Talk to her. Don't assume you know what's best for her. Don't let fear keep you from telling her how you feel."

As the others arrived, Jude thought about Ben's words, but he pushed it all aside as he focused on his mission.

"Milo Schmidt sent a runner into town an hour ago," Abram addressed the men after they assembled. "He said the gang overran his farm about five miles west of here." He looked at each man in turn. "They are armed and dangerous. Keep watch and don't be foolish. We've agreed to let them go if they promise to never come back to Little Falls."

There was some grumbling among the group, but the majority agreed.

"Let's head out." Abram and Timothy led the way and the others followed.

No one spoke as they galloped west. Within a half hour, they could see Schmidt's farm at the base of a hill.

Abram brought the group to a stop. "I want to surround the place. There are fifteen of us, so I want to break up in groups of two or three. I have a white flag I'm going to hold up so they know we're coming to talk—but I don't trust these men, so stay out of sight and be ready to fire, if necessary." He glanced around the group. "I'd like Jude, Ben and Timothy to ride with me."

Jude nodded. Hopefully he'd get a chance to speak with Hugh directly.

The others split off while the four negotiators approached the farm on the main road.

White clouds filled an endless expanse of blue sky, and the stubble of grass waved under a gentle breeze. Milo Schmidt's farm was one of the finest in the territory and boasted a large white house, an even bigger red barn and miles of endless croplands, which had been decimated during the grasshopper infestation. He was one who would benefit from the seed Jude would bring back from St. Paul as soon as he made the trip to retrieve it. At the moment, however, Jude's mind was not on the government aid, but on finding Grace.

Abram held the white flag high overhead as they approached the farm. Slowly, gang members appeared in the barnyard and on the front porch.

Mrs. Schmidt stood at the window, her hands twisted in her apron. No doubt the lady was beyond frightened. Hopefully the gang would be gone soon and she could put her mind at ease.

Hugh came to the front door, his right hand wrapped in a bandage.

"We've come to negotiate," Abram called out.

Jude pulled on Lady's reins and came to a halt beside the others. He searched every window in the house, looking for some sign of Grace, but couldn't find one.

Hugh stepped out of the house and let the door slam shut behind him. It was clear he was exhausted and his hand gave him pain. Something about the set of his shoulders also suggested he was ready to talk.

"Mr. Jones." Abram nodded. "I won't make this speech longer than necessary. We want to see you and your men leave town. Immediately. Judge Barnum will survive, so you are free from the threat of manslaughter. If you leave now, we won't press charges."

Hugh looked at each man, his gaze lingering on Jude for a second longer than the others. "I plan to head west, anyway."

"This goes for all of your men," Timothy added.

"I don't care what they all do. We're breaking up." Hugh's jaw tightened as he aimed his stare at Ben. "Before you go, I need a parson."

"Why?" Jude asked.

"It's between me and the parson."

Jude dismounted and stood before Hugh. "I have a feeling I need to be in on this discussion, as well."

Hugh narrowed his eyes, but he didn't refuse. "Fine." He turned and went back toward the house.

Abram looked a bit befuddled as Ben dismounted.

"You can head on back," Jude told Abram and Timothy. "Ben and I will be along shortly."

Ben cast a look at Jude. No doubt he was thinking the same thing. Hugh intended to marry Grace.

It was the honorable thing to do—but would it satisfy Elizabeth? More importantly, was there a chance he could talk Grace out of it?

* * *

Elizabeth quietly closed her bedroom door so she wouldn't wake Gretchen, who was sleeping peacefully, maybe for the first time in years. Rose was also napping in the sitting room, blissfully unaware of Grace's indiscretion. Elizabeth, on the other hand, knew it all too well and knew she would not sleep until Grace returned.

It had been at least an hour since she'd watched most of the posse members ride back to town—but Jude and Ben were not with them. What was taking so long?

She stopped by the window facing the back of the hotel and wrapped her arms around her waist, wishing she could have gone with them to talk some sense into Grace. Instead, she'd stayed where she was needed more and prayed every chance she could get.

The late afternoon sunshine was warm as it came through the window. All the clouds had drifted out of sight and now the sky was a perfect shade of blue. The Mississippi ran along the edge of town and disappeared behind one of the buildings at the end of Main Street.

When would Jude return? And when he did, would he have Grace?

She'd had a lot of time to think through the morning and afternoon. After speaking to Pascal, she'd decided to close the hotel dining room for the day. Martha was very ill and needed as much sleep as possible. With the responsibility to care for Gretchen and Rose, Elizabeth wouldn't have the time or energy required to make all the necessary meals.

The attic stairs creaked and Elizabeth turned to find Martha coming down. Her face was pale and lines edged her eyes, but she looked a little better than she had earlier when Elizabeth checked on her.

"Any word?" Martha asked.

Elizabeth looked back out the window. "Nothing."

"Don't worry, lovey. All will be well." Martha patted Elizabeth's arm. "Let's go have some coffee and pull together something for supper."

"We closed the dining room."

"I know, but we still need to eat."

Elizabeth followed her down the back stairs and into the kitchen. The space was cool and lacked the usual aroma of Martha's cooking.

"Sit down and let me get the coffee," Elizabeth told her.

Martha took out a stool and sat with a sigh. "Even that little jaunt down the stairs about did me in."

Elizabeth stoked the fire in the cookstove then found the smaller coffeepot and took off the lid. "You should still be in bed."

"I couldn't rest knowing Jude and Grace are still out there."

Elizabeth took the coffeepot outside and worked the pump handle until a stream of water came rushing out. She filled the pot, went back inside and set it on the stove. While Martha looked on, she took a cup of roasted coffee beans, put them into the grinder and sat at the worktable.

She ground the beans, inhaling as the air filled with the refreshing scent.

"How is Gretchen?" Martha asked.

"She's sleeping, but she looks much better now that she knows she's safe from Mr. Dew. I told her he's behind bars and will be facing prosecution."

"I wish I could have been the one to help her." Martha clasped her hands together on top of the table. "But, then again, maybe not. I think it was good for you to see that side of Jude's life."

Elizabeth didn't meet Martha's gaze but continued to grind the beans. "I shouldn't have left Grace and Rose by themselves. If I hadn't..." She couldn't bring herself to finish the statement.

Martha reached out and squeezed Elizabeth's hand. "We all make mistakes we have to live with. Some are worse than others. But—" she paused "—I don't think you made a mistake."

"If I hadn't left, Grace would still be here."

"Maybe." Martha shook her head. "Or maybe not. Remember the night Jude and Ben caught her with Hugh by the barn? She could have left that night, or any other night, for that matter. Grace is a grown woman. You're not responsible for her forever."

Elizabeth brought the ground coffee to the pot. "But I made a promise to my mother."

"How long was that promise intended to last? For the rest of Grace and Rose's lives? Even your mother wouldn't have been responsible for that long."

Elizabeth poured the coffee into the basket and put the lid on the pot. Martha was right. How long did her mother intend for her to be responsible for her sisters? Surely, one day Rose would be grown and capable of making her own choices. Would Elizabeth have to follow her around for the rest of her life to make sure she made only good ones? That was preposterous and would be unfair to her sister.

"As much as we hate to see our loved ones make bad choices," Martha continued, "there comes a point when we must let them go. Grace is responsible for what she's done and she'll have to pay the price. Yes, you and Rose will, too, in some ways, but Grace has to walk out her journey. Only God can direct her steps. Not you."

It was true—but it still hurt.

"And what about you?" Martha asked.

Elizabeth came back to the table and sat across from Martha. "What about me?"

"No one can make choices for your life, either, save you and God." Martha lowered her chin and looked intently at Elizabeth. "Have you decided what you'll do concerning Jude?"

The very thought of Jude forced Elizabeth off her chair. She needed to be doing something. She didn't want to sit around all day and mope about what she couldn't have. "What should we make for supper?"

"Don't change the subject."

"What is there to say?" She took a deep breath. "I've decided to leave Little Falls and go back to Rockford."

Martha didn't look concerned, but rather curious. "Why would you do that?"

"To spare Grace her embarrassment."

"And to run away from Jude?"

Elizabeth swallowed and looked down at her hands.

"He loves you, Elizabeth." Martha stood. "Just tell him how you feel. I know you can work things out."

"There's Rose to consider, too."

"He loves Rose, just as you do. Tell him how you feel and let him decide what's best for him."

The thought of being rejected by Jude, just as she'd been rejected by James, left a sour taste in her mouth. But what if he didn't reject her? What if Martha was right and he did love her?

The sound of horses' hooves seeped through the walls of the hotel and Elizabeth's heart picked up its pace.

She raced to the back door and saw the barn had been opened.

With a trembling hand, she turned the knob and stepped out into the alley. Was Grace with him? Had he found her? The questions begged for answers, so she ran across the alley and entered the barn.

Jude stood beside Lady, unbuckling the saddle. His hair was tousled by the wind and his casual clothes made him look as handsome as ever.

But he was alone.

"Did you find her?"

Jude looked up and she wanted to melt into his beautiful brown eyes. They held so many emotions, some good and some bad, but over it all, they were full of pleasure at seeing her. "I did." He walked away from Lady and pulled a letter out of his pocket. "She wanted me to give you this."

Elizabeth took the letter, disappointment tightening her chest. Why wasn't Grace with Jude? "Where is she? Was she with Hugh? Did she look well? Was she scared?"

"I'll tell you all about it once you've read the letter."

She quickly opened the envelope and pulled out the letter. It was written in Grace's handwriting and was less rushed than the one she'd left last night.

Dear Elizabeth,

I'm sorry I left the way I did. I can imagine you're worried for me and rightly so. As I laid awake in a stranger's parlor last night, I had time to think. I realize I made a hasty decision to run away with Hugh, but given enough time, I would have married him either way. I love him and I know that's hard for you to understand. When I look at Hugh, I don't see the anger and recklessness that others see. Instead, I see the pain and sorrow of childhood memories he's shared with me. He made poor choices, just as I have, and he regrets many of them.

He asked me to be his wife and Ben married us just a short time ago. Jude tried to talk me out of it, but when he realized I wouldn't change my mind, he looked on as our witness. We are leaving for Montana now and will break away from all the others. Hugh wants to try his hand at ranching and I want to start over with him.

I pray, given some time, you will come to understand why I chose this path for my life. Don't hold any regret or guilt over me. I knew what I was doing and I'd do it all over again. I'll write when we're settled.

Love, Grace

Elizabeth lowered the letter and found Jude watching her. "She's married?"

He nodded. "Ben performed the ceremony."

Her legs felt weak and the exhaustion from the past twenty-four hours had finally taken their toll. She sank onto a clean pile of hay. "I can't believe she's married. This whole time I thought she'd return to me and we'd leave here together."

Jude walked over and took a seat beside her. "Are you unhappy?"

Elizabeth looked at the letter again and couldn't deny her sister's excitement. "I'm sad that I might never see her again and I didn't get to say goodbye, but I'm happy that she and Hugh are hopeful." She met Jude's gaze. "I pray they have a good life together. Grace and Hugh have a lot to learn, but then, we all do, I suppose."

Jude picked up a piece of hay and played with it between his fingers. "Some of us more than others."

Martha's words floated back into Elizabeth's mind. She needed to speak honestly with Jude, but the words froze on her tongue as nerves bubbled up inside her.

He dropped the piece of hay and reached over to take her hand.

The simple gesture was all the invitation she needed to lean against his shoulder, thankful for his courage and perseverance. "Thank you for finding her."

"You're welcome." He ran his thumb over the top of her hand. "Lizzie." He paused. "I don't want you to go."

She closed her eyes, wishing she could stay close to him forever, but frightened it might not last.

He turned her hand over and traced each fingertip with his own. "I have something I'd like to say to you."

His touch was like nothing she'd ever felt before. "I have something I'd like to say to you, too."

He sat up straighter and faced her. "Please let me speak first."

His face was so dear to her she wanted to memorize every line of his features. "All right."

"I love you, Lizzie."

She inhaled a soft breath. "You do?"

"I know I don't have much to offer. No respectable past, no family and nothing of great value but a hotel that you rightfully own, as well." He smiled, yet she could see the fear of rejection in his eyes. "I don't have much but a heart that adores you and arms that yearn to hold you for the rest of my life."

Tears gathered in her eyes, yet she smiled as she placed her hand on his cheek. “You have more than you realize, my love. You’ve captured my heart and it will be yours forever.”

“Truly?”

“I love you, too,” she whispered. “And I don’t have much, either. But I have full confidence in you and I know we can do whatever we set our hearts and minds to.”

He put his hand over hers, joy in the depths of his gaze. “I feel called to continue helping women like Violet and Gretchen, but I cannot ask you to risk your life like you did last night.”

“I was called last night, too, Jude. I can’t deny God’s will. I want to help.” She dropped her hand from his cheek and paused. “But there is one more thing.”

Concern edged between his eyebrows. “What is that?”

“Rose.”

He grinned and all the worry left his face. “What about Rose?”

“Will you love her like I love her?”

His eyes caressed her face. “I already love her like a daughter and I look forward to watching her grow into a beautiful, capable young woman, just like her older sisters.”

“Do you mean that?”

“With all my heart.” He leaned forward and set his forehead against hers. “There’s just one more thing to discuss.”

Her stomach filled with butterflies. “What’s that?”

“When shall we get married?”

“As soon as possible.”

He shook his head in amazement. "I never imagined I'd ever be so blessed to hold you in my arms and one day call you my wife."

"Are we done talking?"

"Why?"

"I'd like to be kissed now."

He laughed and pulled her close, his eyes full of the love she could no longer deny. His lips touched hers and she melted into his embrace, loving the strength in his arms and the softness in his kiss. She had never felt as warm or complete as she did in that moment, and she marveled that it was just the first of countless kisses that would fill her life.

Chapter Twenty-One

Jude stood at the front of the little white church in his best suit and polished shoes. It had been the longest two weeks of his life since he'd proposed to Elizabeth. The wait to be married had almost been more than he could bear, yet the day had dawned with brilliant sunshine and the promise of perfect weather. Outside the church, the sky boasted a blue sky and a soft breeze. It was even better than he had hoped.

The church was bursting with their friends and neighbors. Back at the hotel, the ladies had prepared a wedding feast that would not be outdone for some time to come. In the evening, there would be a ball to honor the newly married couple.

He looked forward to all of those things, but it was the days that followed the wedding celebration that he most anticipated. When he and Elizabeth would live life together, side by side, day in and day out, for as long as they both should live.

Ben stood beside Jude and grinned. "Are you nervous?"

Jude shook his head. "I'm too excited to be nervous."

The doors opened at the back of the church and the whole congregation rose to look at the bride.

Elizabeth stood there for a moment alone, and Jude's heart beat like a drum. She was the most beautiful woman he'd ever met and he still couldn't believe God had brought her to his hotel. Just the thought of that first night, when she had barged in and accused him of squatting on her property, brought a smile to his face.

She wore a blue gown that Charlotte had made for her. It matched her eyes to perfection and accentuated her slender body. Her brown curls were pinned up, and she wore blue earrings that caught the sunshine and glinted.

Pascal appeared on one side of her to offer his arm. She'd asked him to give her away in place of her father and Pascal had been honored.

Rose stood on the other side of Elizabeth, wearing a pretty new dress and holding a handful of wildflowers she'd picked the day before when Jude had taken her and Elizabeth to the river. Rose caught sight of Jude and waved, her curls bouncing with her excitement.

The three of them walked down the aisle together and Martha motioned Rose to come and sit with her in the front pew.

Elizabeth's gaze rested on Jude and her blue eyes sparkled with love and happiness.

"Who gives this woman in marriage?" Ben asked.

Pascal puffed up his chest, yet his face revealed some of his nerves. "I do, in her father's memory." He nodded, looking relieved that he'd delivered the important message.

Elizabeth smiled up at Pascal and then looked back at her groom as Pascal set her hand in Jude's.

She wore gloves, but he could still feel the warmth of

her skin beneath his and it sent pleasure racing up his arm and into his chest. From this moment forward, he could hold her hand in public, kiss her when he pleased and embrace her without concern for her reputation. In a moment, she would become his wife and the world would know they belonged together.

Jude wrapped his fingers around hers and stood a bit straighter with her by his side.

"Dearly beloved," Ben began. "We are gathered here today in the sight of God and these witnesses to join together this man and this woman in holy matrimony. Marriage is commanded to be honorable among all men, and therefore it should not be entered into unadvisedly or lightly, but reverently, discreetly, advisedly and solemnly. If any person can show just cause why they may not be joined together, let them speak now or forever hold their peace."

Jude squeezed Elizabeth's hand and she glanced up at him and smiled.

"Jude." Ben spoke in a grave voice. "Do you take Elizabeth to be your wedded wife, to live together in marriage? Do you promise to love her, comfort her, honor and keep her, for better or worse, for richer or poorer, in sickness and health, and, forsaking all others, be faithful only to her, for as long as you both shall live?"

There was not a doubt in his heart. "I do."

"And do you, Elizabeth, take Jude to be your wedded husband, to live together in marriage? Do you promise to love him, comfort him, honor and keep him, for better or worse, for richer or poorer, in sickness and health, and, forsaking all others, be faithful only to him, for as long as you both shall live?"

She did not hesitate. "I do."

"Do either of you have a token of your commitment?"

Jude took a gold band out of his pocket and placed it in Ben's hand. It had been her mother's wedding band and she had entrusted it to him the night before.

"May this ring be blessed as the symbol of this affectionate union." Ben smiled at Jude and then at Elizabeth. "These two lives are now joined in one unbroken circle. May these two find in each other the love for which all men and women yearn. May they grow in understanding and in compassion. May the home which they establish together be such a place that many will find there a friend, and may this ring on Elizabeth's finger symbolize the touch of the Holy Spirit in their hearts."

It was the same blessing Ben spoke at all the weddings he performed, and Jude had heard it many times, but this time it sounded different. It was spoken over him and Elizabeth, and carried more meaning and depth than he'd ever realized.

Ben handed the ring back to Jude and said, "Put this ring on your bride's finger and repeat after me. Elizabeth, with this ring you are now consecrated to me as my wife from this day forward."

Jude turned and faced Elizabeth. Behind her, many friends looked on, but he saw no one except her. She looked up at him with such love and adoration, he wished the wedding was over and he could pull her into his arms. Instead, he slipped the ring on her left ring finger and repeated his vows.

Ben continued. "I give you this ring as the pledge of my love and as the symbol of our unity, and with this ring, I thee wed."

Jude held her hand and said, "I give you this ring as the pledge of my love and as the symbol of our unity." He hoped his eyes conveyed all the love he felt. The smile on her face told him it did. "And with this ring, I thee wed."

"By the power vested in me by the Territory of Minnesota and by Almighty God," Ben said, closing his Bible, "I now pronounce you man and wife. You may kiss the bride."

Jude could not contain his joy. He grinned as he pulled her into his arms and placed a tender kiss on her lips.

She wrapped her arms around him and returned the kiss with as much delight. When she pulled away, she smiled up at him. "I love you, Jude."

"I love you, too, Lizzie."

The congregation rose to their feet and applauded the happy couple. Martha, Pascal and Rose clapped the hardest. But others were there to share in their happiness, too. Abram and Charlotte Cooper, Timothy and Pearl Hubbard, Judge Barnum, Dr. Jodan, Roald Hill, Pierre LaForce and many of the other men who had tried, but failed, to win Elizabeth's heart.

Jude took her hand and led her down the aisle and out into the fresh air. Main Street looked brighter and more promising than ever.

They stopped on the top step and he reached into his back pocket. "I have a gift for you."

She put her hand on his cheek and shook her head with wonder. "You've already given me more than I could ever hope for or imagine."

He held out the envelope. "Open it."

She lifted the flap and took out the piece of paper. He watched her closely as she read the contents, her cheeks filling with color. "Jude."

"It's the deed to the hotel, with your name and Rose's added."

A beautiful smile lit up her face. "Thank you."

He took her hand and lifted it to his lips. "Are you ready to go home, Mrs. Allen?"

She nodded, her eyes filling with tenderness. "I couldn't think of a place I'd rather go."

"And do you mind being called Mrs. Allen?"

Their guests began to exit the church, but she drew close to him and for a moment all the others faded away. "I am honored to carry the name you took for yourself. You are the man you have chosen to be, not the man the world said you were. That's why I love you." She stood on tiptoe and kissed him again. "I am my beloved's and my beloved is mine," she quoted from the Song of Solomon. "Nothing else matters."

Jude tucked her hand around his arm and stood close to her as they greeted their guests.

They'd left the hotel as business partners and would return as man and wife, a partnership formed by God.

Martha had been right all along. God didn't make mistakes.

* * * * *

If you enjoyed this story,
look for the first book in the
LITTLE FALLS LEGACY *series,*
A FAMILY ARRANGEMENT

and this other heartwarming
Love Inspired Historical title from
Gabrielle Meyer

A MOTHER IN THE MAKING

Dear Reader,

The Little Falls War was an important moment in the history of my hometown, yet few people are familiar with the story. Since this is a work of fiction, some of the information was condensed or combined, and some of the people involved are a work of my imagination, but many of the people and events I wrote about are true. For more about the real history behind this story (and the others in the Little Falls Legacy miniseries), please visit my website at www.gabriellemeyer.com.

As always, thank you for spending time with me in Little Falls. It is my prayer that this story has entertained, educated and inspired you to dig deeper into the history of your own hometown.

In His name,
Gabrielle Meyer

COMING NEXT MONTH FROM
Love Inspired® Historical

Available September 5, 2017

MAIL-ORDER MARRIAGE PROMISE
Frontier Bachelors • by Regina Scott

When John Wallin's sister orders him a mail-order bride without his knowledge, can the bachelor find a way to move on from his past rejection and fulfill the marriage promise to lovely Dottie Tyrrell, who comes with a baby—and a secret?

PONY EXPRESS SPECIAL DELIVERY
Saddles and Spurs • by Rhonda Gibson

Maggie Fillmore's late husband had one final wish—that their unborn son would inherit their ranch. But when a greedy relative threatens to take the ranch, there's only one way Maggie can keep it: a marriage of convenience to the new Pony Express manager, Clayton Young.

RANCHER TO THE RESCUE
by Barbara Phinney

With their parents missing, Clare Walsh and her siblings could lose everything, including each other—unless she accepts rancher Noah Livingstone's proposal. And though they plan a union in name only, will Clare and Noah risk their hearts for a chance at a true-love connection?

THE OUTLAW'S SECOND CHANCE
by Angie Dicken

When Aubrey Huxley and Cort Stanton try to claim the same land in the Oklahoma Land Rush, they strike a deal: she can have the land for her horse ranch if he can work for her. But will she let him stay on when she learns he's a wanted man?

SPECIAL EXCERPT FROM

Love Inspired® HISTORICAL

Maggie Fillmore's late husband had one final wish—that their unborn son would inherit their ranch. But when a greedy relative threatens to take the ranch, there's only one way Maggie can keep it: a marriage of convenience to the new Pony Express manager, Clayton Young.

Read on for a sneak preview of PONY EXPRESS SPECIAL DELIVERY by Rhonda Gibson, *available September 2017 from Love Inspired!*

"Have you come up with a name for the little tyke?" Clayton Young asked.

Her gaze moved to the infant. He needed a name, but Maggie didn't know what to call him.

Dinah looked to Maggie. "I like the name James."

Maggie looked down on her newborn's sweet face. "What do you think of the name James, baby?" His eyes opened and he yawned.

Her little sister, Dinah, clapped her hands. "He likes it."

Maggie looked up with a grin that quickly faded. Mr. Young looked as if he'd swallowed a bug. "What's the matter, Mr. Young? Do you not like the name James?" She didn't know why it mattered to her if he liked the name or not, but it did.

"I like it just fine. It's just that my full name is Clayton James Young."

Maggie didn't know what to think when the baby kicked his legs and made what to every new mother sounded like a

LIHEXP0817

happy noise. "If you don't want me to name him..."

"No, it seems the little man likes his new name. If you want to call him James, that's all right with me." He stood and collected his and Dinah's plates. "Now, if you ladies will excuse me, I have a kitchen to clean up and a stew to get on the stove. Then I'm going into town to get the doctor so he can look over baby James." He nodded once and then left the room.

Maggie looked to Dinah, who stood by the door watching him leave. "Dinah, I'm curious. You seem to like Mr. Young."

Dinah nodded. "He's a nice man."

"What makes you say that?"

"He saved baby James and rocked me to sleep last night."

"He did?"

"Uh-huh. I was scared and Mr. Young picked me up and rocked me while I cried. I went to sleep and he put me in bed with you." Dinah smiled. "He told me everything was going to be all right. And it is."

Maggie rocked the baby. Not only had Mr. Young saved James, but he'd also soothed Dinah's fears. He'd made them all breakfast and was already planning a trip to town to bring back the doctor. What kind of man was Clayton James Young? Unfamiliar words whispered through her heart: the kind who took care of the people around him.

LIHEXP0817